Teklife / Ghettoville / Eski

Sonics Series

Atau Tanaka, editor

Sonic Agency: Sound and Emergent Forms of Resistance, Brandon LaBelle

Meta Gesture Music: Embodied Interaction, New Instruments and Sonic Experience, Various Artists (CD and online)

Inflamed Invisible: Collected Writings on Art and Sound, 1976–2018, David Toop

Teklife / Ghettoville / Eski: The Sonic Ecologies of Black Music in the Early 21st Century, Dhanveer Singh Brar

Goldsmiths Press's Sonics series considers sound as media and as material – as physical phenomenon, social vector, or source of musical affect. The series maps the diversity of thinking across the sonic landscape, from sound studies to musical performance, from sound art to the sociology of music, from historical soundscapes to digital musicology. Its publications encompass books and extensions to traditional formats that might include audio, digital, online and interactive formats. We seek to publish leading figures as well as emerging voices, by commission or by proposal.

Teklife / Ghettoville / Eski

The Sonic Ecologies of Black Music in the Early Twenty-First Century

Dhanveer Singh Brar

Goldsmiths
Press

Copyright © 2021 Goldsmiths Press
First published in 2021 by Goldsmiths Press
Goldsmiths, University of London, New Cross
London SE14 6NW

Printed and bound by Versa
Distribution by the MIT Press
Cambridge, Massachusetts, and London, England

Copyright © 2021 Dhanveer Singh Brar

A CIP record for this book is available from the British Library

ISBN (hbk) 9781912685790
ISBN (ebk) 9781912685806

www.gold.ac.uk/goldsmiths-press

Terry Greening
1939–2011

Harkamal Singh Hothi
1984–2016

Contents

Acknowledgments

There are lots of people to thank, all of whom took part in some way or other in the making of this thing.

The founding members of Black Study Group (London): Simon Barber, Victor Manuel Cruz, Ciaran Finlayson, Sam Fisher, Lucie Kim-Chi Mercier, Ashwani Sharma.

Philadelphians who took me under their musical wing: Rucyl Mills, Marlo Reynolds.

Le Mardi Gras Listening Collective: Stefano Harney, Louis Moreno, Fred Moten, Fumi Okiji, Paul Rekret, Ronald Rose-Antoinette.

Laura Harris for reading early versions of the Teklife chapter.

All sorts of people at the University of Pennsylvania: Kevin Connolly, Jennifer Conway, Hubert Cook, Jim English, Nicholas Gaskill, Clemmie Harris, Grace Sanders Johnson, Amber R. Reed, Gina Rivera, Oliver Rollins, Ruth E. Toulson, Sara Varney, Chi-Ming Yang, Alden Young.

Similarly at University College London: Tamar Garb, David (Jeeva) Jeevendrampillai, Stefanie Rauch, Alicia Spencer-Hall, Catherine Stokes, Andreas Weiß.

For seeing a book before it was a book: Shana L. Redmond.

Atau Tanaka and Ellen Parnavelas at Goldsmiths Press.

The clan: Mohinder Kaur Brar, Harpawanjit Singh Brar, Arunveer Singh Brar.

Forever: Kezia Likinde Rolfe.

Introduction

desiccated rumbling bass line / furious chopped audio sample / vicious snapping drum patterns

fizzing asynchronous pulse / crystal clear tones / degraded mumble / valves releasing snatched clouds of digitized hiss

throbbing treble / staggered, shifting breaks / knife-sharp neon melody / truncated rapid fire vocal

The slices of writing above are annotations stimulated by the following three black electronic dance music records: respectively, DJ Rashad's 'Ghost', 'Our' by Actress, and Wiley's 'Ice Rink'. Although they are by no means accurate renditions of the originals, and nor do they represent the precision of notated scores, they do attempt to track the unique sensoria internal to these songs, these sonic objects. Yet, each recording cannot be understood according to its internal dynamics alone. Each operates within a circuit, whether it is one shaped by the producer in question, or one shaped by the communal endeavors required to sustain a musical scene. With DJ Rashad's 'Ghost' the circuit in question is the Footwork scene. Based in Chicago's South and West sides, Footwork is a style of sonic production and performative kinesis that mutated out of the local Juke and Booty House scenes during the early 2000s. The defining traits of Footwork as a sound are the synthesis of ferocity and co-ordination which conditions its range of rhythmic elements. To grasp Footwork both objectively and conceptually, one must understand its indivisibility from performance. Despite the primary function of the musics from which it emerged being that of social dancing, Footwork's primary purpose was the incitement of dance as competition. Strategically shifting outside the leisure space of the dancefloor, Footwork was engineered through the setting of the dance battle, conducted between teams who required of producers and DJs increasingly complex patterns with which to test, explore, and expand their repertoires. In this respect, Footwork also constituted a roving venue, covering the terrain of the racialized Southern and Western territories of the city.

'Our' is a segment contained in the album *Ghettoville*, released by Actress in 2015. Rather than a scene in the strictest sense, Actress was part of a network of independent electronic music labels and club nights established across South London during the mid-2000s. DMZ, Hyperdub, Swamp 81 and Niteslugs all had singular identities but emerged in close proximity to each other, and we can locate Actress within this geography, even more so when it comes to *Ghettoville*. The southern boroughs of London have long been considered somewhat psychically and socially adrift from the city proper, by dint of the 'natural' demarcation of the river Thames. Historically, South London has also contained some of the most impoverished, and by extension in a former capital of empire, the most heavily racialized zones in the city.[1] The basis for the production of *Ghettoville* came about for Actress via the act of regularly walking through some of what is now South London's relative sprawl, and taking in the lifeworlds of its most precarious inhabitants. The secret with *Ghettoville* is that he does not present the album as documentary evidence of his encounters, but allows it to become the resource for an intricate redesign of electronic music patterns.

The relation between Wiley's 'Ice Rink' and the circuitry of Grime is so permeable as to make the drawing of a distinction almost pointless. This track was forged in the crucible of East London in approximately 2003. It was here that the sound which eventually came to be known as Grime was cut and spliced into shape, within the context of economic and social isolation from a city experiencing the boom economies of market-driven governance – a dynamic doubled down by the intensification of racialized policing. Like Footwork, Grime was both a musical signature and a means of social organization, finding a highly effective technology in pirate radio. What Wiley (self-identified as The Godfather of Grime) and his endless roll call of peers and rivals designed in the boroughs of Tower Hamlets and Newham, on the streets of Bow, Stratford, and Limehouse, was something on the order of sonic weaponry, fueling their desire to dominate the landscape through broadcast.

These three soundscapes – the Chicago Footwork of DJ Rashad's 'Ghost', Actress' South London engineering of 'Our', and the East London Grime of

Wiley's 'Ice Rink' – are not only indicative of the cutting edge of contemporary black electronic dance music in the first decade of the current millennium, but they signal the capacities of the music of the black diaspora over the same period. That, at least, is the foundational ethos of *Teklife / Ghettoville / Eski: The Sonic Ecologies of Black Music in the Early Twenty-First Century*. Using their sonically formal non-conformity, the situatedness of their environmental production, and their relative obscurity to those outside the networks of electronic music culture – an obscurity which can be ascribed to the combination of complex dissonances and class character of this music – my argument is that Footwork, Grime, and Actress have been involved in the underground production of new modes of black music. What we have here are extreme registrations of aesthetic and social experimentation, taking place within comparable contexts of urban racialization, which, because of their alienating affectivity and site specificity, have issued forth realizations of black diasporic music that, for the large part, have remained unaccounted for because they belong to an insistently autonomous and highly mutational continuum across the Atlantic.

The work of *Teklife / Ghettoville / Eski* then rests in a fold between an entry into the surface dynamics of the recorded musical materials, and the geographic and social co-ordinates of the environments in which they were composed. Such a fold is understood here as a zone of non-equivalent correspondence. It is not so much that, for example, the histories of urban racialization and the current landscapes of South and West Chicago can be 'read off' against the sound design and social practices of Footwork. Rather, what is at stake is a phonic and material conceptualization of Footwork (as well as Grime and Actress) as formed in atmospheres and producing ecologies.

The importance of a term such as *phono-material*, and the notion of *atmospheres* and *ecologies* (as well as the relation between them) will be more fully mapped out in the following chapters, but to briefly sketch their uses now: firstly, the phono-material offers a means for discussing the sensory operations and shapes of black electronic dance music as a continuum which is primarily non-verbal, and relies on the minute yet potent manipulation of audio frequencies to create affects. Whether it is explicitly named by theorists or not, I will show how the phono-material has been the predominant concern in recent discourse on black music (especially so in the work of Kodwo Eshun, Steve Goodman, Paul Gilroy, Fred Moten, and

Alexander Weheliye), as a way to theorize the sonic aesthetics of recordings without the need for the grammar of musicology. Secondly, black social life has been understood within recent Black Studies thinking (by the likes of Katherine McKittrick, AbdouMaliq Simone, Moten, Stefano Harney) as an atmosphere. What is meant by this is that black social life is a really existing environment that is produced under the brutal urban impositions of racial capitalism, but an understanding of it is not reducible to those impositions.[2] In the sense that black social life is an atmosphere (not fixed, but undeniably present, roving beyond its confines), it is also undeniably an aesthetic. Black social life as an aesthetic atmosphere in internal motion produces its own ecologies which generate genuine alternatives to the present violent racial policing of things. Across the history of black social life, such ecological production has tended to be overwhelmingly musical. It is through the social experimentation in the atmospheres of sound that black life (especially in its urban settings) has manifested ecologies which allow for the sensory production of an alternative. As Steve Goodman makes apparent, such features function at a heightened pitch within the continuum of black electronic dance music, due to its use of new technologies and the abrasiveness of the locations in which it is generated. Hence, there are atmospheres of black social life out of which the phono-material specificity of Footwork, Grime, and Actress have emerged, yet simultaneously, as aesthetic projects they are involved in the further generation of sonic ecologies which feed back into and modulate this social atmosphere. Questions of equivalence (whether the phono-materiality, social atmosphere and sonic ecology are the same) or priority (which comes first) are not relevant here – and neither should they be. It is more that there *is a relation*, one which is generative, fraught, compelling and irruptive, and it demands attention.

Our understanding of Footwork, Actress and Grime as new black music must move through the type of non-equivalent correspondences just described because they allow us to conceive of these sounds as sonic ecologies. We also need to keep in mind the effect created by this book in terms of considering such site-specific ecologies together, in so far as what is being proposed through their arrangement as a grouping is an idea of them as a recent manifestation of diasporic blackness.

In this respect, my task here is not documentary. There is no attempt made to provide an exhaustive, source-based account of a scene (Footwork and Grime) or a single artist (Actress). Similarly, the ethnographic observation of group behavior is in no way a feature of the writing. Instead this is an entirely critical and theoretical endeavor. It represents an attempt to consider, speculate on, and conceptualize the phono-material aesthetics of a set of recordings, in order to address the question of their status as ecological instances of black music, generated through the atmospheres of black social life, in territories understood as urban concentrations of poverty and racialization. By paying attention to the fold between the alluringly alienating textures of these recordings, and the environments in which they were assembled, we can begin to theorize how Footwork, Grime, and Actress were generating sonic ecologies of black music that were operating as the obscured, incisive, and roughened edge of black diasporic culture in the early twenty-first century.

Whilst the rejection of the ethnographic method in favor of the critical when analyzing urban instances of black music might seem like an outlier stance to take, when considered through the history of black music writing from the late twentieth century onwards, it is not all that remarkable. From this vantage point, ethnography has long been eschewed in favor of speculating on the aesthetic possibilities of the music without losing contact with its social dynamics. Amiri Baraka was perhaps the touchstone for this tendency, and this book draws on a series of what could be referred to as post-Barakan thinkers on black music (Gilroy, Moten, Weheliye, Eshun).

Teklife / Ghettoville / Eski is organized into two sections. Following a first chapter which situates Grime, Actress, and Footwork within a longer continuum of black electronic dance music production beginning in the early 1980s, we have a chapter which presents the case for the task of *theorizing* black electronic dance music. This begins with a turn to Kodwo Eshun and Steve Goodman as interlocutors who establish the primacy of the sonic as both the means for thinking black electronic dance music's speculative capacities and its urban ecological dimensions. These core ideas (the sonic as it relates to the speculative and the ecological) are then extended through their relations to a set of discourses in black diasporic thought. One such strand concerns the aesthetic, political, and theoretical characterization of sonic experimentation in black music, as developed by Paul Gilroy, Fred Moten, and Alexander Weheliye. Another centers on the ways in which black social life (especially in its urban articulations) has been theorized through an attentiveness to the histories of racialization and collective social improvisation. The primary thinkers in this area of the chapter are Moten (again) and Harney, McKittrick, and Simone. My purpose in the second chapter is to situate the book within a set of longer discussions of black electronic dance music and current Black Studies debates on music, urban geography, and sociality. More than that though, the aim is to signal how Footwork, Grime, and Actress demand a further complication of ideas of blackness, due to their levels of aesthetic intensity as socially improvised forms of black music made at the opening of the twenty-first century.

The second section proceeds directly into an engagement with the music: three chapters, each conducting a dedicated encounter with Footwork (Teklife), Actress (Ghettoville) and Grime (Eski) on their own terms. My aim here is to build an account of them as sonic ecologies of black music which conduct experiments in blackness. The chapters dealing with Footwork and Grime share a great deal in terms of method and structure. The intention is not simply to provide an account of the stylistic features of the music as music, but to consider how specific performative and organizational systems constructed within the scene, and the spatial pressures of racial pathologization, feed into their constitution as open air sonic experiments. In the case of Footwork, the performative-organizational system is the dance battle circle, and the spatial pathologization occurs through the construction of South and West Chicago as a 'hyperghetto'. Using the scene's description of its own aesthetic practice as *Tek* and as a manifestation of *architekture*, I argue that what is at stake in Footwork is a collectivized system of planning which offers the chance to reorder the racial management of the city. With Grime it is pirate radio as an improvised broadcast technology and the range of techniques used to police the cultural production of racialized populations in London. The chapter is thus organized around analyzing the contact between two forms of antagonism which appeared to be central to Grime: its *internally composed antagonistic expansionism* and an *antagonistic mode of external duress* installed by the state. The question I pose in the chapter is whether the external duress of the state limited the capacities of the music or became a part of its generativity. In both chapters my argument is assembled through the process of listening closely to a range of sonic (and occasionally visual) objects. This listening is supplemented by journalism, music criticism, local histories of race and urbanization, and the deployment of relevant conceptual fragments from Black Studies, Cultural Studies, and Sound Studies.

The chapter on Actress differs slightly. Although, as has already been stated, he formed part of a network of South London electronic experimentation (rather than a fully realized scene), the choice to focus on a single artist and a single album is motivated by other factors. What occurs here through a zoom in on *Ghettoville* and Actress' own ruminations on the making of the work (I give his method the name 'quotidian observation'), is an illumination of ways in which the atmospheric effects of the social and the ecological murmurations of the sonic that can shape the generativity of an entire scene, come into play in equally as expansive ways through the production of a single musical object. Thus, this chapter gives the reader a different vantage point on my concerns in this book.

The decision to title the chapters, and the book overall, using the headings 'Teklife', 'Ghettoville' and 'Eski', rather than the more straightforward 'Footwork', 'Actress' and 'Grime', is one that will hopefully become apparent through the process of reading. To briefly sketch out the reasoning now though: such a choice was made in order to signal something of the productive discontinuity within and between each musical project and its setting. In so far as Grime is an outcome of a social atmosphere, and in so far as it modulates into existence a sonic ecology, then 'Eski' stands as a further emanation issued from within Grime, another concentrated demarcation of its capacities. More or less the same applies to the 'Footwork–Teklife' relation, and 'Ghettoville', as we shall see, operates in the interstitial space between concrete registration of an environment and the improvisatory capacities of a seemingly diminished lifeworld. Such is the febrile intensity and generative instability of this diasporic field of experimentation in sound and sociality.

Whether my presentation of Footwork, Grime, and Actress on these terms is viable is of course what *Teklife / Ghettoville / Eski* will stand or fall upon. What follows though has been undertaken with absolute attentiveness and a careful disposition towards a set of black musical projects that were unsurpassed in their underground, obscured, yet spectacularly complex configurations of black music in the diaspora during the first decades of our current millennium.

Part 1

1

Mineral Interiors: House, Techno, Jungle

To claim Footwork, Grime, and Actress have signaled the possibilities for black music in the early twenty-first century is not equivalent to arguing they represent entirely new systems of aesthetic production. The way Grime and Footwork as styles, and the individual outputs of Actress, throb with highly irregular technologically patterned sounds is not a quality unique to them alone. Similarly, the way their styles of social and aesthetic composition are restricted by space, race, and class is not anything new. Furthermore, the fact that as iterations of black music, Footwork, Grime, and Actress cannot simply be read off against the specifics of urbanization in either Chicago or London, but instead irrupt and expand in relation to their environments is not a feature they arrived at independently. In short, black electronic dance music has been in operation for over thirty years, and the qualities I am ascribing to three recent iterations within the setting of this book need to be considered through a longer lens of diasporic formation.

Since the late twentieth century black electronic dance music has been in operation across the diasporas of North America and Britain, constantly shadowed by a Jamaican ghost in the machinery. Stretching across time and territory from Chicago's instigation of House in the early 1980s, to Detroit's deviation into Techno a decade later, and then the hyperbolic Jungle of mid-1990s London, black electronic dance music has been a cross-hatched field of experimentation in black sonic, social, and spatial production. Whilst each of its first iterations possessed specific local flavors, there are a series of shared features which made them into an Atlanticist continuum. At the level of production, they made use of emergent or discarded audio technologies, and did so in ways which necessitated collaboration. Aesthetically, they redesigned the textures of black music, with special attention given to the pliability and range of bass frequencies. Socially, there was an insistence upon unrelenting performance in autonomously organized space. Territorially, House, Techno, and Jungle were forged in cities where previous institutional models of urban containment were undergoing severe flux – thus this musical continuum was created at the height of shifting race–class dynamics. In terms of their realization as a common experiment, these projects were constantly feeding into each other, but to cast such relations as *de facto* nourishing and mutual would be an error. Often the intense productivity that was key to the forging of the continuum was arrived at through antagonism and negation. All of these factors were compressed into, dissipated by, and remodeled through, the very phonic materiality of the music. This is why, since its formation in House, Techno, and Jungle, black electronic dance music has put forward some of the most intensive social and aesthetic realizations of black diasporic culture under late racial capitalism, particularly in terms of the sedimentation of black working-class and surplus labor populations into the urban geographies of major US and British cities.

The question is how to grasp the relationship between the emergence of House, Techno, and Jungle in the closing decades of the twentieth century, as the initial flourishing of black electronic dance music, and the more recent appearance of Footwork, Grime, and Actress? My intention is not to put in place a historical genealogy. It is not simply the case that there are direct lineages out of House, Techno, and Jungle, which can be established as the causes of Footwork, Grime, or Actress. In fact, since the formation of the continuum there has been a whole variety of production under its umbrella (and there is even more taking place now) which does not feature in this book. Rather, the aim to render a set of what music writer Dan Barrow has called 'mineral interior(s)'. Barrow used the term only once, in a review of the record *The Seer of Cosmic Visions* (Planet Mu, 2014), by Hieroglyphic Being and the Configurative or Modular Me Trio. The formulation was arranged as such in the review:

The Seer of Cosmic Visions comes across like a scouring techno version of Picasso's late cubist paintings: planes and bursts of 303 noise, severe and flat, rendered with brutal force, momentarily overlap. The sound is so raw and lo-fi it's as if you are hearing the mineral interior of the circuits magnified and made audible. The rhythmic structures mutate, leading in new elements and shifting the queasy timbre of the keys, with an inscrutable logic; the bass is frequently pitched so high to function as a lead, with low end provided by echo-drenched kicks that conjure up a sense of illusory space.[1]

In this respect, the way in which Barrow uses 'mineral interior' to magnify the relation between the sonic space inside the record and its affective production of space within the world of the listener/dancer helps to make it clear how within black electronic dance music a febrile experimentation in sound, sociality, and ecology has always been at stake since the terms were set by House, Techno, and Jungle. The focus on mineral interiors across the formation of House in early 1980s Chicago, Techno in early 1990s Detroit, and Jungle in London during the middle of the same decade requires us to map out how a set of improvised structures and kinetic patterns allowed these three styles to become a continuum wherein aesthetic innovation, technological (mis)appropriation, organization of social space, and the institutional aggregation of race–class were mediated through the production of soundscapes which were so intense they could never be adequately read off against these constitutive features. By the same measure, I want to undertake this process in order to mark Footwork, Grime, and Actress as distinct, due to their relative contemporaneity, and their response to new conditions of urbanization under the present form of racial capitalism. We could call this the *changing same* of black electronic dance music.[2]

   Such an argument is one which is fundamental to *Teklife / Ghettoville / Eski* overall in that it concerns an illustration of black electronic dance music's function as the roughened (which is to say quotidian), yet lethal (which is to say incisive), edge of urban black diasporic life in the Global North from the late twentieth century to the present. Under its rubrics, we have heard numerous territorial experiments in the production of sonic ecologies which contain not only relatively unremarked upon realizations of black music, but highly intense reconfigurations of blackness. It is important to stress that such reconfigurations of blackness have been produced precisely through the everyday, underground, non-singular, aesthetic practices of black populations operative within precarious urban zones. This reveals a crucial dynamic at the core of my focus on black electronic dance music: namely, a constant reengineering of the social in and as a sensory field through processes of sonic production.

Made by and for (Black) People

The core constituency which drove the development of House in Chicago was always 'poor, black and queer'.[3] Indeed, the major organizer and instigator of the style, DJ Frankie Knuckles, arrived from New York in 1979 with the explicit intention of pushing the queer/black/latin experiment taking place in that city's Loft Party scene into new aesthetic terrain in Chicago.[4] Yet the social and aesthetic composition of House was never seen internally as a limit point, nor was it understood externally as a barrier. Such were the intensities of the sound Knuckles was arranging in The Warehouse, and his rival Ron Hardy in The Music Box, that the city's young, black, working-class and heterosexual populations were quickly drawn onto the dancefloor, into the DJ booth, and took on the task of record production. Jesse Saunders, Farley 'Jackmaster Funk', Marshall Jefferson, Chip E, DJ Pierre, and Phuture were vital to the development of the music, by providing DJs with new sounds that extended the core House template. As Brewster and Broughton note:

With no Studio 54 celebrity scene to fuck things up, and without New York's overbearing industry presence, music in Chicago stayed dirtier, funkier, more about dancing till you dropped. And without any competing scene the house underground managed to spread beyond its gay origins without losing direction or momentum.[5]

The oft narrated story of the 'Belleville Three' indicates something particular about the class composition of Detroit Techno. Juan Atkins, Derrick May, and Kevin Saunderson were all products of a former inner-city black working class who had followed Detroit's car industry and its stable union jobs out into the surrounding western suburbs.[6] Although the laboring conditions on the new robotic lines were marked into the early aesthetic forms of the music, its initial audience in the greater metropolitan area consisted of those peers of Atkins, May, and Saunderson for whom a sensibility for experimental European pop music allowed them to nuance the core elements of Funk, thus finding a sonic expression for their new class character.

Jungle was undeniably black music, yet precisely because it was composed in the council estates of London it was produced and received by both working-class black and white youth: 'But even if you concede jungle's "blackness" as self-evident, this only makes it all the more striking that from Day One more than fifty percent of the leading DJs and producers have been white'.[7] For Kenny Ken, Nicky Blackmarket, DJ Hype, and MC Navigator the determining factor in the psycho-social and material production of Jungle was the street:

You know what types of struggles people go through on the street. Y'know and its mainly street people that go to jungle. People with street cred or whatever you want to call it. At the end of the day it's all about people that come from an urban background and live in communities. Everyone call them working class or whatever, but it's definitely from a street level.[8]

New Black Music / New Technologies

Chicago House, like Techno and Jungle that followed it, maintained a volatile level of generativity through constantly constructing new ways of arranging sound. This practice was not an end in itself, but was driven by a combination of the indivisible relation with the dancefloor and the use of newly available technologies. The Chicago House sound broadly developed in three overlapping stages. Initially, the aim of Knuckles and Hardy as DJs was to employ material which had been central to the New York loft scene, introduce different elements and blend them into a harder, rawer entity.[9] Eventually though, dancers in the clubs required new textures to sustain their capacity for continuous movement. It was at this point that a spate of local young black bedroom producers who had been experimenting with preset sounds on new pieces of hardware (the Roland 808 and 909 drum machines, Korg Poly 61 and four-track cassette recorders) came to the fore. With cuts such as Jesse Saunders' 'On & On' and Marshall Jefferson's 'Move Your Body' they stripped away and intensified the frameworks Knuckles and Hardy had laid down in the clubs:

The stomping four-to-the-floor kick drums would become the defining mark of house music. Other elements – hissing hi-hat patterns, synthetic handclaps, synth vamps, chiming bass loops, drum rolls that pushed the track to the next plateau of pre-orgasmic intensity – emerged when Chicagoans started making records to slake the DJs' insatiable demand for fresh material. Called 'tracks' as opposed to songs, because they consisted of little more than a drum track, this proto-house music was initially played by DJs on reel-to-reel tape and cassette.[10]

The mining for unrealized affordances in music technologies also instigated a further stage in the Chicago sound when DJ Pierre and Phuture's
'mistaken' engineering of a sustained squeal from the Roland TB-303 saw
the emergence of the 'acid trax' aesthetic.

Due to Detroit's relative proximity to Chicago – and Derrick May's
period living in the city – Techno is often considered a mutation of House.
One of the fundamental distinctions between the two styles is that in
Detroit Techno the emphasis was on building new sonic material through
synthesis, rather than modulating presets or using found material:

Eschewing samples of live instruments in favor of raw, mostly atonal machine
noises, techno's vocabulary involved a heightened emphasis on texture and
rhythm and an approach to sound elements as building blocks. This vocabulary
included such elements as the abrupt fading in and out of sounds, the increasing and decreasing of their intensities, and the use of varieties of graininess. The
result was a shifting interplay of sound patterns that were not, however, simply
abstract: for all its conceptual tendencies, techno is first and foremost dance
music, experienced most immediately as an endlessly propulsive rhythm and
almost always subject to the rigid organization that implies.[11]

The ethos behind the Atkins–May–Saunderson project was an attempt
to redesign George Clinton's Funk template through the Korg Poly 800,
Yamaha DX-100, and Roland TR-808 and TR-909. The basis for such a trajectory lay in the Belleville Three's encounter with Kraftwerk, Depeche
Mode, and other strands in European synthpop, via the Electrifying Mojo's
radio shows, alongside an auto-didact's education in the tropes of science
fiction and cybertheory. This gave the initial flourishing of Techno a highly
developed conceptual language to accompany its otherworldly sonic palette. Once Atkins, May, and Saunderson had entered the international
club network, Underground Resistance stepped into the space they had
left behind in Detroit, introducing a harder industrialism to the soundworld of Techno, along with a more stringently militant ethos.

Jungle proves itself the most resistant to the criteria being applied in
this section. This is because it was an agglomeration of multiple styles, and,
by extension, the distinctions between its constitutive elements, its synthesis as a coherent sound, and the developments that immediately followed were never settled.[12] Nonetheless, there was clearly a music defined
by its constituency as Jungle, and its potency came from its operation as

a 'two lane music'.[13] This meant it held in one single field both the irruptions of breakbeats *and* reggae inflected sub-bass frequencies operating 'almost below the threshold of hearing, impacting the viscera like shockwaves from a bomb'.[14] The ability not only to contain two such dissonant effects, but to do so in a way that reorganized the kinetic range of dancers was enabled by new tendencies in hardware and software. Like samplers before it, the Akai S1000 allowed material to be pulled from a range of sources, but when sequenced through programs such as Cubase or C-Lab, the new in-built device known as 'time-stretching' 'allowed the tempo of a sample to be increased without the pitch going up as well. It's not too much of an exaggeration to assert that [Jungle] could not have come into being without this box and its successors'.[15] Reporting from the dancefloor, Kodwo Eshun noted how the resulting 'febrile metallic sound brought a new dimension to [its] palette of sonic surprise: an atmosphere of impending yet unlocatable dread'.[16]

Race–Class and Urban Crisis

As a city dominated by the steel industry and one of the major destinations in the Great Migration of black workers from the American South to the North, the post-industrial transition in Chicago's economic base was an acute experience for the city as a whole. Having said that, ghettoization and segregation had been embedded into the geographical and social composition of Chicago to such a degree that the Black Belt (or Bronzeville) on the South side was considered a natural part of the terrain.[17] What occurred from the 1960s onwards was a change in the nature and dynamics of urban segregation in the city, through the establishment of major social housing projects and the resulting decomposition of the black bourgeoisie as a class fused with black working people and the poor.[18] The relationship between these structural shifts and the assembly of Chicago House has rarely been made explicit, but it is perceptible. In its primary 'trax' form, soon followed by the Dance Mania label's orchestration of Ghetto and Booty House, we can hear how new styles of sonic production marked out the transforming geographies of race and class in the city.

The narrative twinning of Detroit's rapid fall from apparent grace as America's automobile capital and the emergence of Techno has been repeated so often that it is now an orthodoxy.[19] Rather than go over old ground, it is more productive to turn to Louis Moreno's unsettling of such short-hand accounts of Techno's relationship to the city of its inception. Moreno is suspicious of narratives which cast Detroit as a desolate, vacant city after the urban crises of the late 1960s and early 1970s. For him, the effect of such a nostalgia is that finance capital becomes the limit point of an understanding of social and cultural capacity. This was a conjuncture where the failure of Detroit was seen as a sign that labor and social life are problems capital cannot and should not have to sustain, and there was a rejection of any possible alternatives assembled by organized local populations. For Moreno, Detroit Techno was never a melancholic articulation of these effects; instead it was a countervailing renegade project. What occurred initially under the banner of the Belleville Three was not an aestheticization of Detroit as a 'problem', but rather a direct entry into the crises of racialized labor in order to create new possibilities, to countermap a new black future:

What distinguished the Detroit style was, to be sure, the geographical conditions of the city, but also something inherent within the music itself. The international extension of the *techno sound* was not just an opportunity to make careers for musicians, certain artists thought that the music carried within it the seeds to propagate the experience of Detroit on a planetary scale.[20]

Therefore, what occurred through the rubric of the Detroit Techno sound from the 1980s to the 1990s was in fact a transformation of the name 'Detroit' from one marked by racialized desolation 'into a structure of revolutionary feeling. In a city where space and music have become abundant "natural" resources, the power of Detroit Techno lights up a planetary *Metroplex* of tonal and rhythmic possibility'.[21]

The race–class composition of Jungle's constituency has already been discussed, yet what energized the formation of the music were the effects of another crisis in capital on Britain's inner cities:

It was 1993 and the nation was gripped by the worst economic slump in years. The cost of living was soaring, unemployment prevailed and houses were being repossessed after the 'never had it so good' bubble of the 1980s had finally burst....From Goldie's youth in the urban wastelands of the Midlands to Jumping Jack Frost's upbringing among London's tower blocks, most of Jungle's originators grew up in these surroundings, subsequently imbibing Jungle with the same set of underclass values.[22]

Thus, Jungle became a means for the generation of a new race–class consciousness that could be worn with pride: 'Jungle: it means to me something that's come from the street. It means people who are born with nothing found something that they can relate to and something they can believe in' (Kenny Ken).[23] This had implications for the music, as evidenced by the toxic reception it received when arriving on the broader UK electronic dance music circuit. Even within this self-assembled independent network of clubs, parties, labels, promoters, and media, the new sound faced deeply vindictive levels of pathologization: 'All too often, the dislike of jungle translates into a fear of the Alien Ruffneck, of the Rudeboy from the council estate who's supposedly spoilt the peace-and-love vibe and the dream of trans-tribal unity. Jungle, so this racist myth goes, is what killed Smiley, turned every raver's little Woodstock into an Altamount with bass bins.'[24] It is possible to suggest that this dismissive anxiety that Jungle faced (one which only strengthened its internally cohesive ethos) was not solely a response to the postures of the Alien Ruffnecks who came with it, but was equally the result of an inability on the part of those out of sync with its logic to recognize the way Jungle's phono-material force was remodulating yet another crisis in racial capitalism:

jungle's militant euphoria is fueled by the desperation of the early nineties. Composed literally out of fracture ('breaks'), jungle paints a sound-picture of social disintegration and instability. But the anxiety in the music is mastered and turned into a kind of nonchalance; the disruptive breakbeats are looped into a rolling flow. In this way, jungle contains a non-verbal response to troubled times, a kind of warrior stance.[25]

Club Territories

The important thing to remember is that as projects undertaken during urban crises, and as sounds assembled in immediate contact with their audiences, House, Techno, and Jungle needed to organize places where people could regularly gather in movement. In Chicago, the relation between The Warehouse club and the eventual naming of the style indicates the extent to which site, populace, and dance were crucial to its formation. Occupying a three-story former factory in west central Chicago, the club held up to two thousand dancers, was noted for the intensity of its sound rig, and opened across the entire weekend.[26] Following the departure of Frankie Knuckles in 1983 to establish The Power Plant, The Warehouse owner Robert Williams opened up The Music Box as the host venue for his rival Ron Hardy.[27] This led to the proliferation of clubs (The Loft, The Playground, East Hollywood) and regular parties in hotel ballrooms, which indicates the levels of desire for musical and social experimentation amongst certain Chicagoans.

Detroit Techno is something of an anomaly when it comes to practical social organization, as the leading DJs soon had to take up opportunities in Europe due to the lack of support in their home city. Having said that, the brief year-and-a-half run of The Music Institute in 1988 – co-owned by Derrick May and George Baker – was vital to the initial propagation of the sound in Detroit.[28] As Baker makes clear, the template for The Music Institute was the Chicago scene:

Post-high school years, early college years, everybody got turned on by Chicago. Chicago was the exact forerunner of what the music [Techno] is today as far as the concept of really taking some raw spaces, taking some raw systems, taking some raw jocks and raw music and beating the heck out of it, until it just took us over.[29]

Due to the existence of a wide network of club spaces across London, which served as regular one-night venues for numerous dance music styles, Jungle was able to operate as a social music with relative ease. The sound that became Jungle gestated at nights such as Rage, Freedom, Perception, and Telepathy, but it was at AWOL (A Way of Life) at Islington's Paradise Club in 1992 where it formally solidified.[30] Here DJs such as Randall, Mickey Finn, Kenny Ken and Darren Jay played a role in lending coherence to an urban militant aesthetic built upon maintaining the appearance of control rather than hedonistic disorientation. The dynamics of the AWOL club space created a physical proximity between the DJ booth and dancefloor which meant the style of composition had to adapt accordingly:

As a result, the DJ was forced to read the vibe of the crowd and listen to their reactions. Taking many of the styles of the Reggae soundsystem clashes the audience would let their feelings be known in no uncertain terms. Air horns rang out and shouts of 'rewind' were increasingly heard.[31]

A spate of other regular parties soon followed (Jungle Splash in Edmonton, Sunday Roast at the Astoria, Thunder & Raw in Tottenham Court Road), creating an alternative tempo-spatial map of London according to Jungle's designs.

Atlantic Antagonisms

The ways in which House, Techno, and Jungle latched onto already existing diasporic routes and animated a new type of Black Atlanticism needs to be addressed on two different, yet not necessarily distinct, levels. The first is that of spread and dissemination. Despite its relative lack of attention beyond the Chicago metropolitan area, House – in its already multiple guises – was able to travel to Europe and instigate an almost epiphenomenal shift in underground music culture in the form of the UK Acid House scene. Similarly, the very naming of Detroit Techno was achieved through the need for the UK label Virgin Music to mark it out as both related to and distinct from its Chicago neighbor (hence the compilation release on Virgin which gave the Belleville Three's experiment its name – *Techno!: The New Dance Sound of Detroit*). Jungle was always active in the celebration of its impurity. Feeding off of the sonic signatures and postures of New York hip-hop, plugging into the institutional knowledge of Jamaican soundsystem culture, and adapting the machinism of Techno, Jungle was never though a derivative sound.

The second level of Black Atlanticism at work within black electronic dance music concerns the inevitability and necessity of internal fractures. The Black Audio Film Collective's 1996 essay film *The Last Angel of History* perhaps most effectively stages this dynamic through edited exchanges between Goldie (who produced Jungle as Rufige Kru and was founder of the label Metalheadz), Derrick May (of the Belleville Three) and A Guy Called Gerald (who produced the major Jungle album *Black Secret Technology*):

GOLDIE: People ask you the difference between Techno and Jungle....There's no difference. It's just that it wasn't what Techno is, it's what we took from Techno. It's like anything else. It's not what hip-hop is, it's what we take from it. You know all that stuff that Derrick May made, and the stuff that Carl Craig made. Because it was...it came from somewhere. It was something which had a better meaning to me.

DERRICK MAY: Jungle. I hate the way – I hate the word 'Jungle' if you wanna know the truth about it. What the fuck does 'Jungle' mean? OK it was called breakbeat before. Now it's called Jungle. Where does Jungle come from? What is Jungle? What does that mean?

A GUY CALLED GERALD: Jungle actually comes from an area in Jamaica that they call the Jungle. And MCs from there – I think – elaborated on that. So when it came out on soundsystem tapes people latched onto it and started using it as a name.

DERRICK MAY: Gerald. Hm. Sad inside, happy face on the outside. Put all his heart and love into some big record company and they sold him out.

A GUY CALLED GERALD: Derrick May, I mean, to me, is like, y'know, he kicked me off y'know. Without listening to 'It Is What It Is', 'Feels So Real', all of the early sort of like Transmat stuff, I would have been lost. I was lucky to just hear his things on the radio, and think: 'Yeah, that's the direction, that's where I want to go'. Or else I don't know what I'd have been doing now.[32]

The illustrative point here is that the making of black electronic dance music – like many other historical instances of the practices of diaspora – was not shaped simply by an ethics of generosity. Borrowing, stealing, misappropriation, misinterpretation, and hostility were an essential part of its characteristics.

The above is not supposed to represent an exhaustive history of House, Techno, and Jungle. If read using such a lens then, inevitably, gaps will appear. My intention was to achieve a quite different aim: to identify patterns and resonances in order to make apparent the mineral interiors of these late twentieth-century forms of black culture. Deploying thematic headings (addressing issues such as who made the music?, what did it sound like and how was it designed?, under what constraints was it forged?, how was each scene socially organized and related to other scenes?), we were able to draw out a series of common dynamics in House, Techno, and Jungle which meant their appearance over ten years of activity signaled the emergence of a new continuum in black diasporic aesthetics. Broadly, black electronic dance music converges around, and is determined by, some of the following features: a certain race–class character amongst its participants shaped by their status as urban working class and surplus labor, and thus giving the music an impetus of self-determination; a highly charged pursuit of ever intensive affective arrangements of sound, determined by an improvised (as well as internally coherent) use of audio technologies; an impression that the music is a response to, or at least an effect of, a sustained period of urban crises, thus giving each particular soundscape a strong territorial inflection; the importance of forging social spaces in which the music can be performed and disseminated; and a highly mutational and unstable diasporicism.

Now, of course, these are not strict categories to which all black electronic dance music forms must adhere before they can be placed under such a heading. Neither do they even apply uniformly to House, Techno, and Jungle. Due to localized features and their respective temporalities of emergence, there is a marked amount of difference (and in some respects even antagonism) between the sounds. By the same measure, what does appear across House, Techno, and Jungle at the level of mineral interior is a quotidian quality of social experimentation, which takes place within highly pressurized urban geographies of race–class. Thus, the continuum of black electronic dance music was realized through both self-determined sonic ecologies in almost constant production and a fraught generative diasporic field.

This is the ground upon which our engagement with Footwork, Grime, and Actress will proceed. It should be self-evident that the analysis will not function in exactly the same way as it did with House, Techno, and Jungle, because the nature of their emergence in the early twenty-first century means that black electronic dance music has, by necessity, taken up different arrangements. Yet, the process of thinking Footwork, Grime, and Actress on their own terms will be shaped by questions concerning their quotidian practices of experimental assembly, the production of sonic ecologies, and their surrounding social atmospheres. I want to stress once more, uniformity is not the goal here. These are simply parameters which will shape the analysis and can be stretched, taken apart, and reformulated.

Using these parameters, my approach to Actress, Footwork, and Grime opens up a number of questions at the core of this book. On one level, a conceptualization of their soundscapes will show how they respond to and animate the real existing violence of urban racialization for black diasporic populations of the Global North in the early twenty-first century. In combination with this question lies another, regarding how, as recent forms of territorialized social aesthetics, they have reconstituted the category of black music, which, if understood through the lens of its long history, means reconstituting ideas of freedom, being, revolution, and justice for the contemporary moment.

Irreducibly attached to such a line of inquiry is how, as instances of black music as sonic ecology, they contain the undercommon codes, an open set of secrets, about how the very contestation to live freely, together, can be broadcast across the diaspora.

2

The Blackness of Black Electronic Dance Music

In as much as I am concerned with culture and aesthetics, this book is also meant to be theoretically productive. My task is not simply to describe as accurately as possible the combination of alienating sensuosity, social character, institutional autonomy, and networked mutationality that determine Footwork, Grime, and the music of Actress as the latest refashioning of a continuum. Rather, the endeavor is to address the question of how to *think* black electronic dance music.

Hence, my ambitions require us to address two sets of questions. First, how has the spectacular volatility of House, Techno, and Jungle already been shaped into something like a set of aesthetic theorizations? Where do we enter into this grammar and how do we make use of it? Second, is it possible to extrapolate from already existing conceptualizations of black electronic dance music potential resonances with accounts of the more general category of black music? In addition, to what extent does such thinking on black music contain an ecological dimension?

To put it in the most direct possible terms, this chapter introduces the conceptual question of the blackness of black electronic dance music, by feeding it through the question of the blackness of black music in general, and the potential for thinking blackness through the ecological. All of this will serve as preparation for our path through Footwork, Grime, and Actress.

From Futurhythmachine to Black Atlantic Sonic Futurism

There have been some attempts to discuss black electronic dance music from within Black Studies in the US (Jayna Brown, Tavia Nyong'o, Katherine

McKittrick, and Alexander Weheliye being notable figures in this regard), yet the most sustained engagement with the continuum has tended to come from the UK.[1] From the 1990s onward, the cross-cultural conversation between music criticism, Speculative Philosophy, the Black Arts, and Cultural Studies created an environment in which the likes of Simon Reynolds, Mark Fisher, Jeremy Gilbert, Ewan Pearson, John Akomfrah, and Edward George took seriously the task of understanding House, Techno, Jungle, and beyond as new styles of experimentation.[2]

Kodwo Eshun's 1998 *More Brilliant Than the Sun: Adventures in Sonic Fiction* is the standout work of this tendency, and it is through Eshun's text that our task of thinking black electronic dance music begins. Privileging the intensities evident in House, Techno, and Jungle as part of an array of late twentieth-century electronicized black musical projects, he made the case that at stake were fundamentally new propositions for the idea of black music. Such was black electronic dance music's alienating power that it required a fresh analytical grammar, one Eshun brought into view through the neologism 'The Futurhythmachine'. For Eshun, 'The Futurhythmachine' was an identifying marker adequate to the epiphenomenal shifts in black music being generated by House, Techno, and Jungle:

an AfroDiasporic Futurism, of a 'webbed network' of computerhythms, machine mythology and conceptechnics which routes, reroutes, and criss-crosses the Black Atlantic. This digital diaspora connecting the UK to the US, the Caribbean to Europe to Africa, is in Paul Gilroy's definition a 'rhizomorphic, fractal structure', a 'transcultural, international formation'.[3]

It is the combination of its deviant geography and its open syntheticism, that makes black electronic dance music a uniquely 'artificial discontinuum'.[4] Thus, for Eshun, if understood as 'The Futurhythmachine' the experimentation coursing through House, Techno, and Jungle:

opens up the new plane of Sonic Fiction, the secret life of forms, the discontinuum of AfroDiasporic Futurism, the chain reaction of PhonoFiction. It moves through the explosive forces which technology ignites in us, the temporal architecture of inner space, audiosocial space, living space, where postwar alienation breaks down into the 21st C alien.[5]

The Futurhythmachine, as Eshun conceives of it, fractures what up until that point had been a socio-historical imperative which overdetermined discourse on black music. For Eshun, the categorization of black music had been weighed down by an attempt to secure a tradition, coupled with a seemingly unquestionable insistence on the ethnographically real. The multi-dimensionality of House, Techno, and Jungle rendered such approaches unworkable. The music and its producers' insistence on the inventive force of sound for its own sake led to a sacrificing of 'content to throb and politics for pulse'.[6] Eshun pinpoints the ethical and aesthetic predominance of 'the street' ('widely assumed to be the engine of black popular culture, to be its foundation and its apotheosis, its origin and its limit') as the object which disappears in the face of this fierce production of sensory affects.[7] Abandoning what Eshun sees as the reductive 'logic of representation and will to realism',[8] the driving force of The Futurhythmachine is an irruptive 'antisocial surrealism'.[9] One of the central breaks represented by The Futurhythmachine is that its sites of production and dissemination become 'the bedroom, the party, the dancefloor, the rave: these are the labs where 21st C nervous systems assemble themselves, the matrices of the Futurhythmachinic Discontinuum'.[10]

Already we can see that Eshun's view of black electronic dance music as 'The Futurhythmachine' appears to run at odds with one of the central premises of this book. My proposition is that the aesthetic capacities of black electronic dance music operate in an unstable (yet generative) relation to the urban social environments in which they are composed. We shall see how Steve Goodman resolves the question of willed artificiality and urbanism in his extension of *More Brilliant Than the Sun*. It is better therefore to frame Eshun's perspective as part of a polemic he was producing within the sphere of late 1990s black cultural criticism. To the extent that black electronic dance music had received any reception at all, it was interpreted as a risky loss of cultural authenticity. A prime example of such thinking was Nelson George's knee-jerk dismissal of anything with a programmed beat as an inorganic instance of black musical production.[11] Beyond this somewhat reactionary stance was Paul Gilroy's lament at processes of musical de-skilling apparently caused by the take up of digital audio technologies.[12]

Besides polemics there is a more significant impulse at work in Eshun's 'artificial discontinuum' thesis. This being that House, Techno, and Jungle produced a radical break in the epistemological basis of black diaspora music: 'The mayday signal of Black Atlantic Futurism is unrecognizability, as either Black or Music.'[13] The push towards unrecognizability in *More Brilliant Than the Sun* is central to the arguments at work in *Teklife / Ghettoville / Eski* because such a claim does not rely upon a strict formalist analysis of the music. There is an implicit feature of Eshun's thinking that I want to draw out and make explicit. This concerns the categorical incapacitations generated by black electronic dance music in its relation to the shifting tectonics of political economy in the 1980s and 1990s. Buried within *More Brilliant Than the Sun* is a conceptualization of 'The Futurhythmachine' as a black cultural anticipation of, intertwining with, and deviation from racial capital during a crucial moment of its recomposition.[14] The implied question Eshun was putting to his readers in 1998 was whether they were willing to open up to the full implications of House, Techno, and Jungle and take control of the circuitry before capital weaponized it, or let such possibilities slip by due to an insistence upon codified notions of black music. Similarly, I use the unrecognizable syntheticism of Grime, Footwork, and Actress to point to how they represent the latest iteration in this continuum of black musical experimentation. Crucially though, to make the case that sensuous features of the music carry with them modulative capacities which are lethal to the organization of racial capitalism in the early twenty-first century, then we need to also simultaneously break from Eshun and think the music through the urban.

Despite there being over a decade between them, Goodman's *Sonic Warfare: Sound, Affect, and the Ecology of Fear* is something of a companion volume to *More Brilliant Than the Sun* in that he looks to extend much of the groundwork laid down by Eshun. The major distinction lies in the fact that Goodman no longer sees any real need to maintain the distinction between the sonic and the urban.

In *Sonic Warfare* The Futurhythmachine has been recast into 'Black Atlantic Sonic Futurism' as the heading for 'a nexus of black musical expression' ranging from 'dub to disco, from house to techno, from hip-hop to jungle, from dancehall to garage, to grime and forward.'[15] One of the moves Goodman makes to arrive at the urban is to frame the aesthetics of black electronic dance music as a socializing process. Understood as a 'transduction of the alienating experience of the Middle Passage' into 'a cybernetic phase shift' Black Atlantic Sonic Futurism, he argues, has generated styles of sonic invention which had an immense social effect on captive populations in late twentieth-century Chicago, London, Detroit, and elsewhere.[16] Black music, reprogrammed as Black Atlantic Sonic Futurism, went into operation as a 'sensual mathematics', a 'contagious polyrhythmic matrix', and thus when released into the world 'Western populations bec[a]me affectively mobilized through wave after wave of machinic dance musics'.[17] Thus what Goodman is doing is pushing at Eshun's theorization of the specific technological parameters of The Futurhythmachine in order to propose that what was at stake was also an enactment of the music as its own social technology. Although he is able to move his thinking on black electronic dance music aesthetics into the realm of the effects it had upon the dancefloor, Goodman's account of Black Atlantic Sonic Futurism as a socializing process can be taken further still. One of my aims is to use the music of Actress, along with the Grime and Footwork scenes, to propose that black electronic dance music is a social technology which by design carries out speculations on race. The sonic dislocations of this experimentation in sound involve the making of an aesthetics which decompose and redesign racial logic through the social intensities taking place in real time and across multiple sites. In short, black electronic dance music is a social technology of blackness.

To grasp how this case will be made we need to use Goodman's methodological approach to sound as media. Rather than merely perceptible elements of sound, he wants to draw on what he calls 'unsound', or the imperceptible, yet still present, elements which precede and exceed normative understandings of the sonic.[18] The focal point then is on sound as 'force' rather than 'text', specifically tracking 'the use of force, *both seductive and violent, abstract and physical*, via a range of acoustic machines (biotechnical, social, cultural, artistic, conceptual) to modulate the physical, affective, and libidinal dynamics of populations, of bodies, of crowds'.[19] The purpose of sound/unsound as force in Goodman's account of Black Atlantic Sonic Futurism as social technology plays a significant part in this book's nuancing of such a dynamic through the problematic of race and the question of blackness. House, Techno, and Jungle in the late twentieth century, and Grime, Footwork, and Actress at the opening of the twenty-first, form part of a continuum of hyperbolically proliferating styles which should not be understood as systems of signification. Instead my discussion of Footwork, Grime, and Actress is organized around the basis that black electronic dance music functions as a sonic concentration of force, which, when realized at intensive levels, provokes types of sensory and social reorganization which are unavoidably racial. It is this socio-racial animation of sound/unsound which means black electronic dance music generates experiments in blackness.

With an account of the social in place, it is not difficult to see how Goodman is able to reconcile the sonic and the urban in this thinking on black electronic dance music. For him, the sensual mathematics of Black Atlantic Sonic Futurism are indivisible from the environment in which they are produced. More than that, the forceful movement of these musics at the limits of sound/unsound as they spread across this network feeds back into and changes the environments which generate them. The formative relation shaping his analysis is that between 'vibes' (or the repeated collective improvisation of populations in close proximity and the sedimentation of these improvisations into an aesthetic way of living) and 'vibrations' (or the material organization and abrasive textures of the environment). It is through this relation that the 'urban as resonating surface' becomes a constitutive part of black electronic dance music whereby the rhythmic basis of Black Atlantic Sonic Futurism becomes 'as spatial as it is temporal'.[20]

The prominence given to the vibrational tones of the urban allows Goodman to introduce two vital features of Black Atlantic Sonic Futurism. The first he identifies as 'bass materialism', which, although instigated in the soundsystem culture of Jamaica, became the general affective modality of House, Techno, and Jungle. 'Bass materialism' refers to the 'vibrational nexus' that is animated through the site-specific arrangement of people, equipment, buildings, and territory, or as Goodman describes it 'the media of the earth, built environment, analogue and digital sound technologies, industrial oscillators and the human body'.[21] 'Audio virology' is the second feature of Black Atlantic Sonic Futurism as it is realized through the urban. According to Goodman:

an audio virology is a call for an ecological remit. What is meant here is that its map would begin from an inventory of frequencies, bodies, feelings, machines, utterances, emissions, codes, processes, affordances, economies and environments invested in any sonic nexus.[22]

Goodman uses this framework to give shape to his theories on the nature of Black Atlantic Sonic Futurism as a type of urbanism:

Black noise, painstakingly crafted in the context of enforced migration, depressed urbanism and ethnic suppression, becomes a locus of affective collectivity. Feeling around in the dark, in the toxic smog of megalopian pressure, when no hope seems to exist, when no stability persists, rhythmic decisions still get made, collectivities mobilized and potential futures produced. The rhythmic breakthroughs of the electronic musics of the Black Atlantic have been countless.[23]

What he is setting out is an amplification of the implicit features of Kodwo Eshun's schema. With regards to The Futurhythmachine, Eshun understood it as a categorical imperative to redesign black music that came about through an aesthetic adaptation to technological shifts in racial capital. Goodman takes up with this view, but for him such a dynamic needs to go through an account of the urban. The fact of the massive sensory overload which took place in House, Techno, and Jungle occurred precisely because of their production within and between precarious zones of post-industrial Chicago, Detroit, and London from the early 1980s to the mid-1990s. Goodman's Black Atlantic Sonic Futurism is then as much a territorial as it is an aesthetic heading for this type of experimentation. He requires us to not overly aestheticize the soundscapes of black electronic dance music, but to think their technological production through the improvised social organization taking place within co-existing spatial situations of race–class duress.

This returns us to a central feature of our argument concerning the combination of the roughened and the lethal, the quotidian, and the incisive, as key to grasping the blackness of black electronic dance music. Eshun and Goodman show us that House, Techno, and Jungle constituted problems for cultural analysis because they were rigorously improvised and irruptively strategized instances of sonic and spatial production. They modulated into hyperbolic soundscapes concentrations of geographic duress, technological repurposing, and race–class dynamics, whilst also never being reducible to these features alone. My task is to pass Actress, Footwork, and Grime along these channels, but also to draw out the question of their blackness as part of the non-equivalent correspondence between music, sociality, and geography. What is at stake here is a theorization of them as early twenty-first-century instances in the sonic production of black secret technology. To do so it is necessary to hold onto the imperatives of Eshun's Futurhythmachine and Goodman's Black Atlantic Sonic Futurism, as part of the task of taking black electronic dance music *as seriously as your life*, whilst also pushing to the foreground the problematic of race. On the one hand, we have Goodman's insistence that the affective force of the continuum has engrained within it the pressurized relations between the populations who created it and their urban environments. By the same measure, we must place at the center of any analysis of Footwork, Grime, and Actress, Eshun's axiom that to transpose the sensory brilliance of black electronic dance music onto a preconstituted understanding of the socially 'real', is to limit its aesthetic capacities. Simultaneously, the fold between aesthetic capacity and urban environment needs to account for the brutal impositions of racial capital and the generative production of blackness as constitutive features of these experiments. These then are the logics of our engagement with Footwork, Grime, and Actress – both conceptually (how to think the music) and methodologically (how to build an apparatus for the task of thinking) – as three of the most potent contemporary instances in the production of black electronic dance music.

Black Music

If our idea is to take The Futurhythmachine and Black Atlantic Sonic Futurism and push them towards a firmer conceptualization of blackness, then it is necessary to spend some time pinpointing the term blackness as it lends itself to the question of black electronic dance music. This involves drawing upon Black Studies debates on the larger question of black music in general, especially in their relation to the sonic, the social, the technological, and the ecological.

As Eshun and Goodman made extensive use of Paul Gilroy's Black Atlantic thesis, it makes sense to begin this section with his major work of this period. Beyond Eshun and Goodman's reading of it through the lens of electronic music, it is Gilroy's *The Black Atlantic: Modernity and Double Consciousness* (1993) that initiated the present critical discourse on black music. *The Black Atlantic* marked a shift away from folkloric or ethnographic accounts, towards an approach which pulled in the concerns of Critical Theory, Marxism, and Continental Philosophy, to conduct a theorization of black music's *political aesthetics*.

Gilroy's breakthrough move when it came to thinking black music was to reject all forms of essentialism (whether they be external racist ascriptions of biological essence, or internal nationalist attempts to fix a permanent cultural resource), as well as dismantling the then intellectual vogue for framing black aesthetics as an open field of interchangeable signification. In this context, he insisted on the blackness of black music as a mode of difference which moved through the long history of racialized experience. Black music was black not because it was an expression of genetic code, and neither was it an articulation of a strictly policed Africanism. By the same measure, its blackness could not be understood as an anti-essentialist plurality open to any form of self-declared radical significatory play. Instead, for Gilroy, the blackness of black music:

is in fact an elementary historical acquisition produced from the viscera of an alternative body of cultural and political expression that considers the world critically from the point of view of its emancipatory transformation.[24]

To grasp how he assembles this argument, we need to separate out several strands of his thinking. The first lies in his insistence on the primacy of the sonic. Historically, slaves were refused access to written language and textual mechanics as part of the racial codification of the modern subject. Thus, for Gilroy, the phonic and the aural became the engines for communicative and performative practice amongst the enslaved. Gilroy argues such a maneuver had two effects, one was that the seemingly senseless noise-making of the slaves only confirmed the perception of their pre-modernity on the part of those who traded and owned them; two, such presumptions allowed New World blacks to nuance and experiment with the sonic as a field of expression with only relatively minor interference. Such partial autonomy was crucial, according to Gilroy, because it allowed black diasporans to develop a socially inflected sonic technology known as 'antiphony (call and response).'[25] As a technology, antiphony became *the* engine of black music, because it inscribed communality into its very form and production, thus dissolving racially proscribed notions of singular subjectivity.[26] This blurring of the supposed distinctions between self and other, aesthetics and sociality, is vital for Gilroy, because the antiphonal structures of black music signal the way in which its affective charge is always infused by communality.

Twinned with this framing of its formal characteristics is Gilroy's claim that black music functions as a 'philosophical discourse'.[27] Its philosophical imperatives are the result of the relationship between the formation of the music and the historical experience of slavery. In effect, the structural and everyday organization of racial terror constitute the conditional basis for black music. Gilroy is not setting out an all-consuming brutality as the limits of an understanding of black music, but he is instead pointing to what he sees as its unique utopianism. As a philosophical discourse that does not comfortably register in the epistemologies of the enlightenment, black music generates a sensibility of freedom which refuses to seek equal footing in a world assembled by racial modernity, but instead, Gilroy argues, opens up the possibilities for modernity's moral and ethical recoding.

Gilroy makes the case for the political aesthetics of black music by conceiving of this utopianism as indivisible from the antiphonal social form of its soundscapes. Thus, what we have here are a set of ethical drives conditioning the formal experimentation with sound and, conversely, the social improvisation with the phonic issuing forth an ethical impulse:

This politics exists on a lower frequency, where it is played, danced and acted, as well as sung and sung about, because words, even words stretched by melisma and supplemented or mutated by the screams which still index the conspicuous power of the slave sublime, will never be enough to communicate its unsayable claims to truth.[28]

Gilroy is able to track the movement of these historical tendencies into the realization of black music as a recorded object, particularly in the twentieth century when it became capitalism's mass commodity par excellence. The recorded black musical object took on a highly contradictory, elusive, and irruptive status as a popular commodity, because, Gilroy argues, it was able to enter into the market place, yet still had encoded within it the sociality of antiphony and the moral imperatives of utopianism. Thus, black music, in the form of a recorded object, was able to generalize its aesthetic and political dynamics as a pedagogy which was *de facto* sensory.[29]

This then forms the basis for Gilroy's black music as modernity's counter-culture thesis, or what I am calling his political aestheticization of the blackness of black music. For him the blackness of black music has never been a fixed condition, and neither is it an open system of adaptation.

Instead, it is a highly affective site of *political education* molded in the historical experience of slavery, but issues forth images of living beyond the debilitating limits of racial distinction.

The poet and critical theorist Fred Moten shares much with Gilroy's account of black music in *The Black Atlantic*, in that Moten hears in black music the fraught and almost unfathomable historical memory of racialized brutality tied up with the radical experimentation with sound as form. The key distinction between them is that whereas Gilroy uses this scenario to map out a political aesthetic, Moten moves more assertively towards an *aesthetic ontology*, that is to say a theory of black music as both an art form and a way of being in the world. He focuses on the affective charge of the performative moment of black musical production. By paying attention to the social dimensions of its recording, Moten conceptualizes the history of black music as a sensory field which achieves the appearance of ontology but in ways which require a fundamental reorganization of philosophical aesthetics. This is not to say that Moten refuses any political concerns from this account, far from it. For him the aesthetic ontology of such charged moments of black musical production form the basis for black radicalism as a *historical ontology*.[30]

Moten's aesthetic ontology emerges from his theorization of 'the break' in performative and affective operations of black music. For him, black music functions as a propulsive diffusion which gains its energy through the metaphysics of the break. It is not so much that these two processes complement one another, but more that, for Moten, black music functions as a propulsive diffusion which is by necessity entangled with the break. In this reading, 'the break' encapsulates the effects of one of the Western world's constitutive projects: racial capitalism's capture of Africans and their violent transformation into exiled, enslaved, laboring commodities, or black people. This break was experienced by black populations as the historical condition of their existence, yet its effects were manifested across the face of Western modernity, including the economic (generation of surplus value); the philosophical (the enlightenment project of scientific knowledge and the ideology of the self); the political (establishment of state power); and the historical (the making of the 'West').

The propulsive diffusion of the break, for Moten, was formed almost immediately when black populations began to use it as the structural basis for musical performance. It is important to make clear that black music, in

Moten's view, does not represent an attempt to suture the effects of break-through propulsive diffusion, but instead rests on their indivisibility, or 'the extended movement of a specific upheaval, an ongoing irruption that anarranges every line.'[31] This movement as ongoing irruption is something he locates between Frederick Douglass' 1845 accounts of both his Aunt Hester's beating and collective slave singing in woods, and its rerecording, under new conditions, in Abbey Lincoln's vocal instrumentation on Max Roach's *We Insist! – Freedom Now Suite* (1961). Therefore, for Moten, the blackness of black music moves through what feels like the impossibility of the violent entanglement between break (the history of slavery) and propulsive diffusion (the aesthetic practices of black people) to operate as a 'strain' and 'dispossessive force.'[32]

In order to grasp this 'ongoing irruption' of the break as the ontological basis of black music, Moten concentrates on its sonic form and content, or what he calls 'phonic materiality.'[33] Within the very movement of phonic materiality, we can hear the activity of the break in the 'radically exterior aurality that disrupts and resists certain formations of [racialized] identity', whilst at the same time using propulsive diffusion to generate a sensory field Moten wants to call blackness.[34] The phonic materiality of blackness is therefore not simply internal to black music; Moten argues it is possible to track its appearance in the massive exertion of energy deployed across Western philosophy, art, and society to mute its dynamics. In short, the systematic effort to refuse black populations access to subjectivity was complemented by the philosophical excision of blackness in the form of phonic materiality.

The type of sensory richness generated by the break forms the basis for black music. In the midst of the world-historical encounter between racial capital and the African slave, there was forged the very blackness of the black (under almost totalizing pressure), and the blackness of black music (as a dispossessive force). The twinning of these fraught dynamics, according to Moten, is marked in the very activity of black music: the troubling yet compulsive operations of break and propulsive diffusion, the exertion of pressure and the animation of dispossessive force, which has been recorded to such a degree that black music has acquired 'the status of an ontological condition.'[35] What Moten goes on to call, by way of Nahum Chandler, a *paraontological force* animating the production of black music is, at its outset and by necessity, so disruptive, dispossessive, and dispersive, as to place in jeopardy both its own status as black music (thus refusing claims of racial property), and the brutal racial methods of enlightenment rationality that have sought to administer the world in its death-driven guise since the advent of enslavement and colonization.[36]

Despite the resonances between Gilroy's political aesthetic and Moten's aesthetic ontology when it comes to theorizing black music, there are significant differences in how these two thinkers have developed their ideas, especially when it comes to questions of technology and the relation between the social and the ecological. Their respective trajectories therefore have implications for my approach to the blackness of black electronic dance music.

In a number of essays and texts issued in the years since *The Black Atlantic*, Gilroy appears to have grown increasingly disillusioned with the condition of black music and attached his conception of its political aesthetics to an idea of its *moral* function. The idea of moral education he sets up becomes indivisible from both a particular historical moment in the production of black music, and the use of certain forms of audio technology. The period in question for Gilroy is the massive explosion of black popular music that ran broadly from the post-war period through to the end of the 1970s (with Bob Marley, Curtis Mayfield, and Jimi Hendrix at its apex).[37] He argues that the embeddedness of Soul, Funk, Reggae, Dub, and many more styles within the political terrains of Civil Rights, Black Power, Rastafarianism, Pan-Africanism, and Third-World Liberation was no accident. Both these political and cultural trajectories emerged from the organized activities of the black populations across the diaspora, and thus they were organically infused together, even as they entered the mainstream.

The engines of this infusion between music and politics were the technologies artists and performers were using to experiment with and expand their sonic palettes. New instruments and recording devices offered the opportunity to mold original forms of black popular music, but what was key to this practice was the retention of the social–communal imperative in the form of antiphony. Gilroy's 'electric church' found a vital means for its dissemination in the vinyl record. These commodities carried and stimulated not only new styles, but new ideological sensibilities amongst their black publics by retaining an antiphonal structure:

My experience with these objects is part of living through the final commodifica-
tion of the extraordinary cultural creativity born from the slave populations of the
New World. I have watched their oppositional imaginings first colonized and then
vanquished by the levelling values of the market that was once, but is no longer,
stimulated by commerce in live human beings. Any lingering countervalues are
seen today as a pseudo-transgressive adjunct to the official business of selling all
sorts of things: shoes, clothes, perfume, sugared drinks. In a sense, the black ver-
nacular cultures of the late-twentieth century were the death rattle of a dissident
counterpower rooted, not so long ago, in the marginal modernity of racial slavery
from which it had a conspicuous exit velocity. For a spell, plastic discs stuck with
colored paper – 'records' – furnished unlikely and unanticipated vectors for a restless, travelling sensibility. They became part of outer-national culture-making,
and their history extends arguments about the role of communicative technologies in augmenting and mediating forms of social and political solidarity beyond
the imagined communities achieved via the almost magical agencies of print and
cartography.[38]

By the end of the 1990s, Gilroy was clearly in mourning for the loss of his
electric church. The cause of this irreconcilable loss, he asserts, has been
the advent of 'de-skilling' in black musical production and performance,
initiated by the uncritical incorporation of new digital technologies.
A dynamic he characterizes as 'the DJ or hip-hop option…employs effectively deskilled, dehumanized technologies which, along with indifference, laziness and disregard, have reduced a shocking modernist tradition
to a tame lexicon of preconstituted fragments.'[39]

The human activity seemingly dismantled through the widespread
adoption of digital audio technologies is not solely at the level of the aesthetic, but it is also social. Antiphony falls by the wayside, Gilroy argues,
when the prominent figure in the making of black music apparently
becomes the bedroom producer. The result, he argues, is the loss of political charge:

> making that music, that sound, in real time has gone out of style. If it meets at all,
> the electric church has to operate under the disabling weight of computerized
> dance music that is easily commodified and privatized so that it can afford the
> simplest of routes into the simulated ecstasy of togetherness.[40]

There are a number of problems with Gilroy's post–*Black Atlantic* thesis. Firstly, when making the claim that the adoption of digital technologies (aside from samplers, these are never specified) has *de facto* led to

the flushing out of the social aesthetics of black music, and thus precipitated its political demise, it is never clear whether Gilroy is referring to the organic intellectualism of hip-hop, the culture industry's incorporation of that same musical culture, the continuum of underground black electronic dance music shaping this book, or all of the above. Such an absence of specificity illustrates a lack of attentiveness to the particularities of some of the cutting-edge enactments of black music from the early 1980s onwards. As has been mapped out in the previous chapter the emergence of black electronic dance music as a continuum occurred in concrete social settings, shaped by shifting conditions of urbanization in the US and UK. With Chicago House, Detroit Techno, and Jungle in London, there was forged a concentrated experimentation with the sonic form of black music – via the selective repurposing of digital technologies – in communal relation to an immediate dancefloor community. These experiments could never remain local affairs, and they spread via vinyl, but equally through a myriad of complementary technologies. In this context, Gilroy's lament for the loss of the 'responsible troubadour' becomes immaterial, because as we shall see with Grime, Footwork, and even Actress, electronic music producers are not a 'priestly caste', but rigorously attuned modulators who play a heightened – but not exclusive – role in the production of a sonic ecology which then gets transposed into singular compressions of black music.

Secondly, Gilroy's insistence on a proscribed notion of black music's moral aesthetics reveals something of a temporal trap. His account of black music's ethical function has a very particular historical dimension linked to the combination of post-war black politics in Britain, Civil Rights–Black Power in the US, and Third-World Liberation. Whilst there is nothing wrong with hailing this 'problem-space', Gilroy has something of a restorationist attachment to the black music of this period.[41] In effect, Gilroy loses contact with the methodological and intellectual insistence on the 'changing shame' which propelled *The Black Atlantic*. As the likes of Stuart Hall, Kobena Mercer, Richard Iton, and Robin Kelley noted to varying degrees, with the epochal transformation in the mode of capital at the end of the 1970s, and the accompanying reorganization of labor, the state, civil society, and urban geographies, alongside the transformation of the cultural industries, the assembly of information networks and their attendant subjectivities, the terrains of both black diasporic life and black culture shifted.[42] Kodwo Eshun and Steve Goodman were able to realize that the continuum of black electronic dance music initiated by House, Techno, and Jungle through the last decades of the twentieth century molded those shifting pressures into the social production of a new sonic ecology of black music.

Alexander Weheliye's 2003 *Phonographies: Grooves in Sonic Afro-Modernity* offers a more nuanced path out of the impasse set up by Gilroy on the question of black music and digital technology. Weheliye does not see the use of digital technology as an imposition on the aesthetic, social, or political force of black music as a project compelled to decompose racial ideology. He begins from the basis that the discourses on the 'human' and technology in the West have failed to account for the processes of racialization at stake in the narratives of technological progress. Into this matrix Weheliye inserts black cultural production, not only as an original and improvised encounter with technology, but black culture as a technology of its own propagation. He argues that black popular music has been the primary mode for the realization of this dynamic.[43]

Thus, for Weheliye, the interface between black music and technology, or the fabulation of black music as a technological interface, has been the site of production for 'singular modes of (black) modernity'.[44] Specifically, he positions the sonic as the means for understanding this interface. He foregrounds the sonic in black music and/as technology because it operates as 'the principle modality in which Afro-diasporic cultures have been articulated'.[45] Furthermore, the way in which the sonic has been mediated by and becomes a site of mediation for the blackness of black music, means that sonic blackness stands as 'an unwieldy compound comprising all the discourses (black and nonblack) that imagine and circumscribe racial formation within Western modernity'.[46]

For Weheliye, the task of thinking the sonic blackness of black music requires an attentiveness to the permeability between 'the ephemerality of music (and/or the apparatus) and the materiality of audio technologies/practices (and/or music)'[47] The outcome of such a line of inquiry leads Weheliye to not only redesign Gilroy's project for a new conjuncture, but also take up a position which carries traces of Goodman and Eshun in that he argues black music as a sonic technology has allowed for intensely irruptive, open and yet cohesive experiments in the very form of blackness:

The nexus of black culture and sonic technologies tenders notions of temporality, spatiality and community unlike those that insist on linearity, progress and the like, but without renouncing these *tout court*, thus enabling black subjects to structure and sound their positionalities within and against Western modernity.[48]

With Weheliye we have a far more productive approach to the question of black music's political aesthetics and ontologies through the materiality of digital technologies. For him, there is an experimental impulse determined by the historical status occupied by black diasporans, which allows them to take up an idiosyncratic compositional and social relationship to available sonic devices, and to make use of the resulting sensory field to issue novel phonic materializations of blackness.

Moten has sought to extend the aesthetic ontology built upon the break into an account of a generalized *aesthetic sociality* engrained in black music. He sees the social operation moving through the phonic materiality of the music as an effect of the brutal political administration of black life, and thus black music becomes the holding space for an autonomous, yet open, configuration of blackness as a social structure of feeling. Such an insistence upon sociality in and as sound on Moten's part places him within the remit of Goodman's claims regarding the force of Black Atlantic Sonic Futurism as a socialization process which carries an imprint of the very environments in which it was assembled.

Moten's core argument is that there is a way in which the *legal* force used to prosecute black populations as collections of criminally deviant entities, and the *social* force operative within the communal organization of black diasporic life as a fecundity that frustrates policing, becomes an equally saturative *sonic* force in black music, one he describes as 'the animaterialisation of the fantastic in chromatic saturation'.[49] The mediation between the legal, the social, and the sonic manifests itself as something internal to the organizational form of black music, whereby the production of sound is infused with an insistent, fractured, exorbitant collectivity:

The soloist is unalone; the soloist is not (all) one....He is the Unit that is more than itself, greater than itself, stronger than itself, precisely insofar as he attends to the internal (and more than simply) phonic difference of phonic material.[50]

As Moten and his duettist Stefano Harney have made clear, such radically infused strategies which realize the operations of black social life in and as black music can be found almost anywhere across the field:

Thinking about a certain kind of song, a soul song that you might get in Curtis Mayfield or Marvin Gaye, where somethings going on, let's call it the experiment with/in the general antagonism, and then the song starts. You can hear the audience, you can hear the crowd, and then he begins to sing or music begins to start. So, the thing I'm interested in is, without calling something to order, how can you still sing?[51]

Black music as a means of compressing and remodulating this sociality into sound illuminates not so much refusal, but the absolute necessity of strategic improvisation that comes from informal composition:

So what emerges is not music in some general way, as opposed to the non-musical. What emerges is a form, out of something we call informality. The informal is not the absence of from. It's the thing that gives form. The informal is not formlessness.[52]

What we have here is a questioning of the idea that the genius is a singular source for black music. Instead, the musician, producer, performer, is an emanation of a carefully crafted informal sociality. By extension, the artist and the music generated as part of a sensory field represents a formal aesthetic proposition that has been conducted within an environment. Moten and Harney's theorization of the blackness of black music as an aesthetic ontology therefore has a strong ecological character. Not only is the artist considered to be constantly weaving in and out of a saturated sociality so that the blackness of their music (constituted using whatever technology is to hand) can never simply be considered entirely their own cultural property, but the recorded object stands as a compression device, a momentary phono-image of a ferocious and compelling production of blackness as atmosphere.

Hence, this is why 'black social life' is so crucial for Moten. The blackness of black social life, realized as black music, Moten argues, is a 'terribly beautiful open secret' ready to be distributed:

Blackness, which is to say black radicalism, is not the property of black people. All that we have (and are) is what we hold in our outstretched hands. This open collective being is blackness – (racial) difference mobilized against the racist determinations it calls into existence.[53]

Constant exposure to blackness, through the constant production of black music – in so far as it is animated by black social life – seems to be the imperative here, but Moten does strike a sobering warning note. One of the defining political problems of the racialized world, particularly in the late twentieth and early twenty-first centuries, has been the inability, or downright refusal, to attend to this open secret, to propagate this paraontological force. Such has been the power of ideologies of racial distinction and their attendant subjectivities, that they have served as enough of a block upon the distillation of the blackness of black music amongst those who, historically, have not been racialized as black. There have, of course, been innumerably potent – often underground, sometimes spectacularly public – moments when forms of black music have overpopulated the structures of racial antagonism. These have been some of the most compelling enactments of the collective dissolution of sovereignty and the displacement of surplus value, through the production of social aesthetics which rearticulate capacity. Such tarrying bursts of activity indicate the constant, evasive generativity of black social life, even when many remain deaf to its generalizing operations as black music.

Moten's theorization of the blackness of black music is more audible in the lower frequencies of *Teklife / Ghettoville / Eski* because of the ways in which it meets up with Eshun's The Futurhythmachine and Goodman's Black Atlantic Sonic Futurism. For him, the deviant, non-exclusionary improvisation of aesthetic ontology in black music (Eshun's unrecognizability thesis), needs to be framed through the settings of its production as an ecology (or what Goodman calls the relation between vibes and vibrations). The departure from Gilroy lies in the fact that Moten's aesthetic ontology is aesthetically open, it does not have the same historical baggage weighing it down, and thus it is not limited to specific technologies. What will become evident when we consider Grime, Footwork and Actress is that the music is a production of the saturated atmospheres of black social life and it seeks to technologically transform those atmospheres into aesthetic ontologies of blackness which function as sonic ecologies. Such is the inventive force of its soundscapes that these early twenty-first-century forms of black electronic dance music generate an artificial phonic materiality of blackness which socializes populations as part of the reorganization of desire.

Blackness, Geographies, Ecologies

At a conceptual level, I have secured the basis for thinking the blackness of black electronic dance music along ecological lines through the discourse on black music. However, more work needs to be done to tighten the relation between blackness and the ecological in its relation to the urban, as the production of black electronic dance music is intertwined with the concrete forms of an environment. Recently within Black Studies there have been moves to think along these lines, particularly with regards to the lived atmospheres of black social life and its operations within urban settings.

Katherine McKittrick's work on blackness and the geographical constructs a relation between the historical institution of racial enslavement and the contemporary racialization of the urban. McKittrick is not concerned with assembling strict teleologies from the seventeenth century to the present, but rather her focus is on mapping structural intimacies and generative possibilities between these spatial methods of arranging black diasporic life.

Beginning with 'the geographical mechanics of the plantation economy'[54] McKittrick argues that if the plantation generated the wealth which materialized the metropolis in the Global North during the period of slavery's greatest intensity, then the persistence of racial governance as the dominant feature of Western modernity, indicates the continued presence of plantation residues in the contemporary city.[55] Her notion of plantation residues in the urban is not organized around an idea that the planation was a totalizing zone of black debilitation. First and foremost, for McKittrick, the plantation needs to be understood as the site where collective black behaviors, aesthetic practices, and social arrangements were improvised in ways which actively antagonized – through their sensory 'incoherence' – the dominating spatial force of the plantation. Using this sense of entanglement whereby black life operates within and against zones designed to orchestrate black death, McKittrick turns to the 'seemingly natural links between blackness, underdevelopment, poverty and place'[56] in the contemporary city, a dynamic she identifies as 'urbicide.'[57] McKittrick, though, poses a question of urbicide, particularly with regards to the positing of its apparent structural indivisibility with black social life:

If some places are rendered lifeless in the broader geographic imagination, what of those inhabiting lifelessness? And what of the worldview of those who occupy the wretched category – is this worldview also lifeless because the geographies surrounding the marginalized are rendered dead?[58]

Addressing such a question requires a refusal to accept the direct correlations between conceptualizations of ontologically dead black space and ontologically dead black people. Instead, McKittrick is interested in an analytical shift that does not involve stopping at the 'the suffering / violated black body' but moves through to a 'black sense of place'.[59] The intention here is not to forget the particularity of black suffering, but rather it is to tap into the long plantation history of a zonal, fleshy sociality which allowed captive Africans to 'bring forth a poetics'.[60] If the plantation is the structural basis for urbicide, then McKittrick believes a parallel, fleshy atmosphere is being produced in the toxicity of its zonal equivalents in the city.

This is precisely where Moten and Harney have situated their work on the roving site of inhabitation they call 'undercommons'. To describe 'undercommons' as an object or even a concept is to mistake their use of the term. Undercommons operates as a placeholder for a way of considering all social activity as 'thought', no matter how ephemeral or spectacular. The closest Harney and Moten come to defining the contours of undercommons is by saying it is bound in a vexed relationship to 'the general antagonism'.[61] The general antagonism can be understood as the affective, institutional, and organizational dynamics of racial capitalism as they shape officially sanctioned publics. Undercommons is an ongoing experiment internal to the general antagonism and is thus the locus for the 'riotous production of difference' within it.[62] In terms of how this permanent riot is initiated, it is through forms of social practice Harney and Moten call 'study'. Study is their way of marking the constant production of thought in the undercommons, the common intellectual activity that takes place through any form of co-ordinated social action. Therefore, understood together, the undercommons is an atmosphere whereby the incessant activity of the social – study – takes place. Such is the seeming ubiquity of study that it rarely appears within the operations of the general antagonism, and when it does it is regularly diagnosed as a lack of productivity, solipsism, deviance, sullenness, an absence of affect, indifference, or even uncontrollable violence.

It is in the undercommons where black social life comes into play, because within the regimes of capital operative in the Global North, it is the blackened, the impoverished, the stateless, those in flight, who seem to reside within it. Harney and Moten intentionally make use of the paraontological distinction between blackness and black people in order to open up the (under)privilege of blackness as a force amongst those who experience capital as sustained violence. They do this because they believe that what is forged in the undercommon socialities of these temporary holding spaces are fugitive publics built on mutual indebtedness:

They [fugitive publics] are planned when they are least expected, planned when they don't follow the process, planned when they escape policy, evade governance, forget themselves, remember themselves, have no need of being forgiven. They are not wrong, though they are not, finally communities: they are debtors at a distance, bad debtors, forgotten but never forgiven.[63]

The crafting of undercommons as fugitive publics within the midst of a brutally administered world generates a number of contesting affects. For those looking into undercommons from the outside (i.e. from the administered zones of civil society), all they can see is a concentration of pathologies, which represent a demand for correction and an opportunity for the extraction of value. Although this external threat is always present and acknowledged amongst those studying undercommons into existence, there are far more important things that require care and attention:

We saw it in a step yesterday, some hips, a smile, the way a hand moved. We heard it in a break, a cut, a lilt, the way the words leapt. We felt it in the way someone saves the best stuff just to give it to you and then it's gone, given, a debt.[64]

The preference shown here for this type sociality can easily be dismissed as frivolous and even anti-political, but for Harney and Moten that is precisely the point. For them, the only meaningful deviation from the seeming totality of racial capital has been gestated in the long history of material ephemera that makes the blackness of undercommons.[65]

The task for Harney and Moten is not then about resistance to power, but to read undercommons as nebulous practice is to miss the point, because they do assert a clear desire 'to gather together another city right here, right now'.[66] It is more a case of grasping how the very realization of this other city is already taking place. Undercommons, therefore, is not about the material form of the city, which for them is always temporary, but the persistent blackness of a 'real assembly...the gathering of things in the flesh.'[67] In counterpoint to the strategic impoverishment of local resources, or the managed decline of unfit housing stock, there is 'another ecology':

for an architecture of what people outside architecture, outside the house and the city, outside citizenship and subjectivity, outside settlement and sovereignty, do to all of these by living; for an architecture set up to receive aninstrumental, anarchitectural doing, thinging, thinking; for a communal, anarchic, textural environment that is ecological, social and personal.[68]

The urbanist AbdouMaliq Simone, takes up this notion of undercommons as an architectural ecology forged through the very social lives of those who generate it. Yet Simone is seeking a more systematic account of what this might mean when it comes to understanding the contemporary urban environment. His starting point is the latest version of the metropolis under the current conditions of racialized capital. For him, due to what is now an irrecoverable shift towards the abstractions of high finance, the city has been remolded to accommodate these changes.[69]

One of the major impacts of the environmental shift to 'algorithmic governance' is an increase in 'concrete forms of immunization', such as gated communities, privately owned securitized public space, and generic exclusive high-rise accommodation.[70] What this has led to is the formation of a new citizenry, an 'individual urban subject' for whom the city is being redesigned in order to aid their movement, leisure, and inhabitation.[71] For residents who occupied large portions of the city in its earlier economic form, an apparent choice is offered. Either be 'seamlessly folded into homogenized middle class forms of inhabitation', or live in an altered state of precarity, never fully showing up in the city, but permeated into it as a squeezed periphery.[72]

The customary way to read this scenario is to call for principled political opposition, but, using undercommons as a methodological imperative, Simone conceives of the current systems of urban management as counterintuitively useful, in that they work against their own grain to illuminate a set of barely acknowledged urban resources. The resources he refers to can be located through the lenses of *study*. Simone argues that within the contemporary conjuncture there are increasingly productive and precocious qualities apparent in improvised urban life across a number of settings, that signal a new animation of blackness, even if these types of improvisation are not necessarily conducted in areas or by groups of people biopolitically identified as black. Referring specifically to instances in cities such as Jakarta and Yangon, Simone argues that whilst 'there is nothing within any concept of blackness that could draw any sensible explanatory lines between these occurrences' there is something apparent in each that brings questions of race, class, violence, and vulnerability to the fore.[73]

Simone's position is that the patterns are so resonant that they constitute a 'we', a 'we' he wants to refer to as blackness. He is seeking to both retain and repopulate the heading 'blackness' because he believes the historical constitution of certain styles of urban life as 'black' has contained within it the codes of its own generalizability. The blackened 'we' Simone believes is present, if unaccounted for, in the everyday periphery of the city. This 'we' is 'always fuzzy, shaky, hard to pin down, always broken, but also resounding/resonating' and is forged through 'the entanglement of emptiness and seemingly never-ending sedimentation'.[74] It is important to signal here that Simone is not calling for a deracialized emptying out of blackness. Instead his intention is to expose how, when realized as urbanism, blackness is the only adequate means for disturbing the negating effects of racialized capitalism:

Retaining a notion of blackness is thus important as a vehicle for circulating through the scattered remains and temporary resurrections of new forms of racial feeling and action. It is perhaps the most readily available means for creatively re-imagining the 'restlessness' of racial materials. In other words, if racial identity is maintained by finding ways to detract attention from it, to do the work of race without relying on it, then blackness becomes a tool that potentially draws lines of connection between these scattered instances and maneuvers.[75]

Critical of the 'right to the city' discourse due to the trap of 'the very rationalities of private property long instituted in liberal economics', instead for Simone undercommons serves to negate such processes through 'collective acts of indifference' and the generalized deployment of opacity.[76] According to him, 'experimentation on the part of the expendable may have to look as if nothing is being experimented with'.[77] What is made in the enactment of blackness as undercommon sociality are types of autonomous self-organization and 'the commitment to make something without clear maps or certainties' in the form of culture.[78] Like Moten and Harney, he is not making the case for undercommons as formless. Speaking to the historically specific ways in which black urban life was impacted by the sudden, state-sanctioned shift from post-industrialism to finance capitalism, he sees in its aftermath an undercommon aesthetic built upon a crafting of the informal:

And so blackness has learned to live in the implosion of old orders grinding to a halt, or being the example that teaches a populace how to watch what happens when a portion of its citizenry is unmoored from the basic supports of life. It has learned to live with incessant transience, quickly deciding how to recoup opportunity from sudden detours and foreclosures. It has learned to mine the city for beats and polyphony that reverberate across generations and nations, so as to attune bodies to each other from Rio to New Orleans to Luanda.[79]

The echo of Goodman here is notable ('when no stability persists, rhythmic decisions still get made, collectivities mobilized'). In fact, taken together McKittrick, Harney, Moten, and Simone provide the basis for theorizing blackness as territorially encoded atmosphere in ways which complement Goodman's account of black electronic dance music as an ecological style of urban experimentation. With all of these thinkers it is not simply that fragments of life persist in the face of the desolation of urbicide. The blackness of undercommons exposes how sociality detached from the civil and the political has always carried far greater capacity for invention (combined with higher exposure to risk) than capital's ability to contain it. Encompassing the plantation and the algorithmically governed city, their configuration of an atmospheric and architectural blackness that moves through the entanglement of the social and the sensory, is critical to the encounters with Actress, Grime, and Footwork that follow. Conceiving of the aesthetics of these musical projects as instances of intellectuality which are ecological requires us to consider the question of their blackness beyond any sense of its individuation. That this occurs through the production of the social is no coincidence.

Over the preceding pages I have sought to establish a theoretical basis engaged with selected genealogies of thought. These are not hardened positions though (as will be evidenced by the return to Gilroy in the 'Eski' chapter). Still it is important to stress that we shall seek to use black electronic dance music as a continuum, and Actress, Grime, and Footwork especially, to develop a series of claims about experiments in blackness in the early twenty-first century. Since its inception via Chicago House, Detroit Techno, and Jungle in London, almost any instance of sonic composition across this continuum has contained within it the social conditions of black social life within a given urban environment in the Global North, and speculated on those conditions with such intensity that its material form no longer adheres to what can commonly be considered music, but operates as a self-sustaining diasporic ecological system.

The undercommon autonomy that allows socialities and environments to become embedded in the aesthetic form of the music, via its technological mediation, appears as culture in the city with such force, that it has, at moments, opened up cracks in the psychic, political, and economic management of the urban. Within these concrete wounds, black electronic dance music, since the late twentieth century, has sonically potentialized in real time numerous alternative urban ecological systems that have sought to build a set of conditions which would permit them to flourish.

My argument is that, as styles that appeared in this continuum at the turn of the twenty-first century in the Global North, Footwork, Grime and the music of Actress contain within them the phono-material codes for the expansion of undercommon projects which could have overpopulated their respective algorithmically governed cities. For some observers, the South side of Chicago might be a temporary holding cell for a black populace before their inevitable entry into the prison or the casket, but the ferocious choreography of sound and gesture pouring forth from the Teklife crew tells us Footwork constitutes another city awaiting divination. When Actress walks with those who are deemed to be poor in their South London Ghettoville, he fuses together the pieces for a soundscape which might be heard as dystopic, but is really a wealthy world because of its indebtedness. Grime, in its unavoidable encounter with the regime of racial policing that is the colonial metropole, exploded the pathological logics which apparently predetermined the people who made the music, the East London neighborhoods they lived in, and its broadcast technologies.

Our task is to channel the roughened and incisive edges of these respective black music forms, in order to grasp something of the mineral interior of each instance, and to make the case across all three for an ecological grammar of blackness as a sensory intuition for thinking the black social life of cities in the Global North under the most recent conjuncture of racial capitalism.

Part 2

3

Teklife

Is there a distinction to be made between urban dereliction and social overabundance? Indeed, can waste ground be built upon? Are the types of movements (rhythm) and movements (limbs) generated through the manipulation of urban pressure ecological, or even architectural?

These questions form an entry point into Footwork, a Chicago sound that retraces its origins to the 1990s but has truly reordered the field of electronic music in the last decade. Our focus is on the status of Footwork as black music made within conditions of urban racialization that are often given the short-hand 'ghetto'. This is to say that the nature of the relation between the spatial dynamics of race–class and the aesthetic category of blackness, in so far as it can be understood to inform the phonic materiality of the music, lies at the heart of what I shall present.

Produced within the economically precarious neighborhoods of South and West Chicago, Footwork marked its entry into official dance music culture with the 2010 release of the compilation album *Bangs & Works Vol 1* by UK music label Planet Mu. It can be placed within the thirty-year continuum of black electronic dance music production in the city, which began with the formation of House. Yet specific characteristics mark it out as possibly Chicago's most innovative manifestation, and certainly amongst the most irruptive over the last decade in the field of electronic music. Footwork, as a dance music form, is defined by two dominant features: its complex arrangement of rhythmic textures at a rate of propulsion that on initial exposure seem to place the music at the limits of the listenable; and the intense speeds of gesture dancers employ when conducting competitive battles orchestrated by this music across the city's South and West sides.

It is this relation – between the precision and ferocity of its sonic palette and the precision and ferocity of the dancer's movements – that will guide my theorization of Footwork. This relation, however, cannot be understood in isolation as pure performance. In order to think Footwork's status as black music – while grappling with the question of race and 'ghettoization' – the relation between the sound and the performativity of Footwork also needs to be situated in terms of the historical production of lived experience *internal* to Chicago's South and West sides, the built environments of these territories, and the *external* production of knowledge about the terrain and the people who occupy it. It is only by tracking the movements back and forth across these elements – which could be understood as encompassing the social, the sonic, the performative, the architectural, and the pathological – that we can begin to grasp the totality of Footwork's soundscape. Its phonic materiality has been theorized by Footwork artists via the formulation, *Tek*. They self-identify as *Ghettoteknitianz*, they declare themselves to be *Architeks*, and they conceive of their social relations as generative of *Teklife*. Such a method of neologic production by its very practitioners places our task of thinking Footwork under pressure from the start. The constant appearance of *Tek* across the landscape of Footwork troubles and dislocates any simple attempt to filter the music through a logic of urbicide. Instead, what we have here is the improvisatory manufacturing of sonic ecology, a restless *architekture*, assembled through the dimensions of dance and rhythm, race and class.

My aim is to detail these dimensions in four successive sections, each building on the previous. The first three address, respectively, the phenomenon of Footwork, the rendering of the 'Chicago ghetto' as a racialized sociological object of knowledge, and conceptual accounts of the aesthetic sociality of blackness as a territorial formation. This will culminate in a synthesis of all the preceding material into the various realizations of *Tek*, where I make the case that the blackness of Footwork requires us to remain attentive to the way its socially experimental ferocity is also ecological.

Footwork

Footwork is the latest iteration within a longer matrix of electronic music production in Chicago that was mapped out in the introduction.

As a reminder, the city's production of what is now considered Chicago House was determined by a willingness already in the 1980s to experiment with new mass-market audio technologies in search of fresh sonic effects, combined with the competitive drive to gain an edge in satisfying the dancefloor gathering in the proliferation of clubs containing purpose-built soundsystems. As classic Chicago House sound gained international exposure, generating localized hybrids in London and Manchester and garnering attention from major labels, the activity of the first wave within the city eventually came to a halt. Due to a combination of increased legal difficulties maintaining venues and the collapse of sympathetic local radio stations, on the ground the scene became stagnant whilst DJs maintained careers through bookings abroad.[1] Ghetto House was formed in the 1990s as the first wave lost contact with Chicago's South and West sides. Through the continued experimentation with new audio technologies, Ghetto House saw the extension of the 'jackin' rhythms that had been prevalent in Chicago House. The distinction between Ghetto House and the original Chicago sound came in the former's relationship to the world beyond its immediate environment. As evidenced through the Dance Mania label, the sound became increasingly harsh, with a tendency to remove most extraneous elements aside from drum machines and intense, clipped vocal snippets. Again this came about as a combined result of the relations between innovations in production, the acutely local geography within which the music was being disseminated, and the demands of the audience.[2] Juke was an intensification of Ghetto House palettes during the mid-1990s. Whilst the etymology of the term 'Juke' is not clear, what its initial producers such as DJ Gant Man and DJ Slugo did was to increase the tempo and push the eroticism that were already the dominant traits of Ghetto House.[3]

Footwork, as Chicago's latest black electronic dance music, can be located within this matrix and is its boldest manifestation of a thirty-year trajectory. It is unique because it was designed to meet the needs of a particular constituency: dance crews. Although battles between dance crews had been a feature of Juke, by the late 1990s and early 2000s it had largely turned itself into music made for clubs. Footwork was engineered for the demands of dance crews who wanted to battle each other with their feet outside the setting of the club dancefloor. Thus, the significance of Footwork lies in how the exchange between dancers and producers has driven the rates of innovation in terms of its sonic, performative, and social materiality.

Dave Quam, perhaps the leading Chicago documenter of the style, writes of Footwork as a 'faster, uglier and even more hyperlocal' mutation of Juke.[4] It is often understood in terms of its beats per minute ratio, the most common means of determining stylistic differences in electronic music. Nominally operating at 160 beats per minute, or BPM, Footwork is often considered to provide an exacting aural experience. BPM rate, in and of itself, is not the most significant factor in shaping the sound of Footwork and it might not, in fact, even be accurate to think about this style in terms of tempo alone.

R.P. Boo, DJ Clent, and Traxman were amongst the first to assemble Footwork specifically for dance battles. Tracks such as '3rd Wurle' and 'Baby Come On' introduced 'scattered triplets and pulsating bass' which 'expanded the palettes' in South and West Chicago.[5] The resulting early Footwork sound was defined by a scrambled combination of 'roaring sub-bass, minced vocal samples and knife-like claps.'[6] Retaining Chicago dance music's eclecticism synthesized into a tight blend, Footwork operates not only at the extremes of high-end scatter and low-end pulse, but in the degrees of differentiations between those points. It was with DJ Rashad and DJ Spinn that the sound came into its own. '2020' and 'Teknitian' marked them as adept engineers of the key Footwork signatures: 'spell binding call and response vocal loops, primordial synth spasms, and syncopated bass and drum-machine patterns.'[7] Introducing a series of unfamiliar bass configurations, Rashad and Spinn attuned themselves to the manipulative capacities of dancers.

Built for battles between crews, it is important to gain some sense of how these events are organized in Chicago's South and West sides. *I'm Tryna Tell Ya*, a 2014 film made by 'Tim and Barry,' founders of the London-based independent electronic music broadcast platform 'Don't Watch That TV,' is amongst the first and most comprehensive depictions of Footwork.[8] Following the core members of the Ghetteteknitianz and Teklife crews, the filmmakers gained unprecedented levels of access to the scene. The film provides a platform for those embedded in the making of Footwork to present their accounts of its genealogy and dynamics.

A thematic feature built into *I'm Tryna Tell Ya* is that of the forces at work between dancers and producers. Footwork, the interviewees seem to be saying, can only be understood as a set of techniques that are generated *in social relation*.

Defined as an errant strain of Juke's club dynamics, Footwork battles can take place in almost any setting across Chicago's South and West sides, 'a sweaty vacant warehouse, a school gymnasium, a rec center, a house party or an El train platform'.[9] Given titles such as 'Da War Zone' and 'Battle Groundz', battles move across the terrain under duress from the law and due to complicated relationships with those who hold access to municipal buildings. On any given battle two crews will assemble, along with a crowd and a DJ, to compete, with the stakes being reputation, money, or both. The crowd forms a circle, with the two teams facing each other. Individual members take turns to step in and do battle whilst the DJ sets the terms. What makes Footwork battles compelling is the range of furious movements of feet and legs that the dancers produce and demand from each other (See Figure 1).

The important thing to note is the way Footwork dancers produce frenzy by way of an intensification of technique. This is not an aimless flailing of limbs (to the extent that any movement is aimless) in response to music that appears to be moving too fast for anyone to dance to. Instead, it is the honed manipulation of movement within a soundscape produced by high-end scatter, low-end pulse, and warped vocals:

Dancers make up their own routines on the floor, with their shuffling feet following the lower frequencies and their bodies popping to the claps. A good footwork

Figure 1 Dancers from Havoc (left) and Below Zero (right) compete at Battle Groundz.
Source: www.youtube.com/watch?v=_brqdx7kWqQ, accessed 10th August 2019.

routine, full of 'soul trains', 'pochanotases' and 'ghosts' will have symmetry – the patterns that happen on the left side are followed through on the right – and gimmicks are frowned upon.[10]

These choreographed movements are known as 'basics' amongst dancers. For someone like A.G. of the Legends Clique crew, they are the grounding elements anyone must master before developing the sorts of variations that comprise an individual style.[11] These 'basics' can then be arranged into a series of 'combos' which, as Que (also of Legends Clique) makes clear, can produce an illusory effect to the uninitiated:

Combos will be like putting 'erks' with 'dribbles' going to a 'cross'. Then just keep going rapid Footwork. You know what I'm saying? Just straight combos after another. No stopping. You know what I mean? No pausing. It don't look like you thinking. You just going straight through them. Boom, boom, boom. But it's all neat though.[12]

The sustainment of symmetry of this type by dancers, within the setting of the battle circle, where the DJ is playing increasingly intense off-kilter rhythms, is not an accident. Instead it is in the very encounter between dancers and DJs/producers that what we understand as Footwork is generated. This is self-evident to all participants within the scene in Chicago. In *I'm Tryna Tell Ya*, DJ Rashad describes how in the transitions from House, to Ghetto House, to Juke, and eventually to Footwork, the final phase was the outcome of pressure placed upon producers by dancers for more and more complex rhythmic patterns.[13]

There are many who ascribe Rashad's and DJ Spinn's adeptness as track builders to their past experience as dancers. Both began with the House-O-Matics and Wolf Pack crews, and for Rashad the maintenance of these connections is a necessity to the extent that he often has dancers in the room when producing tracks. Whereas Rashad and Spinn use their knowledge as former dancers, it is DJ Manny who actively keeps the distinction open. Refusing to give up on his dedication to both roles, Manny is not only known for stepping out from behind the decks to battle, but he describes the immediacy of dancing to his method of sonic production: 'When I sit there [building tracks], and stop and just do something with my feet.'[14]

The type of permeability Manny occupies is encapsulated by the axiom of Hot (another Legend's Clique dancer): 'You can't do one without the other'[15] The material presented so far points to a vital feature of Footwork's dynamics: namely that its status as music is as much generated through the movements of dancers as it is by its sonic elements. What I mean by this is that the very materiality of this phenomenon rests not in a reification of sound in and of itself, but in an understanding of phonic materiality that is indivisible from gesture. Stepping back slightly from the specificity of Footwork, Imani Kai Johnson's description of the 'aural-kinesthetics' of 'social dancing' is crucial to thinking these relations between body movement and sound.[16] This is especially the case when, for Johnson, the notion that 'the volume has volume' helps us to grasp the way aural-kinesthetics are involved in the production of social dance environments.[17] Pushing this even further is Naomi Bragin's discussion of 'black hood dance':

a conceptual framework for studying dance as a sensory-kinaesthetic modality through which the logic of racial blackness – and the imagination of a form of black power – remains operative.[18]

Seeking to nullify discourses which have rendered black hood dance 'non-technical, spontaneous, disorganized, intuitive, raw, in crisis', Bragin conceives of it is a 'mode of black thought and sociality' that is an objective reflection of the lived experience of race and class in urban America.[19]

Footwork, then, is held in the relation between the way the arrangement of 'basics' into 'combos' animates the engineering of beats, and the imprints of those movements producers carry in their nervous systems. It is an instance of what composer, trombonist, and historian George Lewis has called 'the improvisation of distributed intelligence' that has determined various instances of black diasporic musical production.[20] Thus, when discussing Footwork it is critical that we avoid focusing solely on a set of core objects (tracks and dance battle videos) as self-contained markers of individual virtuosity. Instead, I am approaching Footwork as a concentrated ensemble of sonic, gestural, social, economic, and geographic relations that are rendered through the production of a phonic materiality which is then demarcated as black music. The notion that the phonic materiality of Footwork can be both ruptural and distributive necessitates that we take on an alternative grasp of experimentation. It is one that requires a partial dissolution of the convention of the individual genius as central to musical production. We are not refusing the agency of Footwork producers and dancers, but rather opening up the form of the question of agency as one animated by the experimentation taking place *between* them, in so far as their expressive actions are understood to be productive of a sonic ecology generated through the atmospheres of black social life in Chicago's South and West sides. My intention is to study sonic and performative gestures as tempo-spatial renderings of all the relations that pressurize and sustain Footwork as black music. Footwork has no single source. It is a phono-ecological fabrication emerging from the social atmospheres internal to Chicago's South and West sides.

I introduced the notion of fabricating a sonic ecology by way of social atmospheres in the previous chapter by evoking Goodman's account of vibes and vibrations. Examined in closer detail, his account of 'vibe' offers a means for thinking the relation between 'the patterned physicality of a musical beat or pulse' and the material dimensions of the urban terrain in which the music is generated.[21] The digital sound design that goes into the production of electronic music, Goodman argues, involves a form of molecular rhythmic conduction that generates a 'microsonic turbulence' within an environment which is fundamental to its aesthetics.[22] In the case of a given musical style and its constituency, this means it coheres according to 'a mathematical set of instructions of how rhythm and frequencies, its *vibe* should be organized.'[23] Goodman is therefore clear in stating that 'vibe' is not simply determined in the mind of the producer building the track and then passed out into the world. The 'mathematics' at stake here are atmospheric and ecological. They are engineered through a number of relations, which operate across different dimensions and coalesce around the vibe of the music scene in question. These dimensions include the encounters between dancers attracted to a style and the way their movements animate sonic experimentation from DJs, who in turn generate new gestures from the participants. Then there is the physical and social organization of the immediate space in which these exchanges take place, whether it is the club, street, or warehouse. This activity is further determined by the wider material and psychic histories of the urban geography in which the scene is concentrated. This is how the 'vibe' of an electronic music style comes to be a sonic characteristic of a set of social relations in a given place.

With this in mind, what can be said about the vibe of Footwork? Its vibe is not solely held in the relations between dancers and producers, but that relation also generates and holds the battle circle itself. As the socially engineered platform for Footwork, the battle circle traverses and repurposes the terrain of Chicago's South and West sides precisely because of the constant experimentation taking place between its participants. The battle circle is a container for a generalized intelligence which transforms lived experience and geography into the contestation between gestures and sounds.

Yet such an understanding of vibe does not take us quite far enough. There are two additional, and critically important, dimensions that need to be addressed before we can begin to grasp the dynamics of Footwork. The first centers on the way these zones of Chicago's South and West sides have been intensely racialized by external systems of knowledge production and governance as part of their construction as 'ghettos'. The second is the fact that Footwork draws upon and adapts local histories of black electronic dance music production, thus situating it within a larger continuum of black music. It is these dimensions, one configured through a drive to aggressively pathologize, and the other shaped by the proliferation of aesthetic and social experiments, that need to be considered in relation to the vibe of Footwork. It is the former that we shall address in the following section: the discursive production of the 'Chicago ghetto' as a racialized object of knowledge.

The 'Chicago Ghetto'

The process of locating Footwork within Chicago's South and West sides requires us to recognize the ways in which these areas of the city have been constructed as racialized environments commonly referred to as 'ghettos'. One of the sources for this form of knowledge production has been the field of American urban sociology. Concentrated areas of black inhabitation in Chicago have been employed as a 'laboratory' by its practitioners for a set of debates about the precise definition of ghettos and their racial status.[24] The purpose of turning to urban sociology is not to apply it in order to 'read' Footwork as black music made in Chicago's South and West sides. Instead, my aim is to point to a number of problems that occupy the sociological imagination in its attempts to research these areas of the city as templates for a general theory of ghettoization. Footwork operates in discordant relation to this type of knowledge production as both its unacknowledged driving force and unwitting distortion.

A great deal of energy has been expended in the debates on the precise social scientific definition of a ghetto in North America. Chicago's South and West sides have often functioned as a template for these debates, largely due to the historical dominance of the Chicago School of Urban Sociology.[25] What seems to have occurred in the course of this scholarly activity is the continual reconstruction of the ghetto as an object of research, through the manifestation of Chicago's zones of concentrated black inhabitation as an exemplary case. Alexander Weheliye has noted this as a general problem that can affect studies of black diasporic life. The distinctions between lived experience, research objects (both figured through the category 'black people') and the production of knowledge ('blackness') often get conflated.[26] This is certainly the case with debates that take place in urban sociology concerning the correct scientific definition of a ghetto.[27] Weheliye's argument suggests that ethnographic fieldwork, in its use of South and West Chicago as an ur-object for ghettoization, enacts conflations that allow for the production of a limited account of black social life. These conflations, it seems, place urban sociology in discordant relation to the forces of social experimentation operating under the heading of Footwork.

Having made such claims about urban sociology, I begin by turning to a classic study of black life in Chicago from within this field, albeit one that maintains a productive relation to lived experience, object, and knowledge. Horace R. Cayton and St Clair Drake's 1946 *Black Metropolis: A Study of Negro Life in a Northern City* was the first sustained analysis of Chicago's 'Black Belt' and arguably sits alongside W.E.B. Du Bois' *Philadelphia Negro* as foundational to establishing black urban life in the North in the consciousness of American researchers. Although Cayton and Drake open with an examination of the structural basis for the existence of the 'Black Belt' of the 1940s, the text is notable because they do not restrict themselves to this method of analysis alone.

What they do say about the institutional foundation for the Black Belt in Chicago is that it lay in two overdetermining factors: a) the restrictions placed upon the expansion of the territory which constituted the Black Belt, and b) the restrictions placed upon the free movement of black populations into the world beyond the Black Belt's borders. The inability of the territory to expand or the people within it to move emerged from a combination of formal and informal regulatory measures. These included prohibitive rent covenants, laws passed against selling property to prospective black homeowners in bordering white areas, and overt racial violence. The results of an expanding black population within constricted space were inevitable.

Drake and Cayton were interested in the misapplication of the conditions which set the basis for the Black Belt, and the effects those conditions produced. Racialized logic allowed a perception of the environment as one in decay to get applied to the social standing of the population within it. This only seemed to justify the increased regulation of movement and territory through the tightening of what Drake and Cayton called the 'cordon sanitaire'.[28] Designed to protect the rest of the city from the supposedly noxious effects of the Black Belt, the result was that the very blackness of the population – their 'badge of color' – stood in for the perceived blackness of their environment:

As it becomes increasingly crowded – and 'blighted' – Black Metropolis' reputation becomes ever more unsavory. The city assumes that *any* Negro who moves *anywhere* will become a focal point for another little Black Belt with a similar reputation. To allow the Black Belt to disintegrate would scatter the Negro population. To allow it to expand will tread on the toes of vested interests, large and small, in the contiguous areas.[29]

The Black Belt was therefore fixed in a regulatory bind. It could not be dismantled, neither could its expansion be permitted. The generative threat of decay simply needed to be contained.

To repeat, these territorial – and by extension categorical – constraints were not the only means of studying the Black Belt for Drake and Cayton. *Black Metropolis* was also a study of inhabitation and the sociality it produced. They were concerned with not only the racist functions of the cordon sanitaire, but also the feelings (as opposed to behaviors) generated by living within what were considered to be a set of debilitating restrictions. This was announced by their adoption of the name those who inhabited the Black Belt gave their home:

Throughout the remainder of this book we shall use the term 'Bronzeville' for Black Metropolis because it seems to express the feeling that the people have about their community. They *live* in the Black Belt, and to them it is more than the 'ghetto' revealed by statistical analysis.[30]

The shift in analysis is notable in that it allowed Drake and Cayton to produce portraits of the 'areas of life' which constituted Bronzeville. These included 'Stayin Alive', 'Praising God', 'Getting Ahead', and 'Advancing the Race'.[31] It was in their description of 'Having a Good Time' that Drake and Cayton began to open up what it meant to live within the cordon sanitaire:

Bronzeville's people have never let poverty, disease and discrimination 'get them down'. The vigor with which they enjoy life seems to belie the gloomy observations of the statisticians and civic leaders who have the facts about the Black Ghetto.[32]

The image of vigorous enjoyment points to an analytical tension between understanding the structural basis for the Black Belt and the styles of inhabitation that made Bronzeville. The tension, according to Drake and Cayton, sheds some light on how 'Negroes live in two worlds'.[33]

Despite the historical distance from the Chicago landscape in which Footwork operates, Drake and Cayton's 1946 study is instructive. They maintain the degrees of differentiation between the structural basis for the existence of an urban zone referred to as a 'ghetto' and the black social life at work within what are deemed to be its confines. Their research exacerbates this flux, thus rendering this urban zone a troublesome as a piece of social scientific evidence. What remains in the intervals is a complexity regarding the question of whether the blackness of Chicago's South side is the outcome of external regulative factors or a set of internal generative capacities independent of those factors.

Written in an historical conjuncture more resonant with Footwork, the scholarship of Loic Wacquant, whilst remaining somewhat attentive to the disjunctures between object, research, and knowledge, closes these intervals at crucial moments. Wacquant's importance as a sociologist of black social life in Chicago from the mid-1990s onwards came in his conceptualization of the 'hyperghetto'.[34] The 'hyperghetto' concept not only announced a shift in the sociological response to black social life, but marked how Wacquant's own relationship to his object of study altered over the course of a decade. The hyperghetto was defined in relation to what Wacquant called the communal ghetto of 1960s Black America.

Whereas the communal ghetto had been 'compact, sharply bonded and comprising a full complement of black classes', the 1990s hyperghetto was defined by 'massive depopulation and deproletarianization'.[35] Those left inhabiting this relatively empty zone were 'characterized by behavioral deficiency and cultural deviance'.[36]

Rather than loosening regulative binds, Wacquant argued the depopulation producing the hyperghetto intensified the logics of restraint and control. He ascribes this to a series of misapplications which allowed for the discursive construction of an 'underclass' concept. The underclass concept was used to single out certain social groups as distinct from civil society due to the supposed desolation of their lives. The underclass could only ever be found in the hyperghetto, and were thus able to be racialized without an overt appeal to race logic. By extension the perceived desolation of the population once again became a factor in an analysis of the environment:

a repository of concentrated unruliness, deviance, anomie and atomization, replete with behaviors said to offend common precepts of morality and propriety, whether by excess (as with crime, sexuality, fertility) or by default (in the case of work, thrift and family).[37]

What this diagnosis justified was the further tightening of Drake and Cayton's cordon sanitaire. Over fifty years later the intensification of control took on different characteristics. As Wacquant notes the hyperghetto was defined by depopulation and deproletarianization, so it was no longer the expansion of territory or movement of people that was the focus of regulative logic.[38] Instead it is the very social pathology that the hyperghetto stands for which needed to be cut off and kept at a safe distance. It is no longer a case of black people per se, but the perceived atmospheric blackness of the hyperghetto.

Dismantling the flawed underclass concept, Wacquant argues that the hyperghetto is anything but cut off from American civil society. Instead its lifeworld is a fundamental part of the system in which it is embedded, and the very attempt to mark it as separate indicates 'a transformation of the *political* articulation of race, class, and urban space in both discourse and objective reality'.[39] The hyperghetto operates as an institution and is a 'mechanism of *ethnoracial closure and control*'.[40] Although it might appear to be an alien and monolithic species-territory, the hyperghetto needs to be understood as:

the work of collective self-production...*organized according to different principles* in response to a *unique set of structural and strategic constraints* that bear on the racialized enclaves of the city as no other segment of America's territory.[41]

From the assessments made by Wacquant in the 1990s it is clear he was able to maintain some of the distinction between constraint and inhabitation that was foundational to Drake and Cayton's study. By the turn of the millennium the relation between object of research and production of knowledge had shifted to the extent that those differentiations – of constraint and inhabitation – had closed in on one another. Writing in 2001 (incidentally the peak period of the Ghetto House and Juke scenes which preceded Footwork) Wacquant saw Chicago as an exemplary case of the racialized hyperghetto now standing in 'structural and functional kinship with the prison'.[42] Underpopulated with people but deemed to be overpopulated with pathologies it has, according to Wacquant, become a preparing ground for incarceration to such an extent that the two zones – prison and hyperghetto – are more or less interchangeable.

Wacquant argues this has serious consequences for black social life in the hyperghetto. No longer able to organize according to its own norms, the hyperghetto 'now serves the *negative economic function of storage of a surplus population* devoid of market utility'.[43] As a racialized territory, Chicago's South and West sides have been reconfigured into 'a one-dimensional machinery for natal regulation, a human warehouse wherein are discarded those segments of urban society deemed disrespectable, derelict and dangerous'.[44] Wacquant sees the hyperghetto as a 'mass machine for "race making"' which, because of its institutional embeddedness with the prison, is now 'saturated with economic, social and physical insecurity'.[45]

The political sensibilities motivating Wacquant are clear and some would applaud them. For him, the creation of the hyperghetto needs to be studied because of the political and economic fault lines that it exposes in North America. Yet what he is unable to avoid is an expression of horror. Observing the internal activity of Chicago's South and West sides at the turn of the millennium, he is only able to see a flattened waste ground in which people live the barest materiality. Perhaps what Wacquant did was go looking for constraint without paying attention to inhabitation, or to put it another way: in his search for the Black Belt he blinded himself to Bronzeville.

This is significant because Wacquant is in many ways reflective of a broader type of ecological attribution that shapes the urban sociological debate on ghettoization. In his work in particular, it seems to be caused by the collapse of a set of categorical distinctions between the external production of constraint and an internal set of lived relations, that goes into the intellectual labor of determining the ghetto as a racialized object of knowledge. The simple question is, if Wacquant was correct and by the early 2000s the hyperghetto was acting as a container for the racial detritus of post-Fordist capital, then how does Footwork emerge from within this setting? And how do we account for the continuum of black electronic dance music in Chicago's South and West sides that was productive during the period of the hyperghetto's construction? Or rather the question might be, how does Wacquant's theorization of the hyperghetto work against its own grain to illuminate the conditions of production for Footwork? In the very act of his well-meaning negation, Wacquant opens up the space for a repurposing of his own analytical imperatives. When placed next to each other, such is the level of discordance between his hyperghetto concept and the activity that generates Footwork, that we can begin to ask: What are the capacities of surplus? How do discarded segments socialize? Is that black music being made in the human warehouse?

Despite the historical distance between them, Drake and Cayton's *Black Metropolis* offers us a far more productive framework for thinking Footwork's status as black music. This is because they keep a set of distinctions between lived experience, materiality, sociality, regulation, and discursive construction open as they relate to the Black Belt / Bronzeville. The disjuncture between external constraint and internal relations is never settled in their work, but instead it is engrained into the analysis as a kind of hesitant sociology.[46] Arguably, a similar hesitancy is central to theorizing Footwork as a sonic ecology. The generalized intelligence and mass improvisation that go into the phono-sociality emanating from the battle circle press up against, escape, and resolutely stay within conflicting determinations of ghettoization. The *problematic* – as opposed to the problem – of the question of the blackness of Chicago's South and West sides is not to one to be resolved, but instead reverberates in the question of the blackness of Footwork.[47]

Aesthetic Sociality and Desedimentation

The use of the term 'blackness' as the basis for thinking about the relation between the production of an environment and the production of music is without guarantees. This is because each invocation of the term 'blackness' as a means for thinking the environmental and the musical carries with it multiple registers of lived experience, historical knowledge, and abstraction. By the same measure, each time the term 'blackness' is used to initiate such a discussion, the very grounds of the environmental and the musical are opened in ways which render them unstable. Such methodological concerns have to be kept in the foreground, therefore, when we consider the question of the blackness of Footwork as a style of sonic fabrication through the blackness of Chicago's South and West sides. Working with such an imperative means not so much setting aside the logics of external constraint which have sought to construct the 'Chicago ghetto', but instead dislodging them through our attendance to an idea of the blackness of Footwork as lived sociality internal to its material and psychic surroundings which allows it to generate a sonic ecology that renders the music (and therefore the territory) incoherent to the brutality of racial enclosure.

The cultural theorist Laura Harris' work on the experimental methods of C.L.R. James and Helio Oiticica offers us such a model for thinking blackness as an 'aesthetic sociality' crafted inside what are deemed to be pathologizing urban constraints. Harris pays attention to how James and Oiticica inhabited and were inhabited by two urban zones that are redolent of the Black Atlantic world: the barrack-yards of Trinidad and the favelas of Rio de Janeiro. As structural extensions of the slave quarters, and in kinship with later formations such as housing projects, these urban zones are conditioned by racial, economic, and social exclusion, but there is also a rough privilege at work within them. The favela, barrack-yard and their iterations, are able to operate 'off the grid, mobile and in hiding' in ways which allow 'for the development of a relatively autonomous, alternative way of life, a sociality, a mode of contact structured by its own aesthetic acts and judgments.'[48] Harris calls this 'the aesthetic sociality of blackness...an impoverished political assembly that resides in the heart of the polity but operates under its ground and on its edge.'[49]

The schema drawn by Harris is jarring because it points to the spatial and aesthetic autonomy of a blackness operating under urban constraint, when settlements of this type are commonly understood as being surrounded. This is because what is at issue in her account of the aesthetic sociality is not the imposition of governance. Instead blackness *within* such zones displaces (and in many ways announces) the incoherent authority of racial and class-based constraint.

The aesthetic sociality of blackness is defined by a number of specific features. One is an ever-expanding inventiveness, seemingly without limits. It is also a non-exclusionary zone that functions as a resource for the socially illegitimate. Finally, it generates a mass intellectuality built upon 'corporeal, sensual, erotic and even violent expression.'[50] This is because blackness within such settings functions as a 'constitutive impurity' which is passed around amongst its populations, unsettled in its effects, and thus does not adhere to accepted forms of racial categorization. It is for this reason that zones deemed to be 'ghettos' become the focal point of intense regulation, in an attempt to curb the possibility that what goes on inside there might breach any cordon sanitaire. As Harris notes, the process of brutally containing this sociality only serves to further stimulate its production:

Here, what is understood as motleyness is now hidden and sheltered, even as racialization and criminalization remain in force and continue to expand. People come together here because they are black. But at the same time, they are black because they come together here.[51]

Or to put it another way: the harder they come (into it), the harder they fall (for it). This formulation from Harris is the key to her argument. She pinpoints the breakdown of one register of blackness (born of restrictions due to the racial mechanics of a pathologized color quality ascribed to bodies and then territorialized), and the generativity of another register of blackness (which by way of its spatial and performative determinations exposes the limitations and restrictions of the former). This occurs through the aesthetic sociality of a place. Or rather the aesthetic sociality in a place. We could even be talking about the aesthetic sociality of blackness as a place. What if the aesthetic sociality Harris charts in zones of urban constraint across the Black Atlantic world could be thought of as a black experimentalism that by taking place 'here' becomes an experiment of what 'here' constitutes? What if the blackness observed from the outside and understood as a pathological racial quality of the location, due to the perceived qualities of those who live 'there', not only operated from inside as an aesthetic sociality which rendered blackness available as inhabitation, *but* by way of its ever-expanding inventiveness functioned as an experiment with the very territory of the ghetto?

It is this breakdown of the distinction between outside and inside, 'here' and 'there', operative in Harris' work that we can track into Footwork. If the aesthetic sociality of blackness dislodges racist logics of urban geography, it does so not simply by way of counter-affirmation but through a blackness which – due to its relative autonomy – serves to negate regulative measures. What then can this tell us about the continual reconfiguration between dancers and producers that is a function of the Footwork circle? What can Harris' account of aesthetic sociality provide when it comes to thinking about Footwork's ecological status as black music?

Addressing these questions requires staying with the idea of locational reconfiguration as it relates to blackness, aesthetics, and territory. With this in mind, Nahum Chandler's formulations on racial desedimentation provide a productive point of interlocution for Harris' thinking as it applies to Footwork. When he writes of desedimentation, Chandler argues it is a function of black diasporic life in that it marks the 'problematic' of that collective existence. By referring to it as a problematic, Chandler is not pathologizing black diasporic life; instead he is showing us how the lived experience of blackness refuses to reify a set of predetermined racial distinctions and places pressure on racial ontologies as natural systems of categorization. Historically, the very living of black diasporic life 'enacted or enabled the elaboration of a fundamental questioning of the possible character and order of social and historical being in general.'[52]

Chandler argues that what this questioning amounts to is a destabilization of the supposed nature of racial distinctions and the way they are used to organize the world: 'desedimentation...as in to make tremble by dislodging the layers of sedimented premises that hold it in place.[53] Racial desedimentation operates as a 'hyperbolic force', which in its refusal of closure moves through and dislodges claims of racial property:

[It] elaborates itself as or with the kinetic and volatile disjunction of the empirical and the transcendental, of the mundane and the ontological, issuing thereby as a historical yet structural affront to systems of subjection, even as such systems configure the subordinate and supra-ordinate alike within its devolution.[54]

The 'labor of desedimentation' has been, according to Chandler, consistently embedded in black diasporic life.[55] As a 'force' its effects have been most spectacularly felt as the 'practice of an art'.[56] Black art is marked by and enacts the collective labor of desedimentation, due to the way in which each time the practice of black art is realized – if done so effectively – it is understood as not, but also nothing other than, black art. The very force of desedimentation in its production renders volatile its own status as black and art, without completely refusing either ontological categorization.

The features of desedimentation that are of interest in terms of the aesthetic sociality and ecology of blackness in its relation to Footwork are those Chandler draws out in black diasporic music. Specifically, it is in the rhythmic substance of the music that its desedimentary effects can be heard:

A decryptic, elliptical rhythm announces itself, refusing, thereby, to state its theme, remaining, resting, perhaps; only. Within the fold of the practice that yields such, a shudder or a thrill, a graphic amber, an asonic sonority, may gather or arise – as, yet otherwise, than the envisaged, the sounded, and the sonorous.[57]

Desedimentation in this context does not operate as a musical theme, but, for Chandler, is an experimental drive apparent as a dissolution-restatement at the level of form. The question of rhythm in black music is not an innate racial quality of the performer, but an irruption that cuts across the social and lived experience of this hyperbolic force. What is significant about Chandler's account of rhythm, for the purposes of my argument, is the way its sociality can be folded into an understanding of racial desedimentation as a territorial operation. Whilst desedimentation, as Chandler describes it, is a general feature of the rhythmic design of black diasporic music, the history of black musical production shows us that a particular rhythmic iteration marks a sociality produced in a given time and place. Due to the processes of sonic reproduction, a specific style of rhythmic iteration can be considered to be characteristic of a place of concentrated black inhabitation (i.e. it has a 'vibe'). We can see how this notion of vibe as rhythmic desedimentation lends itself to the understanding of the multiple rhythmic features of Footwork (sonic and gestural). Yet in the same way that desedimentary rhythm marks a refusal of racial closure even as it is produced, the collective living of black diasporic life in a given territory also enacts a labor of desedimentation to the extent that:

it might be that there arises a kind of sliding and shifting, a certain dynamis, a certain conjunction of movement and weight, yielding a destabilization of ground, deeply locked and fixed in place, or set into new relief new lines of possible concatenation, or turn up old ground into new configurations of its elements. Such a practice, that is, might turn up new soil on old ground.[58]

It is possible to surmise from Chandler's accounts of desedimentation that the vibe or sonic ecology of black diasporic music is as much a rhythmic improvisation of ground as it is an improvisation of musical substance. The question of the blackness of black music lies in the relation between the communal desedimentation of territory, as it is transformed through – and itself transformed by – the phonic materiality of music generated via social experimentation. It is arguable therefore that the sonic ecology of black music can both be site specific and simultaneously refuse any strict racial rendering of spatial constraint.

The artist and theorist chukwumaa uncovers something similar to desedimentation in his account of 'quadrillage', but in ways which move closer to the domain of Footwork.[59] Reworking Giorgio Agamben's account of the plagued city as moment of inception for modern systems of urban control, via a mode of organization known as 'quadrille', chukwumaa locates in this conception the antagonistic and fugitive production of black electronic dance music in urban settings. The pivotal concepts on which he turns Agamben into an unwitting theorist of black electronic dance music are the etymological and historical traces of 'quadrille'. Using the fact that 'the quadrille' was also a European dance form choreographed through the use of a grid which was then popularized in the Caribbean colonies, chukwumaa shifts between the city as a cartographic grid designed to organize populations and the technological production of black electronic dance music by way of software grids displayed on screens and/or the hardware grids of synthesized instruments. The tension here is between a street-born sociality generating phonic material that threatens to reorganize its own immediate environment, and the supposed requirement to govern a city through colonial logics of containment. With quadrillage then, chukwumaa provides a way of thinking the ecological dimensions of dance and sound as a type of mass territorial experimentation.

My splicing together of Harris, Chandler, and chukwumaa allows us to zero in on something fundamental at work in the phonic materiality of Footwork which the field of urban sociology renders largely unavailable. Through their respective theorizations of blackness as aesthetic sociality, desedimented territoriality, and embattled urban soundscape, they provide the tools with which to study the *internal* dynamics of Footwork. These being the forms of autonomy that operate as the condition of possibility for the social experimentation which produces Footwork. Hyperbolic force appears in the sonic palettes of the music as distorted yet coherent degrees of rhythmic differentiation; it can be seen in the speed of the dancers' micro-rhythmic movements; but more significantly, it is the way that the battle circle is held together by the breakdown of the distinction between producers and dancers that tells us most about this musical style.

Through Harris, Chandler, and chukwumaa it becomes possible to conceptualize the battle circle as a desedimentary formation of the very ground of Chicago's South and West sides. Footwork's vibe arises through an engineering of a sociality in operation in these areas of the city, which allows the music to be given to a discursive understanding of black music. At the very same time, its production of vibe is so forceful it overloads the constrained racial logics of urban population and territory. Which is to say that, as part of the built environment of Chicago's South and West sides, Footwork marks the distinction between 'there' as a post-industrial waste storage facility, 'here' as a place where black music is produced, *and* breaks that distinction by overflowing with phonic and gestural ferociousness. Therefore, whatever is understood as the 'hyperghetto' is not a limitation on the phono-social capacities of the style, but on the contrary is its atmospheric generator.

Of course, these pronouncements on my part require further engagement with the range of audio-visual outputs that render Footwork a thing in the world. The section above represents the final piece of a three-part cumulative analysis, prior to a synthesis that brings all of this material to bear on an encounter with the sonic ecology of Footwork. Such a synthesis centers on making use of the various trajectories that I have developed over the three preceding sections. My task is to repurpose this material in order to generate writing that amplifies the ecological dimensions of the social experimentation operating under the heading Footwork. This means paying attention to the dynamics of *Tek* within Footwork, and how as a self-produced form of *Tek*, its social experimentation is resolutely located within, and dislocates the, terms 'black', 'ghetto', and 'music'.

Architekture

In the footage of the Havoc and Below Zero crews in competition at Battle Groundz the propulsion of feet and legs, combined with the angular arrangement of arms, all co-ordinated by a center of gravity resting like a spirit-level, a self-evident truth begins to reveal itself – it is dubious to say that Footwork is made by producers.[60] Instead, Footwork is the outcome of pressure generated by dancers through their use of the system of conduction which is the battle circle. On occasions where the speakers cut out and the dancers continue without a break in their flow, it becomes clear that DJs Spinn, Traxman, and Earl are amplifiers of the collisions of movement that the likes of Lite Bulb, A.G., and Oreo generate. The core elements of the Footwork sound palette – low-end rumble, mid-range synth stabs, and high-end claps – are the phono-material imprints of battle circle action (See Figure 1).

In DJ R.P. Boo's 'Heavy Heat'[61] with its marshaling of almost continuous bass, its chopped militaristic horns, the piercing yet sparse crackle of drum patterns, all given a coded narrative through the mashed-up arrangement of samples, an equally self-evident truth is revealed: to say that Footwork is made by producers is entirely on point. It is the producers who, through their methods of phono-material engineering, drive the kineticism of the action taking place in the battle circle. Take DJ Rashad's 'Ghost'.[62] Containing all the core elements of Footwork, but arranged with the combination of raw edge and playfulness that was always his signature, it is the vocal on this track which indicates the conductive capacities of the producer. The rapid-fire repetition and desiccation of the phrase 'ghost' – one of the 'basics' essential to the repertoire of any dancer – is not so much a command issued by Rashad, but more a means of generating the speed which dancers transform into movement. In this respect, crews such Terror Squad and Wolf Pack should really be considered outcomes of the production styles of the likes of DJs Manny and Clent.

In the case of the preceding two propositions, it is not a choice between the argument of one over the other. Both of the 'truths' presented are indivisible as objective reflections of Footwork. Therefore, it is *between* the pressure dancers manufacture within the circle, which is then exerted upon producers, and the experiments in the rhythmic microtuning which allows producers to set the templates for dance crews, that we can grasp the sonic ecology of Footwork. As a style of social fabrication taking place in Chicago's South and West sides, Footwork is engineered through the intensification of concentric and cross-hatched layers. One such layer exists between dancers and producers, but there are also those layers pressing on dancers and on producers as they occupy dual roles as competitors and pedagogues. All of these layers are contained by the battle circle. It is the design of the battle circle which tells us that dance crews and producers are not distinct entities, but nodes within a system of distributed intelligence. We can *hear* this on Footwork tracks through the way the elements are arranged at a speed which should render them dissonant, but instead leads to a spectacular anti-foundational coherence. We can *see* this in battle footage, where the movements might appear wild and instinctive to some, but upon repeated viewing the levels of control and improvisation conducted in the moment reveal the labor and knowledge in operation.

The argument I am making here is that Footwork, as a name for the relations between dancers and producers, between tracks and battle footage, between sound and gesture, is a mode of socially strategized overabundance. The battle circle is the mechanism for alchemizing these experiments in relation into a phono-materiality which is relentlessly spilling over. It is the battle circle that returns us to the question of Footwork's grounding in what are understood as Chicago's 'hyperghettos', and by extension, the question of its blackness. The battle circle is not just a conjunction of sound and performance; it also reveals the architectural dynamics of Footwork by way of its embeddedness in the historical production of the city's South and West sides. This means addressing another layer of differentiation that shapes its production: the external making of the 'ghetto' as a racial territory.

The Footwork battle circle is formed within what is *externally* deemed to be restricted terrain. Such *external* constraints are the function of racial pressures that are manifested through the state and civil society's lethal political, economic, and geographic governance. These forces combine to externally designate the city's South and West sides as ghettos, and therefore render them, from an external position, as pathological. As Drake and Cayton show us, duress has never been the defining *internal* feature of Chicago's South side, and this certainly applies to Footwork. Operating *inside* the multi-dimensional function of the cordon sanitaire, the battle circle becomes the site of production for what we could call a series of

Figure 2 DJ Rashad's fingers 'dance' on the pads of an Akai MPC 2000XL as he produces a track.
Source: www.youtube.com/watch?v=2AlJ88YZ3U8, accessed 21st January 2015.

'hyperghetto' blueprints. These blueprints appear across the Footwork continuum, in a range of forms, most often attached to the term *Tek*. A concise neologism compressing into one compact bit of slang the terms and concepts of technique-technical-technician, *Tek* operates as a marker for the distributed intelligence which is a structural feature of Footwork realized as a black *architektural* impulse.

Tek marks the confluence of the necessity of grids in the design of Footwork, in that the producers' fingers dance on the pads of the Akai MPC as they manufacture the music (See Figure 2) and the knowledge of the city as a racially and economically encoded cartographic grid which dancers manipulate through the force of the movements they generate in the battle circle (See Figure 3).

Taking this a stage further, *Tek* is also embedded within the manifestation of dance in the battle circle. The crew members conduct their gestural modulations of the producers tracks on the very materialization of

Figure 3 Cover image from Traxman's 2013 album *Teklife Volume 3: The Architek*.
Source: http://litcitytrax.com/project/lctrax003/.

the city as grid. Locked into that system of urban orientation are a series of race and class determinations that generate the spatial parameters of the ghetto, if not its internal constitution. Such a line of argument opens up two possibilities: (a) the furious rapidity with which dancers' feet and legs move is a collective process of gestural desedimentation enacted upon the local cartography; (b) the accompanying pythagorean alignment of upper limbs and torso operates as a repurposing of turned over ground, to the extent that the battles start to generate choreographic designs for buildings that await realization (See Figures 1 and 4).

These dual possibilities point back to my earlier arguments on the status of black hood dance. While Naomi Bragin's conceptualization of black hood dance as social thought was useful as a starting point, her conceptualization of this type of black performance has its limits. Exposing the uncritical 'celebration discourse', which seeks to elevate black hood dance as a simple affirmation of black life 'under conditions of disappearance and death' without ever attending to the realities of 'everyday police terror', Bragin argues such styles exemplify the way in which black performance reconstitutes the vastness of the crime that was racial slavery without ever transforming it.[63] Black hood dance, according to Bragin, operating under

Figure 4   Dancer at Da War Zone battle.
Source: www.youtube.com/watch?v=ni_SxYjGTH4, accessed 10th August 2014.

structural regimes of anti-blackness, only ever affirms the truth of the paradigm of black social death.[64] The perspective I have developed here shows that Footwork's aesthetic sociality of blackness places pressure on Bragin. That modernity is anti-black is evident, and given the existence of zones of urbicide in the major cities of the Global North, such zones are an outcome of the reality of anti-blackness. But the paradigm of anti-blackness does not explain the totality of the blackness operative within such zones. It only determines its so-called parameters; it never gets to its ecology. When it comes to hood dance forms such as Footwork, Bragin's schema needs reinterpretation. It is not that anti-blackness prefigures the lived *experience* of blackness as one of social death, but that the paradigm of anti-blackness is in constant pursuit of, and seeking to contain, the actual lived *aesthetic sociality* of blackness that is in constant production. By way of chukwumaa we could say that Footwork marks the redistribution of the logic of the grid, that cartographically organizes the scales of racial violence within the city, by way of the rhythmic phono-material force of the blackness created *inside* its territories.

In this respect, and to return to the object of study, DJ Rashad and DJ Spinn's ascription of another name for the style of ecological manufacturing specific to Chicago's South and West sides is telling. *Teklife*, the heading for their ever-expanding crew of dancers, producers, dancers-producers, producers-dancers, acknowledges the way in which Footwork dissolves the racial distinction between place and modality, as well as overproducing both. To talk of *Teklife* is to stay attuned to the relations between limbs and environment, rhythm, and ground. *Teklife* signals a collective realization that the generation of vibe within the circle contains an expansionary impulse into which Footwork's aesthetic sociality of blackness can keep on being loaded. Located in parts of Chicago that some well-meaning high minds choose to diagnose as warehouses for post-industrial capitalism's discarded materials, *Teklife* is one node within the irruptive totality of Footwork as a phonic imaging of black city plans.

Footwork is black music because of the way it creates and manipulates an intensive sociality that cuts across racializations of lived experience, built environment, movement (rhythmic), and movement (gestural). Therefore, it is black music precisely because it chooses to stay in the ever-expanding inventiveness of 'here.' Footwork's vibe is generated through its fixedness in a phono-social-territorial place. To say that Footwork is fixed, site specific even, does not mean it is trapped or imprisoned. Rather, the intensity of the relations between dancers and producers, engineered within the battle circle, animates an experimentation internal to Chicago's South and West sides. It powers forth with an expansionary impulse that such zones of apparent near uninhabitability should not be capable of producing, because of the duress that supposedly determines the atmosphere of the place and those who inhabit it.

Since 2010 this experimental activity has been given the name Footwork. In previous moments its antecedents have been called Juke, Ghetto House, Jackin, Trax, and House. What marks Footwork out as a spectacular iteration within this continuum in Chicago, is its *teknical* scope. It holds together an ensemble of rapid actions, sounds and formations that are potentially dissipative, in order to generate furious propulsions which are such a precise, yet speculative, rendering of location that constitutes an *architekture*.

To make this claim about *architekture*, we must recognize that certain aspects of the normative methods of musical interpretation do not adequately adhere to Footwork. Like most forms of black electronic dance music – but at a degree that makes it impossible to ignore – Footwork is much closer to a collectivized system of planning and design built upon improvised social organization in a given time and place. Thus, what is *architektural* about the practices of dancers and producers is that they take their respective lived experiences of race and class as an atmospheric orientation in Chicago's South and West sides, tap into a cultural knowledge and history of electronic music production in those very areas of the city, and aggregate that information into the ecological nerve center which is the battle circle. *Teklife* is the name for that information, and the battle circle (as a temporary construction that roves the South and West sides) becomes the machinery for the manipulation of this activity into phonic projections for an *architekture* of blackness that dancers and producers inhabit. *Teklife* pulses through Footwork and marks the turning over of ground in the ghetto, ground out of which emanates the blueprint for another ecology, another city.

4

Ghettoville

The music Darren Cunningham creates under the guise of the Actress image demands a reconfiguration of the protocols of listening (to the city). The arrangement of minute sonic gestures for maximal cacophonous effect, which has defined his output as Actress, suspends a set of ideas about the given qualities of, and relations between, black electronic dance music and formal abstraction. Yet it is undeniable that what defines the Actress project is its status as black electronic dance music and the presence of abstract operations. Since the release of *Hazyville* (2008), and with his breakthrough album *Splazsh* (2010), there has been a clear sense that Actress is drawing on genealogies, which gives his music a strong resemblance to Techno, House, and electronic R'n'B. His reverence for producers such as Terrence Dixon indicates an acute knowledge of these as styles of sonic experimentation grounded in specific tempo-spatial urban arrangements of late twentieth-century black social life. In addition, the album-length meditation on Milton's *Paradise Lost* (*R.I.P.*, 2012) signaled an internally determined style of composition that Actress identifies as abstract, and that to a large extent molds the entirety of his output.

Our examination of the aesthetics of Actress' music rests in the notion that it is both black electronic dance music and abstract. The question of abstraction has been a feature of recent discourse on black diasporic culture. Whilst Philip Brian Harper has offered the latest, if ultimately unsatisfactory, engagement with the question of abstraction in black aesthetics, it is Kobena Mercer's account of 'discrepant abstraction' in the black visual arts that proves far more productive for our purposes.[1] More akin to an atmosphere than to a method or technique, his description of discrepant abstraction as 'elusive and repetitive, obstate and strange' provides a way into a consideration of the work of Actress.[2] In tandem with Mercer I include George Lewis' understanding of the experimental drive of twentieth-century black improvised music as a 'technologically mediated articulation of the diaspora', which in the case of black electronic dance music can be taken to mean its mutational capacities realized through the corruption of machinic affordances.[3] I believe Actress forms part of the latest stage of this tendency.

Such a picture is further enriched by the release of his 2014 album *Ghettoville*. Stimulated by repeated walks through his local South London, during which he came across the everyday organization of race and poverty, this album brings questions of sociality and ecology to bear on the Actress palette. It is this relation – between a quasi-obsessive dearticulation of black electronic dance musics tropes, and the concrete action of walking through a given urban environment – that lies at the crux of my engagement with *Ghettoville*. The album takes the registers of abstraction in black electronic dance music through the terrains of subaltern lifeworlds, and stands as an instance in the proliferation of what Harney and Moten call debt and study, whilst noting how those ideas are simultaneously cut by understandings of blackness and abstraction.[4] We can hear a version of fugitive publics engrained into the soundscape of *Ghettoville*, not as ethnographic material but through the aesthetic manipulation of the atmospheres of racialized poverty into a sonic ecology. By generating abstract sounds, whilst eschewing the need to deviate away from the social necessities of black electronic dance music, Actress' *Ghettoville* makes apparent the intricate urban geographies of poverty in South London, in its entanglement with black social life.

Abstraction

The natural place for us to begin thinking about discrepant abstraction in *Ghettoville* is through Actress' reflection on his own practice:

What I hear is what's occurring all the time, and that's what music *is*, essentially. It's sort of our surroundings, digitized through the human, through either a band or a computer, and probably distilled through sounds which aren't necessarily correlated to what's going on at the time, but in effect it's…it's really the same thing. It's just so abstract.[5]

From this excerpt taken from an interview with the journalist Rory Gibb, we can begin to grasp some of the ways in which Actress conceives of his work as abstract. Firstly, there is the emphasis placed on environment, in that he foregrounds the immediacy of his surroundings and the activity taking place around him, as an instigating point for the compositional process. This is followed by the digitization of that environment, initially through an instrument he calls 'the human', and then into more conventional music technologies. What he intimates is of a process involving numerous stages of sonic transformation, and he makes it quite clear that his aim is not to achieve a quality of mimetic reproduction. The sounds he generates appear on the surface to be distinct from the environment that stimulated him to produce them, yet, for Actress, there is something at stake in them materially, in the very way they work, which means they make available, at the level of the phonic, a set of activities already operative in that same environment.

These comments made in conversation with Gibb provide us with an insight into the particularities of not only how Actress conceives of his music as abstract, but the procedures he uses to achieve his intended effects. At the same time, a counter to this claim might be that what Actress sets out could be the thoughts of almost any electronic musician deploying a practice of abstraction at roughly any point of the late twentieth and early twenty-first centuries.[6] In order to attend to the specific account of abstraction he sets out it is important to understand how Actress operates within the scope of his chosen field: black electronic dance music.

The common practice for black electronic dance music producers is to inhabit a style and stimulate mutations within it, or to experiment in the spaces between styles, often by using differences in rhythmic patterns. The successes or failures of innovations are largely determined by the way new sonic propositions are received by dancers. This type of activity led Simon Reynolds to describe a defining feature as the tension between experimentation and 'dancefloor functionalism'.[7] As has already been discussed, the points of orientation for Actress are those styles which sought to re-engineer the textures of Funk through the drum machine and synthesizer, in particular Detroit Techno, the later experiments in House, as well as the popular experimentalism of Prince and New Jack Swing. However, as evidenced on tracks such as 'Senorita' and 'Bubble Buts and

Equations' (both feature on *Splazsh*), his sound operates in an obscured relation to these source materials. Actress conducts something akin to a synthesis of the dynamics produced by the styles informing his work, without it ever being possible to determinedly fix him within a single one, or even the joins between several. The potency of an album such as *Splazsh* lay in the use he made of the driving functionality of the dancefloor, whilst at the level of form and intention deploying enough fuzz to intensify the existing abstractions within this social space.

What this allows for in terms of Actress' conception of his own music as abstract is significant. He is clear about the doctrines and approaches that are alien to his musical project. The type of mathematical avant-gardism exemplified by Iannis Xennakis is not what he is conversing with. Equally, Drone's minimalist clusters and Noise's experiments in the boundaries between music and non-music hold little bearing for Actress.[8] Instead he is adamant:

No I wanna hear form, I wanna hear structure, I wanna hear elasticity and I wanna hear meaning.[9]

This is what the various forms of black electronic dance music that filter into Actress' work provide for him. He is able to draw out the effects already at work in what some, listening in from outside, hear only as the reductiveness of Techno, House, and R'n'B. By stating his preference for sentiment, feel, and texture in opposition to the pure formalism of other twentieth- and twenty-first-century experimental electronic music, Actress is marking out something quite particular about the modes of abstraction his source materials make available to him.

It is important that we develop a firmer sense of how Actress conceives of black electronic dance music as abstract, precisely because of its functionality. Joanna Demers addresses the approach to sound by musicians who operate under the umbrella of 'electronica' (a term she uses to encompass popular and underground dance forms of electronic music). The primary feature she identifies in electronica is a structural duality that shapes the way producers conceive of their music. At one level they think of their music as being made from distinct sonic materials: 'what I mean by material here amounts to the objectified, audible phenomena in electronic music, from notes and rhythm to sound grains, clicks, timbres and even silence.'[10] At the same time, producers do not make the case for the autonomy of this material. Instead there is an overdetermination of these sonic objects in terms of their relationship to external sources. The sounds that can be heard in electronica operate with reference to phenomena, actions, and ideas in the world:

Electronica's sounds...are always heard in relation to something beyond the works in which they are housed, but these linkages to the outside world tend not to be mimetic...the relationship between signifier and signified is not based on simple resemblance but rather on conventions that over time have paired a sound with an exterior concept.[11]

What Demers is stressing here is that referentiality is not achieved as part of an attempt to replicate the quality of field recordings. Instead, at stake is the pursuit of the aesthetic proposition that – via the mediations of electronic music – equivalences of activity taking place in the world can be rendered audible. This is achieved through the use of conventions that have been secured within a given style of electronica due to their success in achieving a similar effect. In making the case for the protocols of electronic music, Demers is reworking the distinction Theodor Adorno made between sounds in a musical work which look to imitate empirical reality and those works containing sounds that are wholly constructed yet mediate empirical reality. The outcome of such an approach, according to Demers, is that the aesthetic protocols of electronica operate on the basis of metaphor. The artists in this field insist that 'electronically produced vibrations not only exist as objects but also carry with them associations and references.'[12]

The modeling of electronic music as metaphorical in terms of its sonic form and content has already been introduced through Kodwo Eshun's theorization of The Futurhythmachine. Within his general reconfiguration of the analytical imperatives of black music in the 1990s, Eshun reserved special attention for the Techno style which Actress acknowledges as his guide. Describing the work of the Detroit pioneers Derrick May, Juan Atkins, and Kevin Saunderson – in addition to Urban Resistance and Drexciya – as the autonomous operation of 'synthetic fiction / electronic thought', he argued it was the metaphorical power of this sound which meant it reworked the then conceptual limit points when it came to discourse about black music.[13] The Detroit producers' insistence upon the agentic capacities of technology and space/time travel meant their music gave 'the overwhelming impression that the record is an object from the world it realizes.'[14]

Through Eshun and Demers we can begin to develop a picture of the nature of abstraction in black electronic dance music. Whilst Demers provides a general scope for thinking the relation between phonic materiality and its intention in electronica, Eshun undertakes a more precise analysis of these processes in Techno. The argument he made is that this musical system used metaphor to drive through a reordering of the constitutive elements of black music to demarcate it as already conducting an internally determined abstraction. In the case of Techno, it was the ability to sonically image space travel and the emotive capacities of new industrial technology which provided the impulse.

In order to locate Actress' practice in terms of this material it is important not to rush and make direct associations with Eshun's conceptualizations of Techno simply due to a stylistic allegiance. There are minute, yet significant, differences in the way Actress is using these influences that require tracking, otherwise there is a risk of missing the specificities of how Actress renders his music abstract. Returning to the interview with Rory Gibb, a portion of their exchange takes place whilst walking through the Crystal Palace neighborhood of South London. A preferred activity of Actress' in the area of the city in which he resides, this prompts him to expand on his compositional process:

'Okay, it's basically like this,' he declares, abruptly stopping in his tracks. We're in a narrow alleyway between wooden fences coated in bright green algae. He gestures downwards to the rotting leaves piled up against the fence. 'How these leaves have fallen in this formation – they're brown now, but amongst that you've still got a bit of green or whatever – and how it rests against the backdrop, and the concrete – how things have just fallen. That's how I think about music.'[15]

There are a number of ways for us to reflect on Gibb's account of Actress' observations. One is to filter them through the framework provided by Joanna Demers. In this sense, what is presented in the passage above is an exemplary case of the sonic materials of Actress' music existing not autonomously, but locked in a non-mimetic relay with already existing arrangements in the world. If, though, Actress' fabulating prowess is as a result of his bonds with Techno, then this scene also reveals that his relation to this dance music style is idiosyncratic. As Eshun makes clear, Techno's metaphorical impulse was driven by a desire for a rupture away from the world and the historical category of the human. The futurism of Techno deployed the dynamics of science fiction to project what its practitioners felt were entirely new planes of existence. Juan Atkins' now famous statement, when describing his 'Model 500' persona as an attempt to land a spaceship on a record, exemplifies this conviction.[16]

Yet in his encounter with Gibb, Actress is almost conducting an inversion of this impulse. He is zooming in on the immediacy of the environment around him in South London. It is the minutiae of the arrangement of leaves, wood, and pavement in an alleyway that seem to stimulate him. There are two features of Actress' abstraction that come to the fore here. Firstly, his use of Techno – and black electronic dance music in general – as a guide needs to be understood as the style providing the capacity for intense *formal* abstraction rather than a mimetic extension of its science fiction *content*. Secondly, the qualities of abstraction he produces through the functional terrain of black electronic dance music can be ascribed to an acutely refined observational technique. Actress' soundscape is rendered through the perception of, and absorption in, a range of activity in his immediate geography, which is then digitized in to sonic effects that are not photographic, but a distillation of the relations between material phenomena. What we have here is a cycle whereby observation, built environment, and electronic manipulations of sound feed into a self-determined system of musical abstraction. What is required of us now is a further exploration of the question of blackness with regards to this process in the making of *Ghettoville*.

Population: Zero

It appears then, that abstraction in the work of Actress can be characterized as an adaptation of Detroit Techno's speculative powers, if only to jettison its unrelenting desire for futurity in favor of an increasingly grounded (which is not the same as fixed) attentiveness to the minute composition of immediate environments. Such an account of Actress' particular style of abstraction prepares us for *Ghettoville*.

Released by the Ninja Tune label in January 2014, the album represented the latest iteration in a series of powerful pieces of experimentation Darren Cunningham had issued through the Actress image. Whereas
previous releases had refracted dancefloor sensibilities (*Splazsh*) or
offered an electronic meditation on Milton (*R.I.P.*), like his first record
(*Hazyville*) *Ghettoville* gestured towards a determination of place. The
choice of the title *Ghettoville* carries with it a number of territorial registers. In order to unpack the multiple registers of territory and place carried in the title *Ghettoville*, we can begin by calling attention to its status
as a neologism built upon a grammatical conjunction. Starting with the
'ghetto' portion, almost any use of the term in the Global North sets off
associations. The status of 'the ghetto' as a contested racialized object
of knowledge within the field of urban sociology has been addressed in
the previous chapter. Instead, through Actress' album, our focus will now
switch to the almost overwhelming impact the term 'ghetto' has had upon
the cultural imaginary since the late twentieth century. Understood historically as an effect of the Great Migration to the Northern United States,
and the subsequent sedimentation of race and class in the formation of
major Northern cities, 'ghetto' has become a potent folkloric short-hand
for black urban social aesthetics in such locations. As Tricia Rose and
Robin D.G. Kelley make clear, the reception of this type of black aesthetic
has been, at best, complicated.[17] At the level of its immediate production, the cultural aesthetics of 'the ghetto', are understood to have generated localized and internally coherent fields of activity, which, whether
consciously or not, have momentarily short-circuited the organization
of political and economic power in a given city.[18] Equally, such has been
the alienating effect of any instance of 'ghetto culture' for those operating
outside its remit that it has become the locus for pathological hysteria.
Precisely because of its racialization as black, and its aesthetic deployment of blackness, the generativity of 'ghetto cultures' aesthetics has led
to calls from the mainstream for increased policing, cuts to social welfare, and has been framed as the cause for the apparent environmental
decay in which it emerged. To add further complexity to this picture, the
culture industry has stepped in to actively exploit such tension, by reproducing what many consider caricatured forms of 'ghetto culture' for the
global entertainment market.

Of course, the lines between these dynamics in the assembly, patholo-gization, and economization of this aspect of black cultural aesthetics are not clearly demarcated, and it is certainly the case that individuals, col-lectives, institutions, and organizations have sought either to detourne or to exploit these processes in order to suit their needs. Therefore, when tracking the entry of this mode of black cultural production into the inter-national media landscape, it is important to recognize how all of these questions concerning its dissident aesthetics, commodity status, and *de facto* criminalization, are at stake. Whilst US 'ghetto culture' can now be seen as an almost dominant presence in television, cinema, and fashion, it is music that has always been, and continues to be, its primary disseminat-ing engine. Seemingly endless rates of musical innovation have allowed what are spatially small zones of North America to have a psychic life far beyond their supposed limits.

Taking all of this into account, it is worth considering the poten-tial effects of Actress attaching 'ghetto' to the term 'ville', a suffix used to describe an entire settlement, whether town or city. Clearly there are two resonances of place being spliced together. Taken on its own, the first (ghetto) is understood as a part, whether framed as decayed or full of vital-ity, that is confined within, or parasitically dependent on, a whole (city). When recast as 'Ghettoville', there is an alternation in definitional terms, whereby the degraded part becomes an autonomous whole. We have to consider the choice of album title on Actress' part in light of how we have already mapped out his musical project. Actress is understood as a pro-ducer who self-consciously makes abstract music, yet does so with the explicit intention of retaining the sensibilities, textures, and functionality of black electronic dance music, the primary forms of which emerged in specific urban geographies across the Black Atlantic. What some might see as an inoperable tension (the speculative capacities of abstraction ver-sus the grounded specificity of urban terrains) is the guiding sensibility of *Ghettoville*. The record is not made up of samples or references to 'ghetto music', yet it does have noticeable resemblance to various gestures associ-ated with such forms. Similarly, Actress does not overdetermine the record through a cultural attachment to a specific location, but – as will soon become clear – it was composed in relation to a given urban atmosphere. The result is that *Ghettoville* sounds like a series of – at points hardened, at others joyous – intensely repetitive studies, part-musical, part-geographic. Putting together a sonic palette which shifts from expressive epics to microscopic attentiveness, Actress inserts flashes that insist on something like a spatial-aesthetic resonance of 'ghetto', but again, precisely what sonic work the term is doing as an idea is never settled.

The common thread running through assessments of *Ghettoville* by music writers is of a decelerated relentlessness that reflects a bleak aesthetic. Patric Fallon describes the lead track 'Forgiven' as 'a seven and a half minute meditation on a loop of detuned guitar pitched down into oblivion, with a slow and single beat carrying the instruments death rattle through the muck'.[19] For Angus Finlayson the rhythm on 'Contagious' is halted to the extent it 'resembles the roar and shriek of tortured metal, like some kind of industrial accident happening in bullet time'.[20] Thus the consensus seems to be that a 'darker nastier tone is the defining trait' of *Ghettoville*, whereby the album 'refuses to commune with anything but itself'.[21] Often accompanying descriptions of this type amongst music writers is the suggestion that what Actress is doing is more akin to building an urban cinematic landscape through sonic material. Ruth Saxelby argues the record 'churns chaotically to the cyclical and often alienated beat of inner city life'.[22] Rory Gibb shifts this a stage further by taking an imaginative leap into *Ghettoville* as a place:

Welcome to *Ghettoville*, population: Zero. The curtain rises on Actress' latest album to find Darren Cunningham wandering alone through a barren neighborhood, past hollowed-out buildings, smashed glass and burned-out cars, everything coated in dust and mud. At first the only real evidence people have been here are the traces they've left behind.[23]

It is important for us to both stay with *and* disturb these associations between descriptions of the album's sonic content as inescapably turgid, the ascription of these sounds to a mood of bleakness, and then the proposition that these elements cohere as a sonic rendering of place. The idea that *Ghettoville* is a place Actress walks through is worth retaining, but I want to argue that there might be more to the soundscape of the album than the 'exhausted present' of a 'broken and disadvantaged world'.[24] With *Ghettoville* Actress is conducting urban phono-material study. He achieves this by not only drawing upon the abstract tendencies already latent within an array of black urban musical experiments, and the assumption that spatially constrained urban life is racialized and poverty stricken, but also by using a method of what I am calling *quotidian observation* to mediate his experience of the social arrangements across the streets of South London into sonic ecologies. This leaves us with the unstable yet highly productive proposition that the album is emanating from a place called *Ghettoville* imagined by Actress, and/or *Ghettoville* is the realization of an atmosphere already grounded in South London as Actress walks through it.

Quotidian Observation

My notion of 'quotidian observation' moves within the orbit of Harney and Moten's use of 'study'. Quotidian observation is acting as a name for Actress' practice of composition through the repeated act of walking the streets around him, and his recognition that any social activity (no matter how much it is considered degraded) is aesthetic and intellectual. Yet, the important distinction to be made – and therefore the reason for not settling neatly into an account of study – is the furious quietude and maximalist precision of Actress' method. Certainly, as a soloist, Actress is unalone, but I feel that what makes quotidian observation a more apt formulation in this case, is that it allows for further consideration of his ability as a producer to combine an ethical refusal of the self, with a strategic disassociation which allows him to lock in on the gestural capacity of vilified social atmospheres in South London.

In the instance set out above, the focal point of Actress' walk was the inert arrangements of discolored leaves, wooden fence, and pavement that he and Gibb encountered in Crystal Palace. The key to quotidian observation lies in not only his filtering of non-sentient phenomena, but also, as mentioned, his attentiveness to an entire sociality. He produces music through the tracking of the complex totality of people's lives in relation to the environment in which they move. Our task is to follow the forms of sociality Actress tunes into, his reasons for doing so, and how this activity was used to assemble *Ghettoville*. To put it in coolly analytical terms, Actress' overriding concern in this record is with the sociality of poverty (as an articulation of race–class) and its sedimentation into the built environment of South London. There is much more at stake though than what such a stunted formulation can reveal.

During an interview with *The Wire* magazine's Derek Walmsley to coincide with the release of *Ghettoville*, Actress pauses to make explicit the association between his method of observation, his concern with poverty as a feature of urban life, and its realization as musical abstraction:

' "Street Corp" to me is about the corporations not being in skyscrapers, but being on the street, in the form of what you would think are homeless people, or tramps', Cunningham explains, referring to a track on the new record. 'It's all interconnected. There's a chain reaction between each of these, you know what I mean. I always give money to people involved in the Street Corp because it keeps the street going. It all comes back out.'[25]

The track he refers to – 'Street Corp' – features the characteristics that dominate much of the first half of *Ghettoville*. It is marked by a relentless machinic motion, but one where the propulsions are askew. This decentering of movement gives the impression that 'Street Corp' is a microscopic study of a much larger process taking place beyond the limits of the track. For Actress, the arrangement of sonic materials on 'Street Corp' are the result of his perceptive observation about poverty. What he sees as he repeatedly walks around Crystal Palace is evidence that poverty is anything but the condition of having nothing:[26]

you don't just see [the other person] – you see yourself. Always trying to look at it from that angle – how they perceive you is important. And I think my way of dealing with that is to bring myself down to that level musically, in a way. Even if you're talking about homeless people, it doesn't mean they have nothing. Someone walking with a trolley that is packed full of garbage, which may not mean anything to a normal person, but would mean everything to the person carrying it – it's those sorts of juxtapositions and parallels that interest me, in life in general. It's about seeing what's around you.[27]

The impression given here is of Actress' use of an alternative lens, one designed to dislodge the common assurances of singular perspective, that allows him to reconceive of poverty as a type of collective self-maintenance providing sustenance, rather than requiring it. Through these refracted, roving lines of sight, he is able to hear in urban poverty an abstract and functional arrangement of black electronic dance music. Such a claim forces us to reconsider the almost uniform position held by reviewers, the interpretation of *Ghettoville* as a flattened dystopia. Certainly, its repeated patterns and pulses are the outcome of an idiosyncratic relationship to a 'real' place and 'real' instances of street dwelling and economized brutality, but some music writers appeared to have failed to enter into the internal logic of the album – to join Actress in his experiment in sight and aurality called quotidian observation – when they rush to cast *Ghettoville* as the soundtrack to a place where life has been scorched out of existence.[28]

In order for us to develop a conceptual grammar for *Ghettoville*, it is important at this point to pause in the close analysis of Actress' output and schematize quotidian observation. The formulation requires careful unpacking, because contained within it is a proposition regarding the relationship between not only the way Actress looks as he walks across South London and the transformation of that looking into music, but how that coverage of ground is rendered as sound. All of this activity – which involves a deconstruction of perspective as well as a grounding in the concrete – is inseparable from the way blackness permeates the atmosphere of urban poverty in South London as both racialized knowledge and the arrhythmic movements of force.

It is Hito Steyerl and Katherine McKittrick who provide the conceptual tools with which to address these concerns. Whilst Steyerl is concerned with biopolitical power as it operates from above, and McKittrick's attention is focused on the production of black geographies from below, what makes these two thinkers complementary is their commitment to desedimenting normative cartographic constructions of the urban.

In her essay 'In Free Fall: A thought experiment on vertical perspective' Steyerl charts a paradigm shift whereby the eye of the sovereign in the visual ordering of the world has undergone a transformation. Steyerl makes the case that one of the mechanisms for the constitution of the modern world and subject was the development of linear perspective. Through the spheres of navigation, painting, philosophy, and architecture, the epistemic construction of linear perspective as the scientific truth of the subject became the ground from which to manage time and space. As a result, the history of linear perspective, Steyerl argues, runs in tandem with the modern projects of slavery, capture, and conquest that were launched from Europe and North America.

Steyerl is careful to stress that racial enslavement and colonization, like linear perspective, were uneven, sporadic, and contingent in their emergence. It was only after their near successful implementation that they were historicized as monolithic. A conjunctural moment she turns to when making this point is J.W. Turner's 1840 painting *The Slave Ship*. In its materiality and moral impulse, this painting marks a collision point between the constitution of the sovereign in its mastery of linear perspective, and modernity as a system of capture and enslavement:

At the sight of the effects of colonization and slavery, linear perspective – the central viewpoint, the position of mastery, control and subjecthood – is abandoned and starts tumbling and tilting, taking with it the idea of space and time as systematic constructions. The idea of a calculable and predictable future shows a murderous side through an insurance that prevents economic loss by inspiring cold-blooded murder. Space dissolves into mayhem on the unstable and treacherous surface of an unpredictable sea.[29]

The eventual disintegration of those particular iterations of racialized capture, control, and surplus value extraction by the close of the twentieth century did not mean that the structural relationship between sovereignty, visual perspective, and administration had ceased to function. Steyerl argues that what took place was a repurposing of the same impulses. In a new conjuncture a combination of military technology, silicon valley speculation, and the entertainment industry has allowed for the introduction of an updated model of surveillance organized from above. Whereas previously the basis for the capture of bodies and land had been the construction of horizon, now drones, closed circuit television, and Google Maps allow for a new biopolitical governance she calls '3D sovereignty'. What these technological changes marked was a shift from a colonial mapping of the face of the world, towards more acute and strategic regulation of territory and populations within urban enclaves along lines of race and class. In effect, '3D sovereignty' redesigned the racial role of ocular mastery for finance capital.

As was the case with *The Slave Ship* and linear perspective, Steyerl presses the point that such flattening regulative practices are as unsettled as they have always been. Or to put it another way, their ubiquity and the incessant assertion of their optic power only masks the precarity of the networks of regulation, administration, and sovereignty they are built to secure:

But if the new views from above recreate societies as free-falling urban abysses and splintered terrains of occupation, surveilled aerially and policed biopolitically, they may also – as linear perspective did – carry the seeds of their own demise with them.[30]

As opposed to the racialized biopolitics of surveillance, the object of Katherine McKittrick's critique is the field of human geography and the ways in which its practitioners determine racialized knowledge about territories and populations. The epistemic reordering McKittrick calls for in *Demonic Grounds: Black Women and the Cartographies of Struggle* is built upon the proposition that the relations between people, land, and infrastructure operative within the black diaspora open up unrealized conceptions of space, place, and corporeality.

The fundamental problem she identifies with human geography is its 'discursive attachment to stasis and physicality, the idea that space "just is" and that space and place are merely containers for human complexities and social relations.'[31] The configurations of spaces-places as empty vessels in which sociality is merely held have been organized through a geographic construction of a 'unitary vantage point'. As a mechanism for the production of geographic knowledge this vantage point:

Naturalize[s] both identity and place, repetitively spatializing where nondominant groups 'naturally' belong. This is, for the most part, accomplished through economic, ideological, social and political processes that see and position the racial-sexual body within what seem like predetermined, or appropriate, places and assume that this arrangement is commonsensical.[32]

The stasis that governs the production of geographical knowledge, particularly as it is racialized, takes on specific forms within a city. Social distinctions that are commonly understood as characteristics of specific bodies become mechanisms for reading entire zones:

Ideas are turned into spaces: phenotype *can* reflect place and place *can* reflect phenotype. Or why *are* all the black people living in that particular neighborhood? The socioeconomic mapping of blackness, the unjust and economically driven naturalization of difference, shows the material base of race/racism, the conditions under which many subaltern populations live and have lived, and the spatial constitution of socially produced categories.[33]

Strongly resonant of Laura Harris' account of the aesthetic sociality of blackness, McKittrick's aims, with regards to black geographies, are twofold. Firstly, she wants to 'expose domination as a visible spatial project that organizes, names and sees social differences (such as black femininity) and determines where social order happens'.[34] Secondly, she does not wish to refuse the idea that zones of a city can be given to an understanding of blackness and/or poverty. Instead her attention is focused upon the contradiction between the *external* geographical ascriptions of a territory as an empty vessel in which poverty stricken black diasporans are held (the unitary vantage point), and the *internal* production of a spatialized blackness that moves within, against, and through various modes of confinement. An internal sociality is generated by those living within these 'static' places that reterritorializes the apparent container-like qualities of such zones, into the means for the realization of blackness in ways that do not cohere with the logic of geographical governance.

The attention McKittrick gives to this contradiction allows her to develop an alternative understanding of ground. Using Edouard Glissant's notion of the 'poetics of landscape', McKittrick deploys the 'expressive' as the vector through which to enter into the lived contradiction between external ascriptions and internal production in black geographies:

Insisting that different kinds of expression are multifariously even, that is, not hierarchically constituted as, for example, 'written' over 'oral', and that landscape does not simply function as a decorative background, opens up the possibility for thinking about the production of space as unfinished, a poetics of questioning.[35]

Rejecting the need for the controlling technology of a unitary vantage point, instead, for McKittrick, with the dominance of the expressive there is 'nonlinearity, contradictory histories, dispossession'.[36] The importance of thinking black geographies in this way is due to the embrace of topographical 'derangement'. This is what leads to, by way of Sylvia Wynter, 'demonic grounds' as a territorial concept which encompasses both the cosmological and the mathematical:

The demonic connotes a working system that cannot have a determined or knowable outcome. The demonic, then, is a non-determinist schema; it is a process that is hinged on uncertainty and non-linearity because the organizing principle cannot predict the future.[37]

Black geographies operate through such forms of derangement, because what is at stake is an irruption of the lines between blackness as a racial property and blackness as undercommon operation. Thinking about this in terms of the city, McKittrick offers a means of reordering the normative containment of blackness and poverty via the framework of urbicide. A demonic practice, rather than correcting the pathological ascription of zones commonly referred to as 'ghettos', enters into this pathology and insists upon the improvisation of territory taking place through its very ground. Such derangement can most often be found in the expressive and gestural life of pathologized urban social life.

Through their respective engagements with 3D sovereignty and unitary vantage point, Steyerl and McKittrick show how the administration of space does have as its target racialized urban populations, but those modes of governance are in a state of perpetually frustrated incompletion. The racialized and impoverished populations in question, supposedly held within empty shell-like zones and monitored in 3D, are what Moten and Harney would call consummate conservers of bad debt. The debt they hold together becomes the very function of their sociality and production of territory, because it places them both at the apex of and underneath the dominant system of credit. Devoid of any serious communal pressure to present themselves to the regimes of credit as coherent 'communities' or 'stakeholders', there is a perverse, irregular freedom to roam free from the commands of civil society, even as racialized capitalism continues to generate material conditions of almost unbearable pressure. The question is one of priority – what comes first? For McKittrick and Steyerl, as with Moten and Harney, the fractured territoriality of blackness and/as poverty is anoriginary, in that it both announces and destabilizes modes of urban governance.

The path from Actress' quotidian observation as it relates to *Ghettoville*, to the language of shattered linearity, demonic ground, and debt, invites further mediation on our part. The relation between the specific (poverty on the streets of South London) and the general (black diasporic geographies) as I have presented it is too broad to cohere. An account, then, of biopolitical surveillance and spatial containment in London might offer mechanisms for illuminating the way in which Actress uses something like derangement to transform the distance between 3D sovereignty and poverty into a method for making music.

Here, David Marriott's account of the race–class panoptics of London may provide a useful point of reference. The location he turns to is Peckham in the borough of Southwark, South East London. The date: 27th November 2000. The event is the murder of Damilola Taylor, a 10-year-old black child who was stabbed and bled to death in a stairwell while walking from the local library to his home. To be more precise, Marriott is concerned with the CCTV images of Taylor's last movements as he left Peckham library, and the entry of this footage into the mediascape as the murder became headline news:

> The entire three sequences are haunted by this symbolic distance between what appears and what remains ungraspable as resemblance: the death of a boy that cannot be seen and which, because of that, appears everywhere in these images, but without which these images remain an empty sign of that event, a semblance in which his death is vanished.[38]

Key for Marriott is how the footage of Taylor, and its reproduction, marks both the economy of the visual and an ocular emptiness that speaks to his blackness. CCTV is part of a technological apparatus in London whereby 'the excessive visibility of the socially undesirable' is both produced and regulated.[39] In the case of Damilola Taylor, Marriott argues, a more brutal truth about the media economy of the visual is exposed: namely, that such biopolitical technologies can only function through the racialized catastrophe of black death in the most economically precarious parts of the city.

The forces of racial hegemony and capital that organize the optical reproduction of black life in a city such as London are, for Marriott, an outcome of the failed resolution of slavery and colonialism. This failed resolution means they have been reengineered into the contemporary methods of biopolitical surveillance. Black images that pass through the circuits of regulation, news, and entertainment, according to Marriott, have a vexed ontology: 'bypassing both presence and the present in a truly negative, destructive act of separation and one that remains, in the end, spectral, haunted by the presences of what it is not.'[40] The result is that even in the case of Damilola Taylor, this murder, precisely because it took place in Peckham (a location at the time historically overdetermined by pathological figurations of race and class), becomes part of a territorial discourse that can only understand blackness as 'the epitome of lawless violence.'[41]

Marriott offers a potent territorial reading of poverty and blackness in post-2000s South London. He deploys a weave of ubiquitous destruction and ontological absence, one that is for him inseparable from the

way black life in London is reproduced through the mechanisms of surveillance, rendering the city an object of geographical knowledge. Due to
the fact that both Actress and Marriott undertake their respective projects
within more or less the same racialized geographies, and were doing so
during the emergence of the full urban flourishing of a particular mode
of finance capital, it would be tempting for us to think them together.
However, I want to suggest that there is instead a sharp contrast between
the scope of Marriott's analysis and Actress' method of sonic composition. The issue with Marriott is that he is not so much providing a hyper-
panoptical account of race and class in neoliberal London as reproducing
the dominant ontology of surveillance. For him, a kind of necropolitical
power lies within what Steyerl would call 3D sovereignty and McKittrick,
unitary vantage point. In contrast, such technologies are anything but the
generative source of *Ghettoville*. Actress deploys quotidian observation to
walk through the social life of South London that Marriott takes in via the
lens of the security camera.

Therefore, to get to grips with Actress' quotidian observation, we need
to return to Steyerl and McKittrick. It is important to recall that in naming 3D sovereignty as the reconstitution of linear mastery, Steyerl argued
the degrees of force used to secure this regime always ran in discordant
relation to the precarity of its mechanisms. Similarly, McKittrick makes
it clear that the unitary vantage point of geography was always in a state
of dissipation due to the demonic practices of blackness. For Steyerl, the
point of emphasis is not 3D sovereignty as the organizational mechanism
of the urban, but instead the imminent truth of its fracturing, something
she names as 'fallenness':

A fall toward objects without reservation, embracing a world of forces and matter, which lacks any original stability and sparks the sudden shock of the open: a
freedom that is terrifying, utterly deterritorializing, and always already unknown.
Falling means ruin and demise as well as love and abandon, passion and surren-
der, decline and catastrophe. Falling is corruption as well as liberation, a condition
that turns people into things and vice versa. It takes place in an opening we could
endure or enjoy, embrace or suffer, or simply accept as reality.

Finally, the perspective of free fall teaches us to consider a social and political dreamscape of radicalized class war from above, one that throws jaw-dropping
social inequalities into sharp focus. But falling does not only mean falling apart, it
can also mean a new certainty falling into place. Grappling with crumbling futures

that propel us backward onto an agonizing present, we may realize that the place we are falling toward is no longer grounded, nor is it stable. It promises no community, but a shifting formation.[42]

McKittrick finds something similar emanating out from the inside of black geographies:

Black geographies compromise philosophical, material, imaginary, and representational trajectories; each of these trajectories, while interlocking, is also indicative of multiscalar processes, which impact upon and organize the everyday. Black geographies are located within and outside the boundaries of traditional spaces and places; they expose the limitations of transparent space through black social particularities and knowledges; they locate and speak back to the geographies of modernity, transatlantic slavery, and colonialism; they illustrate the ways in which the raced, classed, gendered, and sexual body is often an indicator of spatial options and the ways in which geography can indicate racialized habitation patterns; they are places and spaces of social, economic, and political denial and resistance; they are fragmented, subjective, connective, invisible, visible, unacknowledged, and conspicuously positioned; they have been described as, among other things, rhizomorphic, a piece of the way, diasporic, blues terrains, spiritual, and Manichaean.[43]

It is with these two passages that we can begin to grasp Actress' use of quotidian observation in the making of *Ghettoville*: falling, as a means of insecure grounding; the continual staging of the same walk in the impromptu anticipation of another encounter like the last; the aggregation of the mundane; gestures and patterns, gestures into patterns, gestures against patterns. All of this, and more, attaches itself to Actress as the uninitiated, incomplete effects of the apparently derelict sociality surrounding him in South London. He then carefully distills this material through pieces of hardware and software, and uses the results to make electronic music that in its style and conditions is black. Which is not to say *Ghettoville* is an accurate representation of impoverishment, it is not a mouthpiece for a subaltern class who are unable to speak for themselves. Instead, with *Ghettoville*, Actress pitches the listener into a world that is directly in front of them, if only they had the lenses to see it. It is a (sound)world with no need for those outside it, will carry on its phonic production of deranged autonomy regardless, which is why for those lacking the ears and eyes, all they can hear are the caricatured cinematic landscapes of post-apocalyptic urbanism.

Wrap Yourself Around Me

Returning to the assessments Gibb, Saxelby, Finlayson, and others made of *Ghettoville* as a broken and exhausted city, it is important to indicate in greater detail how they do not address the fundamental totality of the album. Their accounts of 'Forgiven', 'Street Corp', and other tracks in the early sections of the record as relentless, oppressive, and bleak are in many respects faithful renderings. I feel though that these are not the full array of colors present in *Ghettoville*. As it reaches a conclusion there are a run of tracks which on the surface signal an incongruous shift in atmosphere.

'Don't', like the tracks which precede it on *Ghettoville*, contains little immediate information. What we can hear though is fine-tuned to almost microscopic detail and the impression is given that we are listening to a section cut from a much larger composition. The dominant feature on 'Don't' is a post-euphoric vocal statement (*don't stop the music*). Half-sung half-spoken, it is repeated over and over again across the body of the track. Given a blissed-out effect by dint of heavy filtering, the vocal glistens with neon moistness. The almost minute-and-a-half refracted looping of the vocal means as a statement it lingers between declaration ('the music must not be stopped') and yearning ('*please*, don't stop the music').

With the following track, 'Rap', a similar compositional schema is retained, but the atmosphere is serving a different purpose. Again, there is a repeated, almost obsessive, studied looping of what feels like a single moment lifted from an unidentified song. The textural mechanics of this clip feature a rhythm track with a minor, arresting stutter, which, when combined with the vocal (*wrap yourself around me*), gives the entire piece the feel of a slow jam, with all its attendant seductive hapticality.

It is with 'Rule' that these concluding statements reach a peak. In this instance the recurring structure of off-kilter movement is in place. A dissected and stretched vocal sample from the London all female hip-hop trio She Rockers' 'Give It A Rest', and the refracted keyboard riff from Crystal Water's 'Gypsy Woman', form the central skewed syncopating devices. This voice and keys, rolling at alternate speeds, run out of sync with a sparse, digitized beat. All of these elements proceed along at a pace, never entirely appearing to cohere, but still operating in relation to each other, whilst increasing in intensity. That is until they all lock together. This is not to say they are evened out and rendered sensible, but rather the off-syncopation that placed them in relation becomes the ecstatic foundation of 'Rule' through the intensification of each individual element.

'Don't', 'Rap', and 'Rule', as pieces which conclude the album, contain notable characteristics of the dancefloor dynamics and electronic R'n'B which are the defining sonic reference points for Actress. These are all styles that can be given to the general category of black music, and they are also musical forms which are materially, socially, and culturally – to varying degrees – determined by a relationship to concentrated areas of economically precarious, racially encoded urban inhabitation in the Global North during the late twentieth and early twenty-first centuries. Such territories have been given various names across the Atlantic world: ghettos, housing projects, estates, shantytowns, tenement yards, favelas, and banlieues, to name a few. I am not paying attention to these tracks in order to conceive of *Ghettoville* as an album of two parts, the first embedded in the debilitation of racialized urban poverty and the second illuminating the lines of flight from such a place. For me there is something much more fundamental at stake in the way he makes use of quotidian observation to assemble *Ghettoville*. 'Street Corp', 'Forgiven', and 'Corner' function on three planes. They can be understood as recordings of the ecological grind of concentrated poverty in a city. It is just that Actress does not interpret this grind as a constraint. Through his improvisational style of studied observation, a kind of relentless roving through the terrain of South London, Actress uses *Ghettoville* to reorder the flattened imaging of finance capital's decayed zones as ones defined by the barest materiality. As he encounters someone pushing along a world in a shopping trolley, and gives to street dwellers what was always their wealth in the first place, Actress is looking to work with a sociality that is in constant motion. This sociality (which one could describe as demonic and fallen) has provided the settings for the urban musical forms Actress draws upon and reassembles through the framework of his observations. House, Techno, and electronic R'n'B from across the diaspora have situated themselves in geographical environments that have a kinship with the zones of South London Actress traverses. The environments, like the musical styles, are not uniform, in that each has its own local traits, histories, dynamics, geographies, and aesthetic functions. Yet they contain the combinations of forms, structure, elasticity, and meaning that Actress requires for his desired sense of abstraction to cohere.

With a record such as *Ghettoville*, it is an error to conceive of it as a phonographical map which can be taken in, in its entirety, through the producer as the ethnographic point of orientation. Instead, what quotidian observation allows Actress to do is to use *Ghettoville* to generate multi-scalar black sonic ecologies. The fracturing lines of movement through the layered environments of the South London he sees and then modulates into sounds, operate in such a way that a relatively minor gesture, action or event is magnified to an epic scale, or conversely, something monumental is shrunken to the extent it becomes a barely audible trace. As a result, when listening to 'Street Corp' it is accurate to describe it as a sonic rendering of social negation, but its negation is the code of the dissonant ecstasy of 'Rule'. The dystopic endzone of 'Forgiven' is a micro-section of the coital lush of 'Rap'. The abandoned industrial grind of 'Towers' has locked within it the teary-eyed bliss of 'Don't'. By the same measure, the songlike reveries and soundsystem bass propulsions Actress feeds into the album are inoperable without those configurations of apparently near desolate un-music.

The brilliance of *Ghettoville* as a piece of black music lies in the indivisibility of the totality of the record. I believe this is not despite its apparent contradictions but precisely because of them. Actress transforms the atmospheric relations of urbanization into a soundscape in a seeming ability to grasp that what is at stake is a (racialized) system, a lifeworld (of the poor) that does not require credit restoration, but instead seeks to continue in its riotous production of difference, the simultaneous possession and dispossession resulting from the general antagonism, that is the open secret of undercommons. Actress digitally distills the microtonal emanations of the ground of South London, from the arrangement of decaying plant life on concrete, to the beautiful labor that goes into the self-maintenance of what some would choose to call poverty. He achieves this by abstracting the engines of Techno, House, and electronic R'n'B, modes of musical production that mark urban environments across the black diaspora. Without ever withdrawing from either the music or the territorial lifeworlds of the poor, instead he synthesizes the two, because they are imminent to each other, even in the texture of their negations.

The spatial account of poverty in *Ghettoville* is therefore not solely one of brutal imposition. It is not about a place where the state has failed, where policy urgently needs to be written and neighborhoods plead to be managed. Rather *Ghettoville* amplifies an intricately assembled resource, a social wealth operating as accumulated debt. Actress appears not to be fetishizing these social relations, but recognizing that the grind of street life which makes the ghetto appear a racial dystopia to some, has been the provision for some of the most sophisticated and compelling mass experiments in sound-making to be heard in the late twentieth and early twenty-first centuries. There is a change of state that takes place, where the vexed ontology of bare existence animates forms of movement that allow for the organized production of sound. What we have in the case of Actress' *Ghettoville* is nothing other than an instance of discrepant abstraction on the move in all its obstinance, strangeness, and repetition. Or to put it another way, we have another case of black music.

5

....

Eski

During the first years of our current millennium, a new form of black electronic dance music was generated in London's eastern boroughs. This music came to be known as Grime. The intensity with which Grime permeated the ad-hoc networks, unofficial soundscapes, and improvised everyday of an ever-present, if largely unremarked upon, lifeworld of London, makes its impact comparable to one of its progenitors: Jungle. For those tuned into its frequencies at the time, Grime was *everywhere.*

There are many reasons as to why Grime was a remarkable project. For one, it engineered a singularly London style and sensibility of MC-ing. Equally as important was its intricacy as a sound, combining the propulsions of London's bass culture with a level of neon sharpness. In addition, there was the fact that this level of innovation emerged from what were the city's poorest and most racialized neighborhoods. What made Grime so exciting, so compelling, was its use of antagonisms. Therefore, whilst MC-ing, styles of production, and social geography, were the means for Grime's composition, each of these elements was riven by antagonisms operating within the depths of the music and across its surfaces. The notion that antagonism is the primary mode of Grime raises a number of questions: In this particular instance, what does antagonism sound like? How is it being generated? Where does it come from? Is it external to the appearance of Grime, enacting something like a suffocating press upon its capacities? Or is antagonism internal to Grime, and thus an effect of the music? Perhaps what is at stake is a volatile twinning of various antagonisms, each inhospitable (and maybe even indispensable) to the other?

Such questions require us to consider a number of issues when it comes to the status of Grime as black electronic dance music. Firstly, there are its core elements as a sound and style of performance, the atmospheres in which it was engineered, and the methods used to disseminate the music. Secondly, there is the fact of what happened when Grime's *internally composed antagonistic expansionism* came into contact with civil society and state, specifically racialized policing as an *antagonistic strategy of external duress*. My engagement with Grime rests on this fractured terrain. Our intention is to unlock the antagonisms operating between the improvisation required to generate Grime as black electronic dance music with territorial capacities, and the racialized policing of it as a dangerous pathogen which needs to be geographically contained.

Our theorization of Grime along these lines involves marking a distinction from some of the existing scholarship on this scene.[1] Whilst this work is invaluable in its analysis of the settings, religiosity, and economics of Grime, I am not attempting to add to this arena. Instead we are sidestepping such concerns by jettisoning the use of 'ethnographic veracity'.[2] By approaching Grime as a social experiment in the ecological dimensions of sound, the analysis here is soaked in what the Trinidadian intellectual C.L.R. James called 'speculation'.[3] When setting out his account of speculation, James insisted that in order to transform the observation of 'matters, events, things, personalities' as they form a 'hard knot' into 'the basis of a new substance', it requires a speculative dimension of thinking, one that is capable of loosening established structures about the presupposed unity of entities.[4] Therefore, in order for us to realize some of what was engineered through Grime, it is not enough, for example, to as faithfully as possible describe Grime's location in the boroughs of Tower Hamlets and Newham in the early 2000s, or to transcribe the accounts of, say, D Double E, Kano, Footsie, and Skepta. Instead the page itself needs to become a potential site of *further* production of what were already Grime's experimental imperatives. Of course, to simply state that one is going to produce an analysis which works like Grime in order to theorize it is somewhat presumptuous, overly ambitious, and open to failure. Yet it is worthwhile speculating on the relationship between geography (tower block and road), technology (Fruity Loops and pirate radio), performance (MC, producer, and DJ), and soundscape (riddim and dubplate), because it allows for an amplification of the ways in which Grime – as a form of black music in London – systematically concentrated and patterned antagonism into a sonic ecology.

POW!

First up are the shuffles, then come the thuds. Alternating between the shaken hiss of the former sound and the hollowed weight of the latter, there is seemingly nothing else to be heard aside from their interplay. Until, after a few seconds, the toxic thrust and metallic drips arrive, washing over and working around the opening elements. Then we have steel-reinforced slams, adding a hint of menace to the increasing vibe of detached angularity. All of these sounds are funneled through the treble channel, exposing the rough, synthetic, and lethal edges of the composition. Despite what might appear to be their disparate relationship to each other, this collection of sounds has been arranged with a bubbling propulsiveness.

Whilst all this is going on there is a voice using the shuffles, thuds, drips, and pulse to conduct a performance. The phrases uttered appear to be telling us something significant about a new music and the people who make it, yet at the same time these 'words' are enunciated in ways which make them indivisible from the accompanying soundscape. The performer is maneuvering their voice through this phonic terrain as if it is under immense pressure, whilst also enjoying the combativeness. Then it all stops. And the opening figures start up again, this time with a different voice in combination. There follows a third version with a further new accompanying vocal, and even a fourth arrangement.

The object described above is MC–producer Wiley's 'Ice Rink Vocal EP 1.' The annotations pertain to the 'Ice Rink' riddim. Kano, Riko Dan, Breeze, and Tinchy Stryder are the MCs whose skills are showcased successively on each of the run-throughs of the track. 'Ice Rink Vocal EP 1' serves as an introduction to the aesthetic sociality at work in the Grime scene for two reasons. Firstly, Wiley is considered the 'Godfather of Grime,' the figure who first shaped its imperatives and attitudes. Secondly, to grasp Grime at its forceful best we need to pay attention to 'Ice Rink Vocal EP 1' as an impression and reconfiguration of the scenarios in which it was made.

With the production of the 'Ice Rink' riddim and its release as a 'Vocal EP,' Wiley was able to conduct a phase-shift from what, retrospectively, can be considered the prefigurations of Grime. As a member of the 'Pay As You Go Kartel' (made up of Maxwell D, Major Ace, Playa, and God's Gift), Wiley had been embedded in the Dark Garage sound (Garage being the House-influenced style which took over Jungle's dominance as the sound of London in the late 1990s), where with the emphasis on heavy bass-lines and a reduction in vocal harmonies, the MC began to take prominence.[5] Slimzee, the crew's DJ, pioneered this development by cutting dubplates made up of slowed down Jungle alongside Dark Garage that allowed 'Pay As You Go' to showcase their 8-bar skills.[6]

Still at this late stage prior to the emergence of Grime, the MCs were set on top of the mixes almost as an accompaniment. In addition, the soundscape they were barring over was recognizably a warped version of the Garage's bubbling, slinky, sensual template exemplified by Dem 2's 'Destiny', with the faint trace of songlike structures, a busy palette, and the use of drums and bass as structuring devices. It was with the 'Ice Rink' riddim that Wiley took a leap beyond the parameters of Dark Garage into what is now understood as Grime. The fact that he redesigned himself as an MC who also produced the track, signaled a shift in status which precipitated the importance of this riddim. An arrangement of clicks and shuffles with a comparative absence of bass-lines, to say that 'Ice Rink' was minimal does not quite encapsulate its sensations. Announcing an 'emaciated' production style with nearly all frameworks exposed, Wiley's decision to strip out the rumble of the lower frequencies left behind an asymmetrical construction. The trick though was in the retention of the propulsions that defined London bass culture, but in the form of a throb which meant 'glinting, fragmentary melodies' were placed in the foreground.[7]

The new terms of order being put forward by this, and the spate of Wiley-released riddims (rhythm tracks) alongside it ('Igloo', 'Ice Pole', 'Colder Bass', 'Eskimo'), had numerous implications. They gave MCs the lead in a reorganized sonic terrain, due to the space now afforded to whoever was holding the mic. With a chrome pulse taking the place of any noticeable bass-lines, MCs could go to work on forging original oral signatures. This is not to say things got easier for them. Instead, Wiley's soundworld forced through the capacity for MCs to generate a new aesthetic imprint. Given prominence by Wiley's productions, the exposure meant the quickest-thinking and adaptable MCs shifted from the status of hype merchants to lyrical stylists, with some even designing their own tracks to suit the changed parameters. Thus, the MC–producer arrived as a new entity through Wiley's prowess. The combination of precision in production and oral bravado on the mic his methods allowed for meant the grain of the new experiments in riddim began to operate as speculative simulations of MCs' and producers' lived experience.

As is indicated by the names he gave his productions, there was a frozen quality to his output that led Wiley to initially name his style 'Eski-beat'. Whilst it is noteworthy to point out how the naming of his sound marked a period of unstable, yet productive, genre identification until several strands settled under the eventual name Grime, it is necessary for us to pay close attention to the psycho-social resonances of 'Eski-beat'.[8] Wiley was able to claim the mantle 'Godfather of Grime' because he was located in what are considered its heartlands: Bow, in the E3 postcode of Tower Hamlets. As a zone two area of inner East London, Bow was cut off from the rest of the city, not so much in terms of distance (the financial and retail districts were a bus or tube ride away), but through the institutional forces of race and class that determine London's geography. The estates branching off Roman Road were organized by a stark functionality, and it is not difficult to hear in the echoes of Wiley's 'coldness and rigor' the domesticated industrialism of these surroundings.[9] More than just architecture, it was Wiley's psychic relationship to the precarity embedded in the estates that generated the form of Eski-beat:

I'm a winter person but the cold…sometimes I just feel cold hearted. I felt cold at that time, towards my family, towards everyone. That's why I used those names. I was going to use 'North Pole' but I didn't even get that far. It was all things that were cold because that's how I was feeling. There are times when I feel warm. I am a nice person but sometimes I switch off and I'm just cold. I feel angry and cold.[10]

Photographer Nico Hogg and the writer (as well as founder of the electronic music label Keysound) Martin Clark have zeroed in on the relationship between Wiley's role in the formation of Eski-beat (as the first iteration of Grime) and the ecology of Bow. Discussing a Hogg image of Clare House tower block (one of Wiley's childhood homes in the area) Clark makes the following comment:

Often called 'the godfather of grime', Wiley spent part of his upbringing in Clare House, so when Keysound put out a 12" vinyl that (with his blessing) sampled one of his works, Nico took these shots of his former abode. Cold, industrial and undoubtedly violent at times, Clare House is a suitable answer to the questions about grime's origins. Sharp angular planes look brutal and foreboding, like inverted prison defenses. Inhuman CCTV cameras cling to inorganic walls, peering down over barren environs distrustfully. Yet between the two iron cages springs life against the odds: small plants growing from the concrete rock face. In many ways that's a perfect metaphor for the genre: a vital, creative culture that despite the odds stacked up against it, grew out of the grime.[11]

Such coldness, equal parts aesthetic and existential, did not mean 'Eski-beat' was an angst-ridden solo project for Wiley. Instead it was put to use by the MC–producer in order to ensure that within its own settings, Grime flourished. Wiley's lethal glass-like riddims did not simply flood the pirate airwaves and local record stores with only his name attached, but they were populated with other MC talents, such as those heard on 'Ice Rink Vocal EP 1'. Reaching the point at which he had established a club night ('Eskimo-dance'), Wiley's desire to become one point within a self-generating experiment reflects the way that, as seemingly alien and frozen as Grime sounded, it was also always a communal endeavor. To peel off and try to go it alone was beside the point. 'Eski-beat' (as one of the many iterations that came to be known as Grime) was so embedded into the social relations and landscape of Bow and its surrounding neighborhoods that it demanded a specific type of ambition from the artist:

I won't come off the road. I never will. I'm happy here, you hear what I'm saying? I go to any ghetto in London and stand up and rep myself, and show them love. You get what I'm saying?[12]

Wiley's was not the only name ringing out in the East London experiment that was Grime. Other MC–producers appeared and urgently took on the task of compressing local geography, collectively generated atmosphere, and the social demand for musical innovation into the invention of new riddims. By 2004 it was Lethal Bizzle's 'Pow! (Forward riddim)' that signaled the capacities of Grime.

If ever a 12″ was designed to function like an assault weapon then 'Pow!' was it. The 'Forward' riddim, taken on its own terms, is deceptively simple, with little variation beyond the 'madly gyrating loop' of a screaming melodic line and blazing drum pattern, interrupted by single percussive kicks.[13] What makes this track is that all of these elements are working relentlessly towards a singular affective purpose: to intensify Grime's pulse mechanism to the level of a forearm smash. The ferocity is not an entirely independent feature of the riddim alone, but also comes about through the sheer weight of MCs loaded onto the 12″. In just over three minutes we encounter Fumin, D Double E, Forcer, Flow Dan, Neeko, Napper, Demon, Jamakabi, and Ozzie B, alongside the producer. Given only sixteen bars to make use of Lethal's template, almost the entire surface area is taken up as the performers hurtle through the riddim.

Similar to Wiley's 'Eski-beat', the symbiosis of riddim and MCs that generates 'Pow!' operates as a phonic manipulation of the environment in which it is made; in this case though it takes on different features of the terrain. To understand the geography of the Grime scene in the early 2000s, it is important to grasp that, as Martin Clark wrote in 2005, it was 'a microcolony within a city so culturally insular vast swathes of Londoners are oblivious to its way of living'.[14] The urbanists Paul Watt and Anthony Gunter have ascribed this sense of isolation which imbued Tower Hamlets and Newham from the late 1990s onwards to a combination of the economic restructuring of the city and a state-led program of neoliberalization which 'brought increased socio-spatial polarization in London…and the enforced concentration of a deprived, multi-ethnic working class into marginal spaces'.[15] Conversely, according to Simon Reynolds, this generated an autonomy, insularity, and acute attentiveness to territory that became essential to the capacity of the sound:

Its absolute heartland consists of a few square miles of in that part of East London not served by the Tube. In truth it's a parochial scene, obsessed with a sense of place, riven by internecine conflicts and territorial rivalries (the intense competitiveness being one reason Grime's so creative).[16]

Grime, as a system of social and musical experimentation might have been born of isolation and taken on the appearance of insularity, but this did not mean it was without relation to the rest of the city. The eastern boroughs in which it was formed were amongst the most economically unstable, but directly across the river, bearing down on the local landscape, was the financial district in Canary Wharf. Pay close attention and it becomes clear how much this monolith of 'futures, champagne and bad debt' is a reference point for the Grime scene:

That's where all the yuppies are. We're just over the road and it's one of the worst boroughs in England.[17]

Canary Wharf is like our Statue of Liberty. It pushes me on. It's like all the money is there and it's an inspiration to get your own.[18]

There is a disjuncture here, resulting from the combination of proximity and distance between Grime's 'microscopically local' landscape and the architectures of finance, that becomes a fuel for the levels of propulsion heard in 'Pow!'.[19] The appositional rub between the metropolitan concentration of finance capital and a seemingly underdeveloped microcolony means that, as Dan Hancox writes of MC Fumin's bars on 'Pow!', the track becomes a space generating mechanism:

'buss' meaning to fire a gunshot, bust a move, or strike out, express yourself – find space and freedom. Grime in its first flash of youth was thrilling because it was claustrophobic, a hectic cacophony of beats and synth stabs, channeling the high-rise tension of tower blocks, the limited horizons and possibilities. But just like real claustrophobia, it demands freedom – and space.[20]

It is this repurposing of claustrophobic tension into a tool for creating territory that illuminates the overloading of MCs in the confines of 'Pow! (Forward riddim)'. Such was the soundscape of 'Pow!' when played in clubs that the record received censure from venues hosting Grime dances. It seems as if the degrees of weaponization encoded into it had a corresponding effect on dancers, producing in them hyperbolically congealed bursts of energy. These responses from audiences and club operators to 'Pow!' give some indication of the ecological scope engrained into the phonic materiality of Grime. It has something to do with the way Lethal Bizzle's track appeared to conjoin Grime's situation on the psycho-social margins of London, the friction of its proximity to the architectures of high finance, and the customary constrictions placed upon the social life of those whom Bizzle refers to as 'East London's finest'. To go a stage further, 'Pow!' sounded like a dynamic reconfiguring of these relations, to the extent that the 12" carried with it the threat of territorial expansion from the microcolony.

For the Ruff Sqwad crew local geography was similarly a factor in their presentation – the regular appearance of Canary Wharf in promotion shots and videos offering evidence of an association with landscape. Yet, the defining features of their sound illuminate something else besides the aesthetic engineering of territory, sonic composition, and vocal performance in Grime. Rapid, Dirty Danger, XTC, Slix, Tinchy Stryder, and Shifty Rydos were barely teenagers when their productions marked them out as a force to be reckoned with. 'Functions on the Low' and 'Pied Piper' are riddims which represent one portion of the Ruff Sqwad palette. Held together by intricately weaved melodies, these riddims carry traces of Wiley's emaciated Eski-sound, in that the drums are skeletal background effects and the bass is all but absent. The difference is that as a production unit Ruff Sqwad chose to assemble bold emotive compositions, where myriad synth lines are projected with such fullness that they appear to sing.

At the other extreme there are the crew's 'Tings in Boots' and 'Raw to the Core' riddims. Whilst some melodic emphasis is present, the dominant features on each of these MC templates are the snaked drum patterns and wobbling, buzzed, bass throbs. Particularly with 'Raw', the staccato nature of the bass means rather than giving weight and structure to the production, it pushes at its limits and threatens to overwhelm the framework.

Riddims with such marked distinctions in characteristics became the bedrock for Ruff Sqwad's reputation as a production–MC collective, especially on their *Guns & Roses* mixtape series. The ability to contain this range of colors within the output of a single crew was due to their unique form of sonic engineering. To comprehend their production style – and by extension those of the wider Grime scene – we need to consider the way Rapid and XTC were experimenting with a range of equipment that was readily to hand.

Rapid speaks of affection for the tools that were vital to his – and other Grime producers – capacity to build riddims. The increasing availability of desk-top PCs to those on moderate incomes was a socio-economic shift he was able to exploit:

It's a sign of how precocious they were, that asked when they first started making beats, Rapid and Dirty can only place it by school year: 'I think [year] eight or nine [equivalent to 7th or 8th grade],' Rapid says, eventually agreeing to tie this to a calendar year (2002). 'We had a parents' evening, and my teacher said: "He needs a PC, to be doing his homework, and research and stuff." and my dad was sort of embarrassed, so a week later he went out and bought me a Packard Bell, which came with all these programmes.'[21]

Once with this piece of hardware, the production device of choice for Rapid, XTC, and Dirty Danger became Fruity Loops, at the time a digital audio workstation which due to the relative ease of online piracy was readily accessible.[22] Although they were not the most hi-spec music production tools on the market, the fact that they were within the financial grasp of black teenagers from East London allowed Ruff Sqwad, and a host of other crews, to make improper use of these devices to suit their specific needs. 'Improper' here refers to a level of technological repurposing that allowed Ruff Sqwad to expand the capacities of such 'low grade' tools. Through the improvised corruption these and other producers developed in concert, programs such as Fruity Loops and Cubase became foundational to the aesthetic grain of Grime as a site- (East London) and socially (black) specific project.

The materials we have worked through so far have functioned as a mapping exercise of the experiment that was Grime in early 2000s East London. Each segment of this map, whether it be Wiley's 'Eski-beat', Lethal Bizzle's 'Pow! (Forward riddim)' or the Ruff Sqwad, represents a central, but by no means exhaustive, marker in the making of the sound. All of the elements were most potently realized through the dynamics of pirate radio. As its primary disseminating technology, pirate radio became decisive in determining the soundscape and performative drive of Grime. Its specificities will be given closer attention as we proceed, but for the moment it is worthwhile detailing some of the practical features of the way Grime and pirate radio were intertwined.

The practice of illegally broadcasting the latest electronic music of London's young and black populations had been solidified through the peak 1990s eras of Jungle, Drum n Bass, and Garage.[23] Due to its legacy in those earlier styles, and structural barriers placed in its path, Grime became embedded in the pirate radio network to the extent that the capacities of the sound and this technological form became indivisible.[24] Over the years of its development as an apparatus for the showcasing of new black electronic dance music in London, a number of core elements had been refined as requirements for the establishment of a pirate. These included a set of decks and fresh dubplates, a transmitter, knowledge of numerous vacant tower block apartments, a roster of MCs and DJs to power the station, and an audience ready to receive the signal. Alongside established operations from the Jungle/Drum n Bass period ('Kool FM'), new signals such as 'Pressure FM' and 'Deja Vu FM' appeared in order to push the new Grime sound. It was 'Rinse FM' though, established by

Geenus, Slimzee, and Uncle Dugs, that became its most intense amplifier. The key operational task with a pirate such as Rinse, according to Slimzee, was to transform tower blocks into broadcast devices through various forms of ad-hoc engineering:

I missed cutting wires, I missed cutting the aerials. Like it was a part of your life, you know what I mean?...I used to love going on the roof, all times of the night, getting dirty, the smell of the roof. You get that buzz from it, you know what I mean?[25]

It was vital though to be flexible and to move at speed, because by invading the FM frequency, pirates became the target of increasingly draconian legal measures by local state agencies, the Department of Trade and Industry, and OFCOM (Office of Communications – the government regulator of broadcasting and telecommunications): 'Pirate radio gives you a buzz. If you got hit, go straight back on. You know what I mean like. You just wanna be on air'.[26] Slimzee himself became a victim of these institutions when in 2005 he received an ASBO (Anti-Social Behavior Order) preventing him going above the fifth floor of any building or face the alternative of five years in prison. By this stage though, as Melissa Bradshaw notes:

when OFCOM bust down his door, Rinse were the biggest pirate radio station in the game, and Slimzee was at the epicenter of a grime scene grappling with the contradictions of being newly celebrated in a world whose institutions – the police, OFCOM, the legal system – were prejudiced against it.[27]

As well as the types of producer–MC–crew–riddim manifestations we have discussed so far, the practicalities of establishing and maintaining a pirate were core to the production of Grime. The work that went into keeping Rinse, as well as Deja Vu, Pressure, Heat, and innumerable others on the air, created an audiophonic venue where fresh riddims were tested out by DJs and new MC talent announced itself.

With Grime, socially improvised activity was being channeled through illegal signals, which were taking a proliferation of sonic experiments generated in isolated areas of the city, and not only broadcasting them back into the immediate environment, but also leaving them open to whoever wanted to pick up the roving frequencies. These are a set of arrangements that demand closer attention, because for us to consider Grime only at the level of music as it is normatively framed is inadequate. Instead, when listening to the rapid arrangement of riddims in combination with the seemingly limitless number of MCs on a pirate signal, what we are tuning into is a self-assembled system that was both locked into and reformulating the vision of a given time, place, and way of living. Grime was doing something with, and to, the lived sociality of Tower Hamlets, Newham, and other eastern boroughs in the early 2000s. Thus, I want to propose that what it was able to capture, as well as speculate on, was the racial, economic, and geographical organization of East London. Grime, in this respect, served as a point of enactment for two types of gestural activity. In one sense, it was a system of generalized intelligence which – like Footwork – was able to realize itself as a sonic ecology. Specifically, though, this ecology was operating on the order of multiple antagonisms which appeared to either reflect or threaten to destabilize the compression of race, economics, and geography in these boroughs.

Form 696

In order to focus on both of these types of activity we need to pay attention to the distinctions between the question of Grime's status as black music and the racial governance of East London. There are many indicators that tell us Grime is black music. Firstly, it can be placed directly within a continuum of black electronic dance musical experimentation that was conducted in London and other major UK cities. Its immediate genealogical and geographical progenitors include the Jungle, Drum n Bass, and Garage sounds that dominated the landscape of London, Birmingham, and Bristol from the late 1990s to the end of the decade. These experiments were diasporic in that they made use of the local presence of reggae soundsystem culture, and combined them with either the breakbeat of US House and hip-hop (Jungle, Drum n Bass), or the R'n'B flavors of Timbaland (Garage). Grime extended this ethos by looking to the postures, performativity, and organizational methods of both US hip-hop and Jamaican dancehall.[28] To think of Grime as a development out of already constituted forms though is a gross oversimplification. It is more useful to say that whilst the sharing of traits with hip-hop and dancehall is an inevitable outcome of a diasporic cultural relation, Grime was also always resolutely singular. There was an acknowledgment of borrowed approaches from North America and the Caribbean – as well as from previous MC styles in the UK – but Grime was a concerted attempt to generate a sound, scene, and comportment, specific to its local neighborhoods.[29]

The other major indicator of Grime's status as black music resulted from its meshing of population and geography. As a system of sonic experimentation Grime is predominantly – but not exclusively – made by black Londoners. This is due to the fact that its aesthetic propositions (both audio and lyrical) draw from, and speculate on, the lived experiences of largely young adults inhabiting areas of the city with the largest black populations. The qualifier 'not exclusively' is intended to mark the way in which, during the initial burst of the Grime scene, the presence of figures who were racialized as white (such as Slimzee and Geenus, as well as Scratchy of Roll Deep) was neither an anomaly nor evidence of external imposters. Rather, it was an organic outcome of the composition of race–class in London. Therefore, one indication that Grime can be considered black music is that it functions as a manifestation of the forces of urbanization encoded into the city.[30]

The question of Grime's status as black music has buried within, and interrupting, it the question of the blackness of Grime. Although there is a relationship between the two, all that I have presented in the paragraphs above regarding Grime as black music is at best cursory description. In order to press this question we need to take the sedimented histories and socialities of Grime (it draws on black musical forms, is made largely – but not exclusively – by black diasporans in areas of the city with concentrated working-class and surplus labor populations) and deploy them to ask more fundamental questions of how Grime – by way of its *blackness* – unhinged the forces which structured the race–class composition of London in the early 2000s. Therefore, the question of the blackness of Grime needs to address how, as a form of black music, it presented itself as a crisis in the territorial and administrative control of the city. Which is to say it generated a crisis in policing. Which is it say it represented a crisis in racialization.

Over the course of the late twentieth century the policing of London has remained a racialized activity. It has enveloped the city to such an extent that it is no longer adequate to think of policing as an isolated institutional practice conducted by a group of state-sanctioned 'officers'.

Rather, policing in London is a totalizing racist strategy which can be used by any governance structure, or any person who wishes to position themselves as a legitimate citizen.[31] Therefore, to grasp the blackness of Grime (as it moves through the question of Grime as black music) involves addressing its entanglement with racialized policing. Pirate radio, as both a venue for, and part of, the phono-material grain of Grime, is embedded in this scenario.

Many of the reasons as to how and why pirate radio became a central mechanism of Grime can be traced into the prohibition that was placed on Grime's performance in officially governed public leisure space. Grime was always intended to be pirate *and* club music. It was built to be *live* in both senses. Not only did MCs need to be heard, they needed to be seen. Riddims were not made solely to be taken in through headphones or car speakers, but were designed to course through a soundsystem. More importantly, in order for all the constituent elements of the Grime scene to cohere, it required the oxygen of gatherings, where the arrangements of sounds and lyrics could be worked out through the movements of a crowd. These capacities were denied by the Metropolitan Police (Met). Their tool of choice was Form 696, a risk assessment exercise introduced in 2004. Form 696 was designed to assess the 'risk' of criminal activity and violence at any music event across the city. The form allowed the Met to pre-emptively gather information about performers and audiences from the promoters of a music event. Failure to comply would lead to the event's closure, with a £20,000 fine and possible jail sentence for the license holders. Journalist Dan Hancox has written extensively on Form 696 since 2009, progressively detailing the effects it had upon the performance of Grime in London. At first there was a blanket enforcement of the form across all music venues and events. Amongst its most disconcerting elements was the request that all license holders provide information about the racial make-up of the expected audiences, and if any performers held criminal records. Added to that was the need for promoters to detail the genres of music to be played at their event. The suggested examples listed on this section of the form would generally be regarded as black music (Bashment, R'n'B, and Garage).

The Met were initially heavily criticized over Form 696. Naturally, there were legitimate accusations leveled of racially profiling music fans and performers. Yet the most vocal opposition came from the established elements in the music industry which considered themselves safe, legitimate, and resented the additional administrative complications the form presented. The decision was made to produce a second version of the form, which as Hancox reported, was more subtly crafted:

They went away. They came back. They announced that actually, sorry chaps, they would stop bothering live music fans across the board, instead narrowing their focus to 'large promoted events between 10pm and 4am which feature MCs and DJs performing to recorded backing tracks'. Or 'grime nights' as they are sometimes known.[32]

He continues:

It's no exaggeration to suggest that the period 2004–09 represents a systematic and deliberate attempt by the Metropolitan Police to remove music performed largely by young black men from the public sphere…It's bureaucracy as a weapon.[33]

JME, an MC with Boy Better Know crew, was amongst the most vocal artists within the scene on this issue. In 2014, he produced a short film, 'Form 696: The Police vs Grime', which provided a platform for fellow MCs, producers, DJs, and promoters to vent their frustrations with the Met.[34] The consistent line that emerges from the film is a lack of transparency as to why Grime nights faced such levels of scrutiny and likelihood of enforced cancellation. Form 696 became more or less successful in excluding Grime from public space in London before it was officially scrapped in 2017. Its success was not necessarily a direct result of the technical procedures laid out by the Met. Rather, the very existence of the form generated a sense of suspicion around Grime. Venues became increasingly nervous about putting on Grime nights, and some even went to the extent of self-policing by banning the music entirely. The fact that some performers did have criminal records, however minor, gave the Met license to stop and search them as they arrived at or left shows.[35]

The lack of justification on the part of the Met Police for what Hancox quite aptly calls a bureaucratic weapon is hardly surprising. The absence of dialogue allowed the racialized features of Form 696 to remain an effective policing tool precisely through the use of confused and arbitrary measures that are stealthily linked to the racial categorization of artists and audience, as well as the blackness of the musical style. In this sense what Form 696 did so effectively was to step into a wider circuit of racialized policing which, for a number of years, has cultivated a pernicious relationship to black music in London, and by extension to impinge on the ability of black populations in the city to move freely without the threat of state duress. There is a sliding scale of racialized policing that seeks to encircle black social life in the city, into which a piece of policy such as Form 696 can be inserted. At one end of the scale we have moral panic dressed up as social commentary, whereby historians, journalists, and politicians sought to make a causal link between whatever they determined as locally produced 'gangster rap' and the reported rise in knife crime amongst young black Londoners during the early 2000s.[36] The other sharp end of the scale is the direct use of institutional police power. This includes the everyday brutality of stop and search and 'hard stop' tactics, which have been consistently used to target young black people, extending to the more lethal strategies of Operation Trident, the Met's plan to dissolve gun crime through the use of its own firearms on black populations.[37]

We can see then how Form 696 worked as a technique of racialized policing. It did so by acting as a pivot between discursive pathological claims made about black music, and the co-ordinated institutionalized assault on black populations. What Form 696 did was produce a logic without ever making it concrete: *Grime cannot be performed in public because it carries with it the capacity for ungovernable violence. This ungovernable violence is a quality the music acquires from the people who make it and is generated in the areas they inhabit.* The strategy of racialized policing enacted by Form 696 provides an opportunity to discuss the relation between Grime and violence, as this was the operational basis of the Met's strategy. Such a discussion requires to us side-step the urge to conduct a moral defense of the music against the hysterical claims of the commentariat and the pernicious actions of the police force. Instead we are better served by the nuance and thoroughness of Derek Walmsley's engagement with the question in his essay 'Deconstructing Violence in Grime'. Walmsley breaks down violence in Grime into different chambers, which are all intertwined but require a concentrated ear, one embedded in the internal logics of the scene, to decipher how they operate.

The first chamber he identifies could be called the performative scenario of Grime. As an MC-driven music, particularly one which was taking its models from *both* dancehall and hip-hop, the 'battle' was a key driver for Grime. Not only did the prospect of MCs involved in a 'war' become an effective generator of hype, but competition fueled innovation and pushed forward new talent. It is for this reason that Walmsley acknowledges conflicts are an undeniable part of Grime, but he argues it is important to recognize to grasp their function. 'Beefs' in Grime are nearly always internal, they occur only between artists and, furthermore, they tend not to take place at live events (when it is possible to organize one). Instead the primary battlefield is the radio or the recording studio. In effect, what is being fought over is the MC's reputation, a vital commodity in Grime: 'War is a state of mind: a state of constant awareness of the need to protect your reputation against those in the rest of the scene wanting to take it'.[38]

This then takes Walmsley to the second chamber of violence in Grime: lyrics. If MCs are seeking to protect or amplify their reputation, the words they use are 'simultaneously a matter of fantasy and reality'.[39] The fantasy comes through the way in which 'references to guns, knives, beefs and war are a way of boosting your own image at the expense of others'.[40] There is, therefore, a 'playground' quality to verbal violence in Grime, a feature underlined by Wiley's oft repeated refrain 'lyrics for lyrics'. At the same time an MC is making imaginative use of a set of lived experiences. The fact of growing up in the economic precariousness of East London meant that methods of subsistence deemed to be 'criminal' were often a part of the everyday. Thus, Grime lyrics by necessity reflected 'a setting for the music in which the realities of gang life are never entirely absent'.[41]

Walmsley does not stop here. He uses his analysis of lyrical war to make a more substantive argument about the structural role of violence in the performance of Grime. This means discussing the relation between the MCs' style of delivery and the soundscape of the riddims. Walmsley finds a useful point of comparison with hip-hop, on the surface a style with several affinities to Grime but, as he points out, there are some vital distinctions. The customary 'boom-bap' beat of hip-hop operates at a slower tempo to Grime (around 120 bpm compared to 140 bpm), and this gives the hip-hop MC more space to embellish their delivery with rhymes and recognizable word play. It is this feature which gives hip-hop MCs their customary 'flex', an effect realized in the ABBA rhyming structure often used in this style. In contrast, Grime riddims not only move at a higher tempo, but they have a degree of claustrophobia which means that MCs are propelled forward through a tight space at great speed, with less room for conventional rhyme play. The result is that:

> In Grime, a common lyrical device is the one-line flow, where every line ends with the same word, an AAAAAAAA rhyme pattern like a machine gun.

Therefore:

> because Grime's lyrical structure is so simple and direct, it has the effect of simplifying and abstracting the messy business of violence into a flow of code, boasts and bravado. There are many terms for guns, for instance, usually single syllable words that can be dropped quickly: heat, skeng, shotty, pumpy, glock, gat and so on.[42]

Walmsley brings all of these chambers of violence together into his analysis of MC Dizzee Rascal's bars, when his Roll Deep crew took a turn on Wiley's 'Eskimo' riddim:

> each line contains a sum, and if you do the math, each of those sums is a reference to a different caliber gun. 3+2+3+1 equals a 9mm; 3x10+7+1 is a .38 caliber; 9+8+3+2 equals a .22 caliber. He drops all of these sums yet the whole thing rhymes. It's a brilliant piece of lyric writing – dense, fast, yet subtle.[43]

Walmsley argues that in this concentrated thirty seconds of recording, Dizzee Rascal encapsulates the role of the Grime MC. He simultaneously protects his status, threatens the reputation of any potential rivals, uses the imagery of his immediate social world, and does so whilst experimenting on the move within the confines of the riddim. All the way through, 'violence has generated the form, the structure and the contours of the lyrics'.[44]

It is clear Walmsley believes violence is an indivisible part of Grime, yet the violence at the center of his analysis bears no relation to the coordinated rush to diagnose the music as a social pathogen. The truth of racialized policing as a totalizing strategy is exposed by the distinction between Walmsley's careful listening to the grammar of violence in Grime's performativity (one where the artists aesthetically manipulate their relation to an environment), and the positivist uncritical judgments of public figures who cultivate their own ignorance. Such a discord leaves an opening, one which allows us to ask: if there is a colossal gap between Grime's weaponized operations and the mainstream perception of its inherent anti-sociality, then what was taking place under the name of this experiment which demanded such stringent levels of racialized policing? How was it possible to create a dovetail between the production of Grime and the seeming necessity of the response from the hegemony of police, policy, and media? In short, what can Grime tell us about the relation between racial pathologization and blackness?

Developing adequate answers to these questions requires a return to the subject of pirate radio. If we detail the mechanics of pirates then we can begin to think about how they gave shape to, disseminated, and amplified, the types of violence in Grime mapped out by Derek Walmsley. Therefore, what we require is a similar analysis of the *operation* of pirate radio in order to lock into the blackness of Grime.

Although writing just prior to the emergence of Grime, when the airwaves were dominated by Jungle, Drum n Bass, Garage, and breakbeat, Matthew Fuller's claim that London has a particular 'style' of pirate radio still rings true. For him, 'pirate radio' is never a singular entity. Instead, it is an ensemble of elements ranging from what might be understood as technical ('transmitter, microwave link, antennae'), instrumental ('turntables, mixers, amplifiers'), and institutional ('record shops, clubs, parties').[45] All of these elements, working at varying degrees of intensity, make 'pirate radio' a 'zone of experiential combination.'[46] It is a practice defined by 'connective disjuncture', whereby broken up parts are synthesized ad-hoc to generate a signal that carries with it a manufactured 'unity...brought into being by disequilibrium.'[47]

The first point in this zone that Fuller tracks relates to the occupation of space and the deployment of equipment. The social capacity of pirate radio is determined by the landscape in which it is assembled. Thus, in the case of housing estates compacted into the geography of London as hub for finance capital, it was the tower block that became the 'incubator' and 'antennae' for pirates.[48] Once on rooftops, the issue for operators became establishing and maintaining a signal. This not only required a level of self-taught technical competence but the acceptance that all the equipment could be seized. The pressing concern then for a pirate radio outfit was not fidelity, rather it was disposability: 'At what level of cheapness will things still run? How disposable can the gear be made in order that when it is seized another can be put into play as soon as possible?'.[49] For Fuller this indicates a level of 'pragmatic-conceptual work' in the running of a pirate, a 'sense of techno-aesthetic life inventing and reassessing itself through the process'.[50]

One such 'pragmatic-conceptual' worker is the MC. Whilst this figure is coded into several forms of black music, the MC on pirate radio operates at a heightened state of instrumentality. Fuller argues that due to the constant improvisation that takes place in the pirate, the MC both announces all the joints – making clear the spliced artificiality of the signal – and also becomes one of the joints: 'the corporeally anchored voice...loses itself as a separate category of sound' due to the way in which it also needs to function as part of the equipment.[51] Therefore, with the pirate radio set-up, no one point is given complete primacy over another. The MC is as much a transmitter as any seemingly non-animate sonic device, no more so than when delivering hype:

Hype is that moment when the transmission of information in the strict sense reflexively incorporates information about the fact of transmission as part of that transmission. It is not simply information, but the way in which it moves.[52]

Fuller's turn to the audience identifies another vital laborer in the pirate radio circuit. Due to the fact that they interrupt but do not seek out the regulated channels of official broadcasting, pirates are, according to Fuller, caught in a double bind. On one side they operate on the basis that they are in a vacuum, with no one able to tune into the signal. Conversely, the incessant stalling of the performance, in order to announce each communicative interaction with a listener (whether by telephone or SMS), means that a pirate is always declaring its outlaw status. This 'mutual excitation' is necessary not so much to boost egos, but to sustain the signal: the 'audience induces sound' in the pirate ecology.[53]

The name Fuller gives to these numerous relations generating the pirate signal is a 'machinic phylum'.[54] What he means by this is that it is the very interface between hardware and software, electronics and flesh, concrete and voice, which creates the phonic materiality of pirate radio:

This sound not only exists at a level independent of the technical and social assemblages that are mobilized around it; it also articulates them, gives them sensual, rhythmic and material force.[55]

In many ways Steve Goodman takes up with Fuller on pirate radio as 'machinic phylum', and through a direct engagement with the Grime scene, pushes it towards a more severe urbanism. For Goodman, the pirate allows Grime to become involved in a practice more akin to invasion than interruption. Alluding to the combination of pulse and shudder of the early Grime soundscape, alongside the MCs self-weaponization under intense vibrational pressure, he describes pirate radio as:

A veritable sonic war machine temporarily occupying a slice of radiophonic territory, hacking the national grid in a logistics of infection. Ofcom – a centralized radio disease control agency monitoring outbreaks of 'viracy' in the frequency spectrum.[56]

Goodman is building upon Fuller's account of pirates being involved in an 'arms race' designed to effect a 'process of pragmatic deformation of control', control here being defined as 'a whole interrogative field of social, juridical, legislative, political, economic formations'.[57] Goodman, though, hears in Grime, as it synthesizes and expands through pirate radio, an ability to weaponize itself at the level of the bio-chemical. Populations locked into the Grime signal 'attract and congeal':

Instead of merely making connections between individual cells, [it] probes the mutational potential of pirate media, asking what aesthetic transformations, what new modes of contagious collectivity and what rhythmic anarchitectures such microcultures may provoke.[58]

In their complementing analyses Fuller and Goodman highlight two key features of pirate radio. The first is a highly intense degree of sensuousness. This occurs at multiple levels in the manifestation of the pirate, whether it be the continuous adaptation of all the constituent parts, the breakdown of the distinction between aesthetics and broadcast, or the viral generation of audience. Second, the way the sound-signal of Grime–pirate radio moves through the material and psychic grain of its immediate environment produces a conflict with the institutions of governance designed to regulate airwaves, territories, and populations.

Within the account of pirate radio Fuller and Goodman provide lies the basis for thinking the antagonistic relationship between Grime and racialized policing, though even they do not explicitly account for the racial constitution of civil society, state, and capital. Drawing this out from their work requires turning to dynamics of Grime–pirate radio that Fuller and Goodman to varying degrees raise: that of the relation between black music and blackness. If pirate radio, as it has functioned in London since the advent of Jungle, has been a means for the realization of black electronic dance music, and Grime was the latest manifestation in this continuum, two things become clear. One, that which Fuller called 'machinic phylum' is an alternative name for blackness. Grime was an emanation of black social life in Tower Hamlets, Newham and other East London boroughs, and the massive concentration of experiential energy required to produce it operated as an experimentation within a given terrain that was realized through the fugitive assembly of pirate signals. The very movement of this force is the blackness of Grime, a blackness that was encoded into the phonic materiality of the music which was also a signal. Two, the conflict Grime and pirate radio induced existed between the movement of its blackness, and the totalizing strategy of racialized policing. The Grime–pirate radio conjunction was orchestrating a viral deformation of control (as Fuller and Goodman might have it), and it was doing so by animating (and being animated by) a blackness that antagonized racialized policing through its techniques of evasion and invasion.

Therefore, to conceptualize Grime as an enactment of sonic warfare is useful, but only if we think the sonic in this instance as a troubled conduit for the racial. The argument I am making here is not that Grime was the site of invocation for a race war. It is not the case that an understanding of Grime can be reduced to a staged battle between white governance on one side, and black social life mediated through black music on the other. Instead, the blackness emanating from Grime–pirate radio was placing in severe jeopardy the terms and conditions of race as a spatial epistemology in London, and it was doing so by way of its carefully crafted use of violence. This is why, as a form of black music, Grime induced such intense levels of racialized policing, because it represented a spectacular breach in a previously sedimented order. Through the textures of pirate radio, Grime manifested itself as a war machine of blackness whose primary object was its own continual flourishing. The effect of this internal activity was to so potently threaten the way race–class demarcations were engrained into the architectures and psyche of the city as to force the law and media institutions to frame its blackness as an alien intrusion, thus requiring an irrational declaration of race war on their part.

Colony Culture / Bass Culture

So far we have established a link between the aesthetic sociality of Grime, and the way in which the scene was the target for racialized policing that sought to pathologize the cultural and social life of young black people in London. Violence and blackness were the issues at the heart of this. The racialized policing of Grime worked on the basis that there was an unspecified, yet apparently detectable, capacity for ungovernable violence operative in the soundscape of Grime, in the black people who made it, as well as amongst those who gathered to listen to it. The truth of violence in Grime was the genius of collective experimentation that saw MC-producers aestheticize their lived experiences in an urban situation, in order to generate new sonic ecologies of feeling local to the areas of London they inhabited. The effect of this tension over the work of violence was that Grime was criminalized precisely because of its blackness. Pirate radio became the means to amplify this disjuncture over violence, blackness, and criminality. The assembly of pirate signals, their use as a performance technology, and its broadcast capacities, sparked off a conflict that, for the state and civil society, necessitated the tightening of the police cordon enacted by Form 696 and other measures. The fact that Grime was black music functioning in this way represented a threat to the race–class administration of the city.

I want to argue that as an outbreak of blackness in its eastern boroughs, Grime pointed to a colonial legacy embedded in London's geography. In order to make such claims substantive it is important for us to develop a historical schematic for the racialized policing of black populations in London. Situating the production of Grime, and the response to it, within a longer continuum shaped by empire will provide a stronger conceptual grammar for considering its blackness. This is particularly the case when the aim is to consider the blackness of Grime as an exacerbation of a colonial legacy that determines the political, economic, and geographical form of the city.

It is with cultural theorists Stuart Hall and Paul Gilroy that this task begins. If considered a collaborative undertaking from the early 1970s through to the mid-1980s, we can find in their writing the intellectual realization of black populations as an autonomous class within the landscape of post-imperial Britain. This autonomy took the form of a *colony culture* that was simultaneously a *bass culture*, which through its territorial, aesthetic, and social practices, exposed the racial nature of capitalism, and thus incited the use of policing to control and occupy through force, newly formed areas of black inhabitation in urban Britain. Although Hall and Gilroy are often understood as thinkers of the problematic of race and nation, it is as thinkers of race and the city that we will take them up here in order to grasp some of the deeper resonances informing Grime as an aesthetic mechanism of antagonism within London at the turn of the millennium.

1978's *Policing the Crisis: Mugging, the State, and Law and Order* sees Hall and his collaborators at the Birmingham Centre for Contemporary Cultural Studies present a masterful account of the shifting terrains of capitalist production and political consensus in Britain, to find at its apex the social life of young black populations. It is in a later chapter ('The Politics of Mugging') that we find them mapping out the colony culture that becomes decisive to the formation of black populations in Britain as a class. The solidification of the colony in the 1970s was the result of the combined effect of external forces pressing upon black people, and the internal production of dissident socialities that had been in the collective memory prior to migration, yet were urgently put to use under new conditions of duress.

Addressing the external factors, Hall and his co-authors note how 'mugging', as a barely coded discursive marker for racial pathology, was understood through the identification of 'trouble spots', where those deemed to be more naturally inclined to cause social unrest resided:

Overwhelmingly, in the large cities, they are also the black areas. And the black population stands at the intersection of all these forces: an alienated sector of the civil population, now also a significant sector of the growing army of the unwaged, and one vulnerable to accelerating social pauperization.[59]

The racialization of such zones was the clearest sign of a 'colony' formation in the organization of urban working-class populations in Britain. On an immediate level the 'residential concentration' of black populations in this way was the result of institutional and everyday xenophobia in the workplace, rental property market, and public leisure amenities.[60] Hall is clear though that racism of this type was not an aberration, but a structural feature of Britain's history of colonial exploitation. At its peak British imperialism created a division between the 'metropolitan working class' and 'the colonial workforces' which: 'imprinted the inscription of racial supremacy across the surface of English social life, within and outside the sphere of production and the expropriation of surplus.'[61]

The national independence movements in Africa, Asia, and the Caribbean which forced through formal decolonization, and the subsequent arrival of immigrant labor into Britain, saw the transportation of these colonial relations to the metropole. The distance between administrative center and frontier that held the idea of Britain in place collapsed, and its terms were hastily reorganized onto the ravaged post-war geography of cities such as London, Birmingham, and Bristol.

Hall et al. observe how the formation of the colony was a process that sedimented over time in post-war Britain, but by the mid-1970s economic crisis, the group at the heart of Britain's internal urban colonies were second generation black youth. Accustomed to educational exclusion, unemployment, and often precarious living situations, they understood their status within the colonial landscape of the British city:

Black youth, in each generation, does not begin as a set of isolated individuals who happen to be educated, to live and labor in certain ways, encountering racial discrimination on the path to adulthood. Black youth begins in each generation from a given class position, produced in an objective form, by processes which are determinate, not of their own making: and that class position is, in the same moment, a racial or ethnic position.[62]

The lived experience of blackness as a class position became a consciousness of subordination for black youth in 1970s Britain. Thus, it became an objective category of identification in colony culture.

It is important to stress though that racism was not the only condition under which colony culture in Britain emerged. It was also *made internally* by the very black populations who were the targets of state and media hegemony. Once again, Hall et al. locate the emergence of such geographical and social forms in migration from the Caribbean to Britain in the 1940s and 1950s. In this setting colony culture came about as a result of the desire to reproduce 'a little bit of the West Kingston shanty town or native Port of Spain.'[63] This took the form of shebeens and blues dances, which ran counter to the set working day pattern, and thus allowed money to circulate from the black wage earners with work outside, to the organized unemployed inside the colony.

By the 1970s the colony as a distinct form was in full existence. The dissolution of any veneer of assimilation in the face of the brutal logic of repatriation necessitated the internal formation of a 'colony society'. Whilst in some sense it was a defensive measure, the 'ghetto colony':

meant the growth of internal cultural cohesiveness and solidarity within the ranks of the black population inside the corporate boundaries of the ghetto: the winning away of cultural space in which an alternative black social life could flourish.[64]

What occurred in this newly self-determined living space through the force of 'positive alternative cultural identities' was the development of 'new strategies of survival amongst the black community as a whole.'[65] As discussed above, it was second generation black youth who became the bearers of this colony culture. It being the closest to a home they had experienced, they understood themselves as a new black population from 'an embattled position at the heart of white society'.

Both Hall and Gilroy noted how, once the colony became a site for the flourishing of black consciousness and sociality, the police became an occupying force:

The extent of police supervision of the 'colonies', the arbitrariness and the brutality of the 'hassling' of young blacks, the mounting public anxieties and the moral panic about 'young immigrants' and crime, and the size of the welfare and community projects designed to relieve tension and 'cool' the problems in the ghetto, serve only to reinforce the impression, both inside and outside the 'colony', that, in some as yet undefined way, a 'political' battleground is being staked out.[66]

The political battleground in this instance was a function of the black populations status as surplus labor. In the absence of access to wages, and the ability of black people to improvise social reproduction through the economy of the colony, policing took on the characteristics of control and coercion – in effect the colonial nature of policing revealed itself. According to Gilroy, this renewed battle line between 'the solidarity and political strength' of the colony and the racialized police function served to further 'determine[d] a specific *territorialization* of social control.'[67] As a result, the colony was marked into the form of the city as a psycho-social expression of the conflict being fought to sustain the imperial logic of Britain against its internal negation by subaltern black populations.

The question of the colony culture's specific constitution was set out by Gilroy in the early 1980s. For him, the black consciousness forged internally within Ladbroke Grove, Notting Hill, Brixton, Handsworth, and St Paul's was realized through a *bass culture*. The technological, institutional, aesthetic, and performative adaptation of Jamaican soundsystems became one of the most heightened flash points in the black refusal of external governance. Gilroy carefully detailed how it was not only the gathering of black masses around soundsystems that induced policing, but equally the very experiments in phonic materiality with which they emotionally carved out a new environment.

Focusing on dub as a genre-process, he describes how soundsystem selectors would seek to dismantle the mechanisms of an 'original' record in order to illuminate its artificial status and 'expose the musical anatomy of the piece, showing how each layer of instrumentation complements the others to form a complex whole.'[68] As a method defined by its dissipation of seemingly solid song forms, and the pursuit of expansive resonances, dub found an ethical accompaniment in the Rastafari ethos being transported from Jamaica on records and sparking a new consciousness in the UK. Although dub was by no means an exclusively Rasta aesthetic, the moral imperative to refuse the 'ism' and 'schism' of any proscribed political ideology, in order to take in the truly constructed nature of a world shaped by racial division and economic exploitation, was intensified by the formal improvisation taking place in the soundsystem session.

Thus, a key figure in the soundsystem crew, complementing the use of wall-shaking bass to isolate and stretch the revelatory potential of a track, was the toaster. Gilroy saw in the toaster – who had to maintain the interest of the crowd, negotiate a unique lyrical style through the soundscape, and offer a commentary on life in the colony – a class of organic intellectual who could speak on behalf of 'the rising generation of blacks gathering in darkened dancehalls'.[69] Key for Gilroy is that the interplay between equipment, bass frequencies, and voice was always taking place *live* in the dancehall with *recorded* material. As the point for the sustainment and reproduction of blackness within the colony, it had to occur with the manipulation of records in real time for the full scale of its experiments to be transmitted as a social practice that, through its intensity, went about dismantling the control logics of a racist society:

> records become raw material for spontaneous performances of cultural creation in which the DJ and the MC or toaster who introduces each disc or sequence of discs, emerge as principle agents in dialogic rituals of active and celebratory consumption. It is above all in these performances that Black Britain has expressed the improvisation, spontaneity and intimacy which are key characteristics of all new world black musics.[70]

Bringing together Hall's and Gilroy's thought on black social life, racism, and the city during the 1970s and 1980s allows us to reflect on the valences of 'colony culture / bass culture' as a formulation. To think colony and bass as imminent to each other gives us a structural grasp not only of black culture during this period, but of black culture in its formation as an aesthetico-territorial expression in the post-colonial British city. Colony culture / bass culture – in effect another name for black social life in its phonic and spatial relation to blackness – is perhaps limited if understood as something that unfolded in linear stages. Whilst of course tracking a historical genealogy of how soundsystems were points of evolution for new genres (ranging from Lovers Rock, to Digi-Dub, to Ragga) is valuable, restricting our understanding of the sheer anti-singular intensity of soundsystems to methods of periodization alone means we risk losing something crucial. It is more generative to conceive of 'colony culture / bass culture' as 'colony-bass culture' – which is to say to consider it as a concentrated ecological type of technological production, that simultaneously contained all of the distinct styles which emerged from it, and carried the capacity to generate further, as yet unrealized, configurations. To break this down a little more: rather than stating genre 'a' developed into genre 'b', and was soon followed by genre 'c', we should be arguing that each time a new style (and thus a new type of social composition) was issued, such was the level of volatility that we can hear the potential for all the subsequent styles which were to come, all those which preceded it, and the potentiality for sonic innovations which await us. If we are able to get to grips with this latter conceptualization, then it becomes possible to argue that colony-bass culture, as a territorial rendering of blackness, was fully demarcated the very first time a bass line came shuddering out of a speaker at a blues dance in a Notting Hill basement. From this moment, the experiments in valves, air pressure, and chest cavities have persisted as an exercise in spatial production, which have always contained within their grain a relation to racialized duress, but cannot be understood as black music on those terms alone.

The question for us to ask now is what do Hall and Gilroy allow for in terms our chapter's focus on Grime? How useful is colony-bass culture in thinking about the synthesis of Grime and pirate radio as the means to induce a war over the sonic, technological, and spatial determination of race engrained into the psychic architectures of early 2000s London? Through Hall and Gilroy's analysis of black social life as a colony formation in urban Britain, we can begin to think about a sensory knowledge coded into the structures of Grime. As soon as the colony was concretized as *the* geographical unit of black urbanism in London, bass culture became *the* organizational way of living. What was initiated in the making of colony-bass culture was the technological adaptation of sonic practices in their mediation with social practices. This had two effects: firstly, it meant the symbiosis of colony-bass became the primary territorial operation of black social life in British cities; and secondly, the affective force of soundsystem culture – the ferocious autonomy of its improvisation – was toxic to the sedimented spatial structures of race–class in the wider society.

Therefore, when Grime appeared it already possessed a sensory knowledge of embattlement against a hostile external world, which meant not only that territory became a determining factor in its constitution, but that as black music, Grime already understood itself as a site of conflict. By extension, the general intellect that went into the formation of Grime also knew the necessity of adaptation to the changing coercions of state and civil society. We can hear this in the seductive friction between the scene's heartlands and the monolith of Canary Wharf; the chilling distance of Wiley's productions and his refusal to leave the road; the transformation of 'Pow!' into an early twenty-first-century Trojan horse; the repurposing of the entertainment industries' technological detritus by Ruff Sqwad; and the aesthetic invasion of the FM signal by innumerable pirates. These features of Grime, and the immediate racialized response of the state and media show us that the colony was still in existence in the early 2000s. By extension, Grime was evidence of the persistence of London's colony-bass culture – a claim which becomes concretized when we consider that Wiley's, Jammer's, and Footsie's fathers were all in the same reggae band.[71] It was a soundscape which was carved out of (but never simply reducible to) the atmosphere shaping Tower Hamlets, Bow, Newham, and Limehouse. Turned into a sonic ecology that could be adapted for illegal broadcasts, Grime came to be used as a tool to expand the borders of the colony, and thus it incited a conflict with the imperial function of the metropole. The condition of possibility for these capacities in Grime (capacities understood as its blackness) was its status as black music.

Jammer's Birthday Bash: Deja Vu FM 2003

The proclamations that have populated this chapter have reached a limit point. If, through the blackness of its pirate radio broadcasts, Grime was initiating a conflict over the administration of London, then we need to understand how its soundscape came to be a battleground. This requires zooming in on an instance when the blackness of Grime was being assembled inside the colony. It is here that we can begin to unpick the racial mechanics of border demarcation through sound and signal. One such instance is the recording of *Jammer's Birthday Bash*, broadcast on Deja Vu FM in 2003.[72]

A camera opens at around dusk in what is most likely the storage room on the roof of a building. It is a functional space, with exposed piping, tiny air vents in the upper corners and bars over the windows. The off-white walls marked with streaks of dark paint push it towards the run down. This room is the nerve center of the pirate Deja Vu FM. Located somewhere amidst the landscape of Stratford, the room has probably been secured due to a combination of ease of access and its nondescriptness. Everything can be hidden in plain sight. The antennae, transmitter, turntable, amps, and more have been soldered and connected with all the power stolen from the local grid.

The room is tightly packed with around ten men and one woman. More people can be seen through the open doors, roaming on the roof outside. They are all there not solely to listen to the music that can already be heard pulsing out of the speakers, but to become part of the Deja Vu signal. The men represent a roll call of leading Grime MCs of that moment: Wiley, Crazy Titch, Dizzee Rascal, D Double E, Kano, and Escobar, each affiliated to variety of crews including Boyz in the Hood, Roll Deep, and N.A.S.T.Y. These were the names seen on dubplates, printed on flyers, and most importantly, repeated across local airwaves. Visible in snatches on the edge of the screen is Mak 10 who is stood over the decks. Although there is an easy familiarity between them, evidenced by the camaraderie with which they greet a new arrival, the most discernible trait the MCs have in common is a deep, stern concentration. They are rocking side to side, listening with almost monastic intent to the riddims Mak 10 selects to carve his set.

These descriptions of *Jammer's Birthday Bash* constitute an exemplary social image of a Grime–pirate radio broadcast. Using the building as an incubator, the Deja Vu crew are manufacturing a phono-material substance that is partly weaponized. The strategy involves deploying a fugitive disposability at the level of equipment to generate – through their signal – a field of mutual excitation that we might otherwise call black music. Stretching out from the eastern colony and bleeding into the metropole, the Deja Vu signal also induces the racialized policing that has been defined by its constant pursuit of bass culture in London. This induction (which we can also think of as conduction) becomes such an engrained part of the signal that we have to conceive of Deja Vu as a sonic war machine of blackness.

It becomes clear from taking in *Jammer's Birthday Bash* that the MCs are not an afterthought layered on top of this activity. Instead they are indivisible from the conflict embedded into this system of talking media. As much as Dizzee, Kano, Wiley, and Tinchy Stryder are listening with intent to Mak 10's selections, finding space in the riddim for their burst of bars, they are also sparring with each other. The condition of possibility for MC-ing in Grime is the protection of reputation through war – where lyrics gun down lyrics. When you have the levels of personnel as seen and heard on the Deja Vu recording, the terms of order shift dramatically. The deep encryption of violence into their delivery, operating at such speed of thought and under pressure, means that the MCs in this broadcast are weaponizing themselves not only to do battle with each other, but to go to war with whatever is looking to hunt down this social systemization of black music.

In the case of *Jammer's Birthday Bash* there are three notable MCs who provide us with a panorama of Grime's self-weaponizing capacities. Take D Double E, already by this stage a commanding figure in the scene. Shoulders hunched, head down, he has somehow both latched onto, and detached himself from, the vibe pulsing around this tight room. There is an economy and calculation to his delivery, which he uses to maneuver himself around the tempo of the riddims. Not only does this allow him to create the impression that he has somehow bent Mak 10's sonic palette to his will, but there is a sense that the cold precision of his bars is built to contain a more lethal force bubbling underneath the surface.

Escobar has to work much harder to stay on his feet when he is passed the mic at the back of the room. Eyes locked tight shut in concentration, he shifts rapidly from one foot to the other, as he pieces together his reflexive lyrics. As the overamplified gun blasts and metallic drips of a Wiley Eskibeat production threaten to run him over, he grips both hands around the mic seemingly using it as both shield and firearm. The relief when Mak 10 cuts the sound for a pull up is tangible, as Escobar's lines ease up, and he shows it was all no problem for him in the first place.

It is with Crazy Titch that the sparks start to fly. In contrast to D Double E and Escobar, he steps into the heat of the scene around him and tries to bring it to the point of combustion. For Titch, swagger and shudder become his method of choice, as he mimes a walk through the simulated gun blasts that ground the riddim. Audio bullets bouncing off him, he responds with such a terrifying volley that the game faces of everyone in the room drop, and they demand Mak 10 edges the tune so that Titch can do it all over again.

Through the furious activity operating in *Jammer's Birthday Bash* – as one single instance in the pirate production of Grime – we can begin to grasp the antagonisms that were shaping London in 2003. To repeat, as a new mutation of bass culture, Grime showed the continued existence of a colonial relation in the city, because its production, and especially its use of pirate radio, incited a brutal strategy of racialized policing. *Jammer's Birthday Bash* illuminates for us the types of performance and organization, the pragmatic and conceptual work of musical and social production, that sparked such a massive state project of racial containment. The repurposing of derelict architecture, the invasion of regulated airspace, the synthesis of crystalline audio propulsions with lethal word bullets – all under the heading of 'Grime' – represented a capacity for blackness as imagination and organization that the hegemony of government, police, and media needed to restrict to Tower Hamlets, Bow, and Newham, if not completely starve of oxygen.

The claims I have made above open up two insights into the territorial experiment in sound that was Grime. Firstly, as a black musical style it was able to exacerbate what Barnor Hesse argues is a long held nervousness that frames black life in London as a 'racialized alien intrusion, a difficult cultural virus'.[73] Listening in from the outside, Grime represented that latest stage in a late twentieth-century 'spatial anxiety about race' that has fixed black sociality (and its production of blackness) as a mechanism for marking 'the terminus of the white city's limits'.[74] We can understand this demarcation as part of the recasting of the colonial antagonism within the heart of the British metropolis. Through acts of national amnesia about racial slavery and empire building, the inner-city colony in mainland Britain was held in place as a pathological site of inhabitation via stringent policing. As a result, for Hesse, racial violence in London can never be framed as an aberration from a harmonious civil norm, but it is rather the structurally consistent 'victimization of a communal location...[it] is better analyzed as a scenario'.[75] In short, Grime showed up the persistence of the racialized scenario in early twenty-first-century London.

Although Hesse's work is offering a great deal here, there is something slightly unsatisfactory about his analytical lens when it is used to think about Grime. Something remains unaccounted for if we rely solely on the racism/anti-racism paradigm as a way of mediating an encounter with the sonic ecology of Grime as black music. To understand its capacities solely in their relation to the racialized violence of the British metropolis means we lose out somewhere. The potency of the project named 'Grime' lay in its ability to synthesize, and contain within a single system of musical organization, a set of aesthetic propositions which reorganized its environment. To be able to compress the psychic architectures of housing estates, finance capital, the disjunctures between them, and the accrued communality of black social life in East London, into a soundscape created through the repurposing of everyday technology, that then synchronized with a style of vocal performance channeling multiple non-lethal dynamics of violence, whilst at the same time expanding upon an existing broadcast network, indicates that Grime possessed an improvisatory drive which requires us to put into severe question our accepted epistemological norms regarding this strange composite we call 'race', in its relation to that other thing known as 'blackness'. The line of argument running through this chapter is that the movement of all of these forces under the heading 'Grime' was fueled by its own internalized expansionary antagonism. Therefore, despite the attempts to understand Grime as autonomous from racialized policing, it is perhaps better to think of it as prior to and surrounding it. Framed this way, we can say that the blackness of Grime, as a form of black music generated in East London, surfaced with such intensity it could do nothing else but attract the levels of duress that it did. Form 696, the hysterical causal links made with knife and gun crime, the use of local and national state agencies to cut off pirates, were part of an effort to refuse the continued flourishing of Grime's ever-expanding antagonistic field. It was a coercive attempt to shut down the type of massive concentration of experiential and experimental energy that was resonating between D Double E, Escobar, Crazy Titch, Mak 10, all of their crews, and the equipment, as they were compressed into the Deja Vu studio.

Unfortunately, arriving at some sort of resolution over the issue of Grime's autonomy only leads us to a further series of questions. We do not have the space to fully explore them here, but they are worth posing nonetheless, so as to trace another set of propositions which have been appearing at the edges of all that I have set out in this chapter. They concern the necessity of *any* possible relation between the internal forces which generated Grime in the early 2000s, and the suffocating practices of racialized governance enacted by state and civil society:

If the blackness compressed into Grime allowed it to induce and encircle the seemingly totalized strategy of policing, then what could have this black musical project have been capable of in the absence of any warfare from the state? How might have the transfiguration of an array of socialities internal to Tower Hamlets and Newham into a sonic ecology indivisible from its means of transmission, worked out, if a metropolitan coloniality had not tried to force its way into the frame? If unhindered, would the grand experiment we now call Grime, have been able to reconstitute the racialized geographies of the entire city? In the first years of our current millennium, did Grime contain the phono-material codes to turn London into a bass colony?

Conclusion

The moment shaping *Teklife / Ghettoville / Eski* has now passed. Running from the early years of the new millennium through to the mid-point of the century's first decade, triangulating the eastern boroughs of London, Chicago's South and West sides, and back to the transpontine zones of Britain's capital, Footwork, Grime, and Actress do not necessarily correlate any longer with the arguments I have set out in the preceding chapters. This is in no way to say that the scenes or artists in question have experienced a dwindling of their experimental energies, far from it. Instead, it is more that the nature of the roughened alignment between the bursts of aesthetic sociality which allowed for the production of sonic ecologies, and a set of atmospheres molded in specific racial situations of urbanization, has more or less receded. Again, my judgments are not imbued with a sense of mourning about unrealized possibilities for these musical projects. Rather, they signal an attempt to recognize the rate and intensity of a type of urbanization, and by the same measure they are built on an understanding of black cultural aesthetics of the type discussed in this book as always on the move and undergoing adaptation.

Beginning with the former, the algorithmic governance which is dominating cities in Britain and North America has been twinned with the dislocation of local black and subaltern populations. It is within the social life of these populations that we find the generation of undercommon atmospheres which function as holding spaces for the production of sonic ecologies. Taking London as an example, black social life is attacked by a kind of tripartite exertion of duress, as exemplified by the killings of Rashan Charles and Edson Da Costa following contact with the police, the regularity of unannounced immigration raids, and the 72 deaths at Grenfell Tower, a tragedy directly attributable to corporate and governmental malfeasance. A similar story can be told of Chicago, and almost any other major urban center of black social life across the diaspora.[1]

Invariably, the capacity for experimentation in the aesthetic sociality of blackness is shaped by these dynamics. Which is in no way to say that is diminished. It is more that the modality of aesthetic sociality – the impulse to generate sound, movement, groupings that respond to, but are not the equivalent of, an atmosphere – goes on under different guises, takes alternate forms. With that in mind, what can we say now of the projects which have driven the analysis in this book? Footwork has followed the path of House-derived dance music forms from Chicago before it, in that it has become a sustainable career option for those producers and dancers who are able to connect to international electronic music networks and their economies. In this way, Footwork as a style has rapidly reorganized the aesthetics of electronic music, stimulating nearly everybody who has come into contact with it. It is evident though that the Teklife crew are still feeling the effects of DJ Rashad's premature loss, but a signal of where Footwork has gone lies in the realizations currently being generated by one of its outliers, Jlin.[2]

With Actress, his impulse towards an abstraction that is indivisible from the social force of his chosen sonic tool kit has grown exponentially, which is an exceptional feat considering how potent his output had already become with *Ghettoville*. For a ruffneck individualist, Actress' capacities for collaboration have also expanded, with re-edits of Wiley riddims, and joint productions with the London Contemporary Orchestra. Still, the 2017 release of *AZD* shows that the combination of neon sheen, cool detachment, and seductive pulse are still at the core of Darren Cunningham's phono-imaging techniques.

Invariably the situation with Grime is complicated. The first flourishing of the Grime scene set out in the previous chapter was more or less nullified at an institutional level by the Met, local state infrastructures, and the interests of the nighttime economy. This did not mean that Grime 'died'. The social energies of the music persisted, both by returning to its locales and by traveling through new networks. In this supposedly fallow period, the established players and new talent were able to plan for what took on the appearance of a co-ordinated assault upon the popular mainstream.

This set of circumstances now gives us Skepta as Mercury Prize Winner, a number one album for Stormzy, and Dizzee Rascal's homecoming concert in Stratford.[3] The second arrival of Grime has taken place during a violent period of social reorganization in East London. I want to suggest that there is perhaps some correlation between the music's return and the redesign of the area for a new class of inhabitant. To take such a proposition seriously though will require others to systematically engage with Grime in its current guise as well as the new racialized hysteria surrounding UK Drill.[4]

Although Footwork, Actress, and Grime have been the determinants for a series of claims about the social production of black music in the early twenty-first century, *Teklife / Ghettoville / Eski* is not a completist endeavor. Which is to say that the theorizations of blackness I put forward in this book are temporary. They are organized around what I felt to be strong correspondences between each musical project when it came to questions of urbanization, aesthetic sociality, and sonic ecology, but such correspondences are inescapably imbued with knots and complexities. What I have sought to avoid in the book is a presentation of sonic cultures (and therefore cultural aesthetics in general), as preformed systems with fully fledged patterns. As with anything made by people, there are always anomalies which mean the cultural dynamics and aesthetic operations cannot be grasped in their entirety, because such anomalies are evidence of culture in movement, in a state of incessant adaptation. In the early stages of its composition this book could have taken numerous alternate pathways. In one version, my intention was to displace the chapters on Footwork and Grime in order to include two sections of writing on the artists Cooly G and Dean Blunt, to make this a book about singular modes of blackness as sonic ecology in London. In another iteration, there was the possibility of setting aside the work on Actress in order to undertake a study of New York's modern Ballroom scene, thus giving the book a more concerted roving diasporic orientation. Such changes in content would, of course, have required a recalibration of the book's intellectual trajectories – we would have been talking about an almost entirely different project. The reason I am making such structural decisions clear is that whilst all that has been written in *Teklife / Ghettoville / Eski* is hopefully intellectually coherent, it does not represent a set of totalizing claims. Rather, the hope is that it has been read as a provocation, an attempt to incite a shift in critical work on black cultural aesthetics, not simply by introducing new content, but by asking how such material demands that we rethink theoretical production. The success or failure of such a task is for the reader to judge.

If the moment when Footwork, Grime, and Actress were active in the production of blackness as sonic ecologies has passed, then the best way for me to bring *Teklife / Ghettoville / Eski* to a close is by speculating on black electronic music in its present and emerging forms. What has been in generation in the years since the release of *Ghettoville* in 2014? What might such music tell us about its entanglement with social life and its mediating production of blackness now that we are well into the disaster that is the twenty-first century? Of course, I do not have the room to compose a full response to such questions, but it is possible to lay out some co-ordinates.

What come to the fore in the contemporary soundscapes of experimentation in black electronic music are several notable tendencies: one is that of a shift away from coherent 'scenes' with fully realized sonic imprints that are geographically specific; instead there has been an emergence of auteurs (for example Klein, Yves Tumor, Mhysa) who, whilst clearly raised on the dancefloor, have moved towards a bleeding out of the craft of song composition;[5] alongside this the likes of Nkisi, Nazar, and Jlin have been in pursuit of modes of rhythmic reprogramming which seek to directly intervene in the mechanics of the psycho-social.[6] Perhaps, between such internally derived invention of song forms and the outward looking scale of rearranged desires, we might begin to interrogate the sensoriums of other, newer, sonic ecologies of black music.

Notes

Introduction

1 Sukhdev Sandhu, *London Calling: How Black and Asian Writers Imagined a City* (London: Harper Perennial, 2004).

2 Cedric Robinson, *Black Marxism: The Making of the Black Radical Tradition* (Chapel Hill, NC: University of North Carolina Press, 2000); Gaye Theresa Johnson and Alex Lubin, eds., *Futures of Black Radicalism* (London and New York: Verso, 2017).

Part 1

1 Mineral Interiors: House, Techno, Jungle

1 Dan Barrow, 'Hieroglyphic Being and the Configurative or Modular Me Trio / *The Seer of Cosmic Visions* (Planet Mu, 2014)', *The Wire*, no. 369 (November 2014).

2 Amiri Baraka, *Black Music* (New York: Akashic Books, 2010).

3 Bill Brewster and Frank Broughton, *Last Night a DJ Saved My Life: A History of the Disc Jockey* (London: Headline, 2000), 335.

4 Tim Lawrence, *Love Saves the Day: A History of American Dance Music Culture 1970–1979* (Durham, NC: Duke University Press, 2004).

5 Brewster and Broughton, *Last Night a DJ Saved My Life*, 326.

6 Simon Reynolds, *Energy Flash: A Journey through Rave Music and Dance Culture* (London: Faber and Faber, 2013), 4–5.

7 Ibid., 247.

8 Rachel Seely (dir.), *All Junglist: A London Sum Ting Dis* (Channel 4, 1994), quote from MC Navigator.

9 Reynolds, *Energy Flash*, 17.

10 Reynolds, *Energy Flash*, 18.

11 Ben Williams, 'Black Secret Technology: Detroit Techno and the Information Age', in *Technicolor: Race, Technology and Everyday Life*, ed. Alondra Nelson, Thuy Linh N. Tu, and Alicia Headlam Hines (New York: New York University Press, 2001), 162.

12 Martin James, *State of Bass: Jungle – The Story So Far* (London: Boxtree, 1997), 5.

13 Reynolds, *Energy Flash*, 242.

14 Reynolds, *Energy Flash*, 242.

15 Chris Sharp, 'Jungle – Modern States of Mind', in *Modulations: A History of Electronic Music: Throbbing Words on Sound*, ed. Peter Shapiro (New York: Caipirinha, 2000), p139.

16 Kodwo Eshun, 'Jungle! Jungle! The Last Dance Underground', *I.D.* (May 1994), 45.

17 St Clair Drake and Horace R. Cayton, *Black Metropolis: A Study of Negro Life in a Northern City* (Chicago: University of Chicago Press, 2015).

18 Audrey Petty, ed., *High Rise Stories: Voices from Chicago Public Housing* (San Francisco: McSweeny's Books 2013).

19 Mike Rubin, 'Days of Future Past: Techno', in Shapiro, *Modulations*; Gary Bredow (dir.), *High Tech Soul: The Creation of Techno Music* (2006).

20 Louis Moreno, 'The Sound of Detroit: Notes, Tones and Rhythms from Underground', in *The Acoustic City*, ed. Matthew Gandy and B.J. Nilsen (Berlin: Jovis, 2014), 105.

21 Ibid., 106.

22 James, *State of Bass*, 19–20.

23 Seely (dir.), *All Junglist*.

24 Eshun, 'Jungle!', 44.

25 Reynolds, *Energy Flash*, 239.

26 Brewster and Broughton, *Last Night a DJ Saved My Life*, 314–315.

27 Reynolds, *Energy Flash*, 17.

28 Dan Sicko, *Techno Rebels: The Renegades of Electronic Funk* (New York: Billboard Books, 1999), 92–93.

29 Bredow (dir.), *High Tech Soul*.

30 James, *State of Bass*, 13.

31 James, *State of Bass*, 24.

32 John Akomfrah (dir.), *The Last Angel of History* (Channel 4, 1996).

2 The Blackness of Black Electronic Dance Music

1 Jayna Brown, 'Buzz and Rumble: Global Pop Music and Utopian Impulse', *Social Text* 28, no. 1 (Spring 2010); Tavia Nyong'o, 'I Feel Love: Disco and Its Discontents', *Criticism* 50, no.1 (Winter 2008); Katherine McKittrick and Alexander Weheliye, '808s & Heartbreak', *Propter Nos* 2, no. 1 (Fall 2017).

2 Jeremy Gilbert and Ewan Pearson, *Discographies: Dance Music, Culture and the Politics of Sound* (London: Routledge, 1999); Simon Reynolds, 'The Wire 300: Simon Reynolds on the Hardcore Continuum', *The Wire*, no. 300 (February 2009); Simon Reynolds, 'The Hardcore Continuum or (a) Theory and Its Discontents', http://energyflash-bysimonreynolds.blogspot.co.uk/2009/02/hardcore-continuum-or-theory-and-its.html, accessed 27th February 2018; Mark Fisher, 'The Abstract Reality of the Hardcore Continuum', *Dancecult: Journal of Electronic Dance Music Culture* 1, no. 1 (2009); Edward George, '(ghost the signal)', in *The Ghosts of Songs: The Film Art of the Black Audio Film Collective*, eds. Kodwo Eshun and Anjalika Sagar (Liverpool: FACT/Liverpool University Press, 2007).

3 Kodwo Eshun, *More Brilliant Than the Sun: Adventures in Sonic Fiction* (London: Quartet Books, 1998), -006.

4 Ibid., -003.

5 Ibid., -003.

6 Ibid., 132.

7 Ibid., 117.

8 Ibid., 117.

9 Ibid., -004.

10 Ibid., -001.

11 Nelson George, *The Death of Rhythm & Blues* (London: Omnibus, 1998).

12 'The control of multi-national corporations has been loosened and music-making and distribution have become less capital – and labor – intensive, while public musical performances are becoming more and more expensive to produce. The most depressing aspect of this historical shift is the process of radical de-skilling which had destroyed the magical authority of instrumentalists. But the revolution of digital technology is not a wholly negative development: the destructive impact of de-skilling must be seen in relation to its clear implications for the demystification and democratization of the culture. Producing music without an element of performance to mediate its creation and its social use feeds the privatization of cultural production and can isolate the music-makers from the social exchanges and disciplines of alternative public spheres which have nurtured black musical sub-cultures for so long. The Bomb Squad's Hank Shocklee has warned that live performances may soon be a thing of the past and asks what the consequences of this change will be for the evolving tradition of black music-making. However defiant and insubordinate its muses are, most of the music produced in the bedroom on samplers and drum machines lacks the moral authority that once grew from the informal negotiations between performers and crowds. Antiphony is not structured into it from its inception. Indeed, this new black music is increasingly not produced at all but playfully and creatively recycled from a standard lexicon of break beats and other sampled sounds.' Paul Gilroy, *Small Acts: Thoughts on the Politics of Black Cultures* (London: Serpents Tail, 1993), 5-6.

13 Eshun, *More Brilliant Than the Sun*, -001.

14 It is possible, in this sense, to situate *More Brilliant Than the Sun* through the debates that took place between Stuart Hall and A. Sivanandan concerning 'New Times'. See Stuart Hall, 'The Meaning of New Times (1989)', in *Selected Political Writings: The Great Moving Right Show and Other Essays* (Durham, NC: Duke University Press, 2017); A. Sivanandan, 'All That Melts into Air Is Solid: The Hokum of New Times', in *Catching History on the Wing: Race, Class and Globalization* (London: Pluto Press, 2008).

15 Steve Goodman, *Sonic Warfare: Sound, Affect, and the Ecology of Fear* (Cambridge, MA and London: MIT Press, 2009), 2.

16 Ibid., 2.

17 Ibid., 2.

18 Ibid., 9.

19 Ibid., 10.

20 Ibid., 112.

21 Ibid., 76.

22 Ibid., 169.

23 Ibid., 192.

24 Paul Gilroy, *The Black Atlantic: Modernity and Double Consciousness* (London: Verso, 1993), 39.

25 Ibid., 78.

26 Ibid., 79.

27 Ibid., 38.

28 Ibid., 37.

29 Ibid., 38.

30 The way in which historical ontology enters into Moten's work is via his reading of Cedric Robinson's 1983 *Black Marxism: The Making of the Black Radical Tradition*, and in

particular an essay which bridges the two halves of the book, 'The Nature of the Black Radical Tradition'. The central claim Robinson puts forward in this essay is that since the prefigurative moments of the black radical tradition, through to its full formation and subsequent adaptations, it has been shaped by a set of evolving collective desires on the part of slaves and their descendants, forged from their experiences of the rapaciousness of racial capitalism: 'The renunciation of actual being for historical being; the preservation of the ontological totality granted by a metaphysical system that never allowed for property in either the physical, philosophical, temporal, legal, social or psychic senses.' Whilst the notion of an ontological totality and its preservation can jar on initial reading, it is Robinson's insistence on a *historical* mode of being that illuminates the potency of his insight. For him, the enslaved Africans who became New World blacks were simultaneously alien to *and* the means of realizing a system of economic, political, and psychic organization that was built to sustain their continual destruction. Hence, what developed amongst black populations was a collective imperative to maintain and further animate this alienation, to be in the West but not entirely of it, to be its living critique. Thus, whilst slave insurgency may – as an initial form – have been designed as an attempt to preserve the memory of what was left in the memory, during conjunctural shifts in the operation of racial capitalism, black populations have historically sought – by dint of a highly differentiated collective consciousness that became a culture and a politics – to defend and propagate the very fact of their distinctions from it, even if they were its targets. Such a process introduces a key dynamic for Robinson. Whilst black radicalism, as the name for the insurgent political culture of black social life, was forged within the crucible of racial capitalism, it is not in its totality, reducible to an understanding of it: 'This was a revolutionary consciousness that proceeded from the whole historical experience of Black people and not merely from the social formations of capitalist slavery or the relations of production of colonialism.' At each stage of its reformation, the question of the nature of the black radical tradition, or the question of the blackness of black people, was determined by this lack of complete compatibility, the refusal of full incorporation, which provided the interval from which to repose the question of black radicalism internally under a new set of conditions. Cedric Robinson, *Black Marxism: The Making of the Black Radical Tradition* (Chapel Hill, NC: University of North Carolina Press, 2000), 168–169.

31 Fred Moten, *In the Break: The Aesthetics of the Black Radical Tradition* (Minneapolis: University of Minnesota Press, 2003), 1.

32 Ibid., 1.

33 Ibid., 1.

34 Ibid., 6.

35 Ibid., 14.

36 Nahum Chandler's elaboration of 'paraontology' is amongst several concepts (such as 'exorbitance' and 'desedimentation') that are composed through his meditation on existence under the heading 'Afro-diasporic'. As a result of his rigorously original reading of W.E.B. Du Bois' own approach to the same matrix, Chandler begins from the basis that the inauguration of the black through racial enslavement and its gradual codification through the sciences of knowledge and political institutions, has always been accompanied by the persistent imposition of debilitation upon black life. Such features of Afro-diasporic existence have been philosophically determined through the positing of an absolute ontological separation between the African and the European, the slave

and the master, the colonized and the colonizer, the black and the white. The white is presupposed as operating within an unquestionable ontological remit; for the black such assurances are out of reach. Whilst it is undeniable that to consider black existence is to illuminate 'the structure of possibility of subjectification', a mode of living shaped by availability to crushing force, Chandler also locates in black existence 'a kind of gift, a distillation of ostensible horizon as a limit'. The gift appears through the very operations of the blackness of the black on the outer edges and internal fault lines of what is racially determined to be the rational mode of being in the world: 'The kind of force, or better violence, that is in place in the domain of this problem – the violence by which the historical conditions of the emergence of the Negro or African American as such makes the very historical emergence of this entity the scene of an ontological question.' This 'question' is the domain of the paraontological in Chandler's work. It is clear for him that Afro-diasporans generate presence, in so far as they exist, act, think and communicate, but because the racialized ontology of Western enlightenment, with its continual operations, refuses to acknowledge this presence in action, the enactment of black existence functions as a dehiscent, ghosting, trembling, or shuddering (hence 'para') of the assuredness of the properly ontological. It is important to stress that for Chandler this paraontological affect of black life is not to be resolved or sutured in pursuit of the assurances of the ontologically proper. Instead, paraontology is to be amplified as the imperative for formations of thought, aesthetics, and social organization that do not structurally depend on exploitation and violence: 'This historical form of origin would be the very opening of exorbitance with their sense of being; of an inelectable and threshold displacement of the origin *and* of the always renewed opening to that which is beyond any given form of being.' This is why the paraontological is generative of exorbitance in that it takes the form of 'displacement' and 'irruption'. What becomes significant for Chandler in his reading of Du Bois through these frameworks, is that Du Bois was able to locate the dehiscent movement of the paraontological in the enactment of black social life: 'Du Bois privileged the theme of *negro capacity*, the way in which an infinite horizon of possible forms of becoming opens up with their own *existence*'. Thus, in his examination, defense and amplification of black social life in texts such as *The Souls of Black Folk*, Chandler believes Du Bois arrived at formulations which not only gave a name to the effects of racialization, but announced the possibility of its annulment through the very form of collective black existence. Nahum Chandler, *X: The Problem of the Negro as a Problem for Thought* (New York: Fordham University Press, 2014), 34–36, 57.

37 Paul Gilroy, *Darker Than Blue: On the Moral Economies of Black Atlantic Culture* (Cambridge, MA and London: Bellknap, 2010), 121.

38 Paul Gilroy, *Between Camps: Nations, Cultures and the Allure of Race* (London: Routledge, 2004), 272.

39 Paul Gilroy, *Darker Than Blue*, 128.

40 Paul Gilroy, 'Between the Blues and the Blues Dance: Some Soundscapes of the Black Atlantic', in *The Auditory Culture Reader*, ed. Michael Bull and Les Back (Oxford: Berg, 2003), 394.

41 David Scott, *Conscripts of Modernity: The Tragedy of Colonial Enlightenment* (Durham, NC: Duke University Press, 2004); Gilroy, *Darker Than Blue*, 123.

42 Stuart Hall, 'New Ethnicities', in *Stuart Hall: Critical Dialogues in Cultural Studies*, ed. David Morley and Kuan-Hsing Chen (New York and London: Routledge, 1996); Kobena

Mercer, *Welcome to the Jungle: New Positions in Black Cultural Studies* (New York and London: Routledge, 1994); Robin D.G. Kelley, *Yo' Mama's Disfunktional! Fighting the Culture Wars in Urban America* (Boston, MA: Beacon Press, 1997); Richard Iton, *In Search of the Black Fantastic: Politics and Popular Culture in the Post-Civil Rights Era* (Oxford and New York: Oxford University Press, 2008).

43 Alexander Weheliye, *Phonographies: Grooves in Sonic Afro-Modernity* (Durham, NC: Duke University Press, 2005), 2–3.

44 Ibid., 3.

45 Ibid., 5.

46 Ibid., 5.

47 Ibid., 7.

48 Ibid., 8.

49 Fred Moten, 'Jurisgenerative Grammar (for Alto)', in *The Oxford Handbook of Critical Improvisation Studies Vol 1*, ed. George E. Lewis and Benjamin Piekut (New York and Oxford: Oxford University Press, 2016), 1.

50 Ibid., 7.

51 Stefano Harney and Fred Moten, *The Undercommons: Fugitive Planning and Black Study* (Wivenhoe, New York, Port Watson: Minor Compositions, 2013), 126.

52 Ibid., 127.

53 Fred Moten, 'The Subprime and the Beautiful', *African Identities* 11, no. 2 (2013): 238.

54 Katherine McKittrick, 'On Plantations, Prisons and a Black Sense of Place', *Social & Cultural Geography* 12, no. 8 (2011): 948.

55 Katherine McKittrick, 'Plantation Futures', *Small Axe* 17, no. 3 (2013): 2.

56 McKittrick, 'On Plantations', 952.

57 McKittrick, 'Plantation Futures', 7.

58 Ibid.

59 McKittrick, 'On Plantations', 948.

60 McKittrick, 'Plantation Futures', 5.

61 Harney and Moten, *Undercommons*, 76.

62 Ibid., 76.

63 Ibid., 64.

64 Ibid., 62.

65 Stefano Harney and Fred Moten, 'Michael Brown', *boundary 2* 42, no. 4 (2015): 81.

66 Ibid., 86.

67 Fred Moten, 'Collective Head', *Women & Performance* 26, no. 2–3 (2016): 1–2.

68 Ibid., 9.

69 AbdouMaliq Simone, 'Urbanity and Generic Blackness', *Theory, Culture & Society* 33, no. 7–8 (2016): 4.

70 Ibid., 5, 11.

71 Ibid., 5.

72 Ibid., 5.

73 AbdouMaliq Simone, *City Life from Jakarta to Dakar: Movements at the Crossroads* (London: Routledge, 2009), 278.

74 AbdouMaliq Simone, 'It's Just the City after All!', *International Journal of Urban and Regional Research* 40, no. 1 (2016): 2.

75 Simone, *City Life*, 284.

76 Simone, 'Urbanity', 18.

77 Ibid., 5.

78 Simone, *City Life*, 296.

79 Simone, 'It's Just the City after All', 7–8.

Part 2

3 Teklife

1 Hillegonda Rietveld, *This Is Our House: House Music, Cultural Spaces and Technologies* (Aldershot: Ashgate, 1998), 114.

2 Jacob Arnold, 'Dance Mania: Ghetto House's Motown', *Resident Advisor*, 15th May 2013, www.residentadvisor.net/feature.aspx?1806.

3 Sonali Aggarwal (dir.), *From Jack to Juke: 25 Years of Ghetto House*, http://vimeo.com/36275353.

4 Dave Quam, 'The Evolution of Footwork', *Resident Advisor*, 19th November 2010, www.residentadvisor.net/feature.aspx?1235.

5 Ibid.

6 Dave Quam, ''These Feet Were Made for Workin': Inside Chicago's Explosive Footwork Scene', *Spin*, 5th July 2012, www.spin.com/articles/these-feet-were-made-workin-inside-chicagos-explosive-footwork-scene/.

7 Ibid.

8 Tim and Barry, *I'm Tryna Tell Ya* (Don't Watch That TV, 2014), www.youtube.com/watch?v=2AlJ88YZ3U8.

9 Dave Quam, 'Battle Cats: From the Rise of House in the 80s to Today's Juke and Footwork Scenes, Chicago's Circle Keeps Expanding', *XLR8R*, 9th August 2010, www.xlr8r.com/features/2010/09/battle-cats-rise-house-music-80s.

10 Quam, 'The Evolution of Footwork'.

11 A.G. in *I'm Tryna Tell Ya*, 13.17.

12 Que in *I'm Tryna Tell Ya*, 25.45.

13 DJ Rashad in *I'm Tryna Tell Ya*, 6.20.

14 DJ Manny in *I'm Tryna Tell Ya*, 22.42.

15 Hot in *I'm Tryna Tell Ya*, 14.38.

16 Imani Kai Johnson, 'Music Meant to Make You Move: Considering the Aural Kinesthetic', *Sounding Out!*, 18th June 2012, http://soundstudiesblog.com/2012/06/18/music-meant-to-make-you-move-considering-the-aural-kinesthetic/.

17 Ibid.

18 Naomi Bragin, 'Shot and Captured: Turf Dance, Yak Films and the Oakland, California R.I.P. Project', *TDR: The Drama Review* 58, no. 2 (2014).

19 Ibid.

20 George Lewis, 'The Timeless Blues', in *Blues for Smoke*, ed. Bennett Simpson (Los Angeles, CA: Museum of Contemporary Art, Los Angeles, 2012), 76.

21 Angus Finlayson, 'Interview: Kode9', *Red Bull Music Academy*, 13th July 2013, http://daily.redbullmusicacademy.com/2013/06/kode9-2013-interview; Goodman, *Sonic Warfare*, 83.

22 Goodman, *Sonic Warfare*, 83.

23 Finlayson, 'Interview: Kode9', emphasis added.

24 Robert Sampson, *Great American City: Chicago and The Enduring Neighborhood Effect* (Chicago: University of Chicago Press, 2012), viii; Allan. H. Spear, *Black Chicago: The Making of a Negro Ghetto 1890-1920* (Chicago: University of Chicago Press, 1967), vii.

25 Robert E. Park, Ernest Burgess and Roderick McKenzie, *The City: Suggestions for the Study of Human Nature in the Urban Environment* (Chicago: University of Chicago Press, 1925); E. Franklin Frazier, *The Negro Family in Chicago* (Chicago: University of Chicago Press, 1932); Martin Bulmer, *The Chicago School of Sociology: Institutionali zation, Diversity and the rise of Sociological Research* (Chicago: University of Chicago Press, 1984).

26 'Instead of assuming that black studies reflects an already existent series of real objects, we need to draw attention to the complex ways this field of inquiry contributes to, or articulates, the creation of objects of knowledge such as the black community, black culture and indeed black studies.' Alexander Weheliye, *Habeas Viscus: Racializing Assemblages, Biopolitics and Black Feminist Theories of the Human* (Durham, NC: Duke University Press, 2014), 18.

27 Ray Hutchison, 'Where Is the Chicago Ghetto?', in *The Ghetto: Contemporary Global Issues and Controversies*, ed. Bruce D. Haynes and Ray Hutchison (Boulder, CO: Westview Press, 2011); Loic Wacquant, 'A Janus-Faced Institution of Ethnoracial Closure: A Sociological Specification of the Ghetto', in *The Ghetto: Contemporary Global Issues and Controversies*.

28 Drake and Cayton, *Black Metropolis*, 211.

29 Ibid., 211.

30 Ibid., 385.

31 Ibid., 385.

32 Ibid., 386.

33 Ibid., 396.

34 Loic Wacquant, 'The New Urban Color Line: The State and Fate of the Ghetto in Postfordist America', in *Social Theory and the Politics of Identity*, ed. Craig Calhoun (London: Wiley, 1994), 234.

35 Loic Wacquant, 'Deadly Symbiosis: When Ghetto and Prison Meet and Mesh', *Punishment and Society* 3, no. 1 (2001): 104.

36 Wacquant, 'New Urban Color Line', 232.

37 Loic Wacquant, 'Three Pernicious Premises in the Study of the American Ghetto', *International Journal of Urban and Regional Research* 21, no. 2 (1997): 345.

38 Wacquant, 'Deadly Symbiosis', 104.

39 Wacquant, 'New Urban Color Line', 234.

40 Ibid., 236.

41 Wacquant, 'Three Pernicious Premises', 346.

42 Wacquant, 'Deadly Symbiosis', 103.

43 Ibid., 105.

44 Ibid., 107.

45 Ibid., 107, 117.

46 W.E.B. Du Bois, 'Sociology Hesitant', in *W.E.B. Du Bois: The Problem of the Color Line at the Turn of the Twentieth Century: The Essential Early Essays*, ed. Nahum Dimitri Chandler (New York: Fordham University Press, 2015); Ronald Judy, 'Special Issue – Sociology Hesitant: Thinking with Du Bois', *boundary 2* 27, no. 3 (Fall 2000).

47 Chandler, *X*.

48 Laura Harris, 'What Happened to the Motley Crew? C.L.R. James, Helio Oiticica and the Aesthetic Sociality of Blackness', *Social Text* 30, no. 3 (2012): 53.

49 Ibid., 53.

50 Ibid., 53.

51 Ibid., 59.

52 Chandler, *X*, 13.

53 Nahum Dimitri Chandler, 'Originary Displacement', *boundary 2* 27, no. 3 (Fall 2000): 255–256.

54 Ibid., 283.

55 Chandler, *X*, 19.

56 Ibid., 19.

57 Ibid., 10.

58 Ibid., 20.

59 Personal Correspondence with author, April 2015; chukwumaa, 'Quadrillage', lecture delivered at Institute of Contemporary Art, Philadelphia, Pennsylvania, 16th April 2015.

60 'Havoc Vs. BelowZero', www.youtube.com/watch?v=_brqdx7kWqQ, accessed 10th August 2019.

61 RP Boo, 'Heavy Heat', *Bangs & Works Volume 2* (Planet Mu, 2010).

62 DJ Rashad, 'Ghost', *Just a Taste* (Ghettophiles, 2011).

63 Bragin, 'Shot and Captured', 109.

64 Ibid., 110.

4 Ghettoville

1 Philip Brian Harper, *Abstractionist Aesthetics: Artistic Form and Social Critique in African American Culture* (New York: New York University Press, 2015); Kobena Mercer, ed., *Discrepant Abstraction* (London: Institute of International Visual Arts. Cambridge, MA: MIT Press, 2006).

2 Mercer, *Discrepant Abstraction*, 7.

3 George Lewis, *A Power Stronger Than Itself: The AACM and American Experimental Music* (Chicago: University of Chicago Press, 2008), xxxiii.

4 So that 'appeals to internal difference are made in order to disallow instantiation. Abstraction of or from the referent [blackness] is seen as tantamount to its non-existence'. Harney and Moten, *Undercommons*, 48.

5 Rory Gibb, 'Dark Matter: An Interview with Actress', *The Quietus*, 5th February 2014, http://thequietus.com/articles/14423-actress-interview-ghettoville.

6 Shapiro, *Modulations*, 3.

7 Reynolds, *Energy Flash*, xxiv.

8 Ruth Saxelby, 'It's Medicine – That's What Music Is', *Dummy*, 20th April, 2012; Tom Lea, 'Watching Westerns with the Sound Off: Actress Interviewed', *Fact*, 7th February 2014, www.factmag.com/2014/02/07/actress-interview-fact-ghettoville-darren-cunningham/.

9 Lea, 'Watching Westerns with the Sound Off'.

10 Joanna Demers, *Listening through the Noise: The Aesthetics of Experimental Electronic Dance Music* (Oxford: Oxford University Press, 2010), 43.

11 Ibid., 45.

12 Ibid., 64.

13 Eshun, *More Brilliant Than the Sun*, 100.

14 Ibid., 121.

15 Gibb, 'Dark Matter: An Interview with Actress.'

16 Akomfrah (dir.) *The Last Angel of History.*

17 Tricia Rose, *Black Noise: Rap Music and Contemporary Culture in Contemporary America* (Middletown, CT: Wesleyan University Press, 1994); Kelley, *Yo' Mama's Disfunktional.*

18 Murray Forman and Mark Anthony Neal, eds., *That's the Joint! The Hip-Hop Studies Reader* (New York and London: Routledge, 2004); Nelson George, *Hip-Hop America* (London: Penguin, 2005).

19 Patric Fallon, 'Actress – Ghettoville', *XLR8R*, 27th January 2014, www.xlr8r.com/reviews/2014/01/ghettoville/.

20 Angus Finlayson, 'Ghettoville', *Fact*, 24th January 2014, www.factmag.com/2014/01/24/actress-ghettoville/.

21 Andrew Gaerig, 'Actress, *Ghettoville', Pitchfork*, 28th January 2014, http://pitchfork.com/reviews/albums/18946-actress-ghettoville/.

22 Ruth Saxelby, 'Curtain Call: Ruth Saxelby on Actress' *Ghettoville', Electronic Beats*, 23rd January 2014, www.electronicbeats.net/en/features/reviews/curtain-call-ruth-saxelby-on-actress-ghettoville/.

23 Gibb, 'Dark Matter: An Interview with Actress.'

24 Saxelby, 'Curtain Call'; Gaerig, 'Actress, *Ghettoville'.*

25 Derek Walmsley, 'Actress', *The Wire*, no. 361 (March 2014).

26 Fred Moten, 'Empire, Multitude and Commonwealth: Duke Faculty Bookwatch', 11th November 2010, https://itunes.apple.com/us/itunes-u/faculty-bookwatch/id459096499.

27 Gibb, 'Dark Matter: An Interview with Actress.'

28 For a similar discussion of black musical experimentation and its deployment of poverty as a formal resource, see Fumi Okiji, *Jazz as Critique: Adorno and Black Expression Revisited* (Redwood City, CA: Stanford University Press, 2018), 29.

29 Hito Steyerl, 'In Free Fall: A Thought Experiment on Vertical Perspective', in *The Wretched of the Screen* (Sternberg Press, 2012), 20–21.

30 Ibid., 27.

31 Katherine McKittrick, *Demonic Grounds: Black Women and the Cartographies of Struggle* (Minneapolis: University of Minnesota Press, 2006), xi.

32 Ibid., xv.

33 Ibid., 13.

34 Ibid., xiv.

35 Ibid., xxii.

36 Ibid., xxii.

37 Ibid., xxiv.

38 David Marriott, *Haunted Life: Visual Culture and Black Modernity* (New Brunswick, NJ: Rutgers University Press, 2007), xiii.

39 Ibid., xiv.

40 Ibid., xx.

41 Ibid., xx.

42 Steyerl, 'In Free Fall', 28.

43 McKittrick, *Demonic Grounds*, 7.

5 Eski

1 Richard Bramwell, *UK Hip-Hop, Grime and the City: The Aesthetics and Ethics of London's Rap Scenes* (London: Routledge, 2015); Monique Charles, 'Hallowed Be Thy Grime? A Musicological and Sociological Genealogy of Grime and Its Relation to Black Atlantic Religious Discourse' (PhD dissertation, University of Warwick, 2017); Joy White, *Urban Music and Entrepreneurship: Beats, Rhymes, and Young People's Enterprise* (London: Routledge, 2016).

2 John Akomfrah, 'John Akomfrah in Conversation', Sheffield Doc/Fest 2015, www.youtube.com/watch?v=b6Mr2heCoeM.

3 C.L.R. James, *Notes on Dialectics: Hegel, Marx, Lenin* (London: Allison & Busby, 1980), 10.

4 Ibid., 10.

5 Dan Hancox, 'Tarik Nashnush and UKG's Most Important Label, Locked On', *Red Bull Music Academy*, 26th April 2019, https://daily.redbullmusicacademy.com/2019/04/tarik-nashnush-ukg-locked-on; Dan Hancox, 'The UK Garage Committee Meetings and the Garage Wars', *Red Bull Music Academy*, 17th June 2019, https://daily.redbullmusicacademy.com/2019/06/ukg-committee-garage-wars.

6 'A Brief History of Grime Tapes with Michael Finch and Rollo Jackson', *Adventures in Modern Music* – broadcast on Resonance FM, June 2011, www.thewire.co.uk/audio/on-air/adventures-in-modern-music2-june-2011.1.

7 Simon Reynolds, 'Simon Reynolds on The Hardcore Continuum – #7 Grime (and a Little Dubstep)', *The Wire*, no. 300 (February 2009).

8 Martin Clark/Blackdown, 'Eski-Beat: An Interview with Wiley (Part 1 October 2003)', *Riddim Dot Ca*, 23rd October 2009, www.riddim.ca/?p=232.

9 Reynolds, 'Simon Reynolds on The Hardcore Continuum'.

10 Clark/Blackdown, 'Eski-Beat: An Interview with Wiley'.

11 Nico Hogg and Martin Clark, *London: Signs and Signifiers* (London: Keysound Recordings, 2015).

12 Wiley in 'A Day with Wiley', *Lord of the Decks CD & DVD Special Vol 2* (DVD, Hot Headz Promotions, 2004).

13 Reynolds, 'Simon Reynolds on The Hardcore Continuum'.

14 Martin Clark, 'The Month in Grime/Dubstep', *Pitchfork*, 22nd June 2005, https://pitchfork.com/features/grime-dubstep/6073-the-month-in-grime-dubstep/.

15 Paul Watt and Anthony Gunter, 'Grafting, Going to College and Working on Road: Youth Transitions and Cultures in an East London Neighbourhood', *Journal of Youth Studies* 12, no. 5 (October 2009): 518.

16 Reynolds, 'Simon Reynolds on The Hardcore Continuum'.

17 Breeze, in *Wot Do You Call It* (Channel 4, 2003).

18 Dan Hancox, *Stand Up Tall: Dizzee Rascal and the Birth of Grime* (Kindle Edition, 2013).

19 Ibid. The idea of physical proximity to finance capital combining with economic distance in this area of London as an incitement for aestheticization is not restricted to Grime alone. Black Audio Film Collective's 1989 essay film *Twilight City* in many ways sees the scenarios coming which Grime deals with. Reese Auguiste (dir.), *Twilight City* (Channel 4, 1989).

20 Dan Hancox, ' "Pow!": Anthem for Kettled Youth', *The Guardian*, 3rd February 2011.

21 Dan Hancox, 'A History of Grime, by the People Who Created It', *The Guardian*, 6th December 2012.

22 Laurent Fintoni, 'How Fruity Loops Changed Music-Making Forever', *Red Bull Music Academy*, 13th May 2015, http://daily.redbullmusicacademy.com/2015/05/fruity-loops-feature.

23 Lloyd Bradley, *Sounds Like London: 100 Years of Black Music in the Capital* (London: Serpent's Tail, 2013); 'First Sight – Pirate Radio London Kool FM' (Jungle Drum & Bass Documentary, 1996): www.youtube.com/watch?v=d3AQ59y2t-I; 'Welcome to the Jungle – Rude FM' (1995), http://junglednbdocumentary.blogspot.co.uk/2014/11/blog-post_13.html; 'Radio Arena – Pirate Radio London Rush FM' (1994), http://junglednbdocumentary.blogspot.co.uk/2014/11/blog-post_38.html.

24 'Incubated on pirate radio – a network of illegal and hyper local FM stations that were vital to grime, just as they were to dubstep, UK garage and jungle before them – the new sound was disseminated by a new generation of teenage MCs and producers making sparse but devastating beats, often using cheap home PC software or video game consoles.' Dan Hancox, 'Skepta's Mission: Skepta's Leading Grime into the Future by Returning to Its Roots', *The Fader* (June/July 2015).

25 Slimzee, in *Slimzee's Going on Terrible* (dir.: Rollo Jackson, 2014), https://vimeo.com/109801766.

26 Ibid.

27 Melissa Bradshaw, 'Slimzee: Asbos, Breakdowns and Dubplates', *Boiler Room*, 6th July 2015, https://boilerroom.tv/slimzee-asbos-breakdowns-and-dubplates/.

28 Dan Hancox, Tom Lea, and Mr Beatnik, 'Stand Up Tall: A Roundtable Debate about Dizzee Rascal's *Boy in Da Corner* and the Birth of Grime', *Fact*, 22nd August 2013, www.factmag.com/2013/08/22/stand-up-tall-a-round-table-debate-about-dizzee-rascals-boy-in-da-corner-and-the-birth-of-grime/.

29 Martin Clark, 'Interview with Terror Danjah', *Riddim Dot Ca*, May 2004, www.riddim.ca/?p=230.

30 'In the encounter between black settlers and their white inner-city neighbours, black culture has become a class culture. There is more to this transformation and adaptation than the fact that blacks are among the most economically exploited and politically marginal sections of the society, over-represented in the surplus population, the prison population and among the poor. From the dawn of the post-war settlement, diaspora culture has been an ambiguous presence in the autonomous institutions of the working class. Two generations of whites have appropriated it, discovering in its seductive forms meanings of their own. It is now impossible to speak coherently of black culture in Britain in isolation from the culture of Britain as a whole. This is particularly true as far as leisure is concerned. Black expressive culture has decisively shaped youth culture, pop culture and the culture of city life in Britain's metropolitan centres.' Paul Gilroy, 'One Nation Under a Groove', *Small Acts*, 34–35.

31 Alex S. Vitale, *The End of Policing* (London and New York: Verso, 2017).

32 Dan Hancox, 'The Outsiders', *Daily Note*, 11th February 2010.

33 Ibid.

34 *The Police vs Grime Music – A Noisey Film* (Noisey, 29th May 2014), www.youtube.com/watch?v=eW_iujPQpys.

35 Alexandra Topping, 'Police Accused of Discriminating against Urban Music Scene', *The Guardian*, 8th January 2012; Dan Hancox, 'Public Enemy 696', *The Guardian*, 21st January 2009.

36 'Cameron Attacks Radio 1's Hip Hop', *BBC News*, BBC, Wednesday 7th June 2006, http://news.bbc.co.uk/1/hi/uk_politics/5055724.stm; David Goodhart, 'The Riots, the Rappers and the Anglo-Jamaican Tragedy', *Prospect*, 17th August 2011; Paul Routledge, 'London Riots: Is Rap Music to Blame for Encouraging This Culture of Violence?', *The Mirror*, 14th August 2011.

37 Patrick Williams and Becky Clarke, *Dangerous Associations: Joint Enterprise, Gangs and Racism* (Centre for Crime and Justice Studies, Manchester Metropolitan University, January 2016); George Amponsah (dir.), *The Hard Stop* (Ga Films, 2015).

38 Derek Walmsley, 'Deconstructing Violence in Grime', *The Wire* (October 2015), www.thewire.co.uk/in-writing/book-extracts/deconstructing-violence-in-grime.

39 Ibid.

40 Ibid.

41 Ibid. The following comment from Lethal B also supports Walmsley's claim: 'One thing about Grime, the majority of MCs spoke about their surroundings, their areas. Our heroes were the shotters – they had the clothes, the cars, the girls, the money. They was hood stars. We wanted to be them without having to sell drugs. A lot of my friends from school were involved in certain things, I was involved in certain things and so music was a release. I saw a lot of things, so a lot of what we spoke about came from true things – everyday life in East London, there was always something going on'. Lethal B in Hattie Collins and Olivia Rose, *This Is Grime* (London: Hodder and Stoughton, 2016), 24.

42 Walmsley, 'Deconstructing Violence in Grime'.

43 Ibid.

44 Ibid.

45 Matthew Fuller, *Media Ecologies: Materialist Energies in Art and Technoculture* (Cambridge, MA: MIT Press, 2005), 15.

46 Ibid., 13.

47 Ibid., 13.

48 Ibid., 16.

49 Ibid., 16.

50 Ibid., 17.

51 Ibid., 17.

52 Ibid., 31.

53 Ibid., 36.

54 Ibid., 36.

55 Ibid., 18.

56 Goodman, *Sonic Warfare*, 178.

57 Fuller, *Media Ecologies*, 20, 23.

58 Goodman, *Sonic Warfare*, 179.

59 Stuart Hall, Chas Chritcher, Tony Jefferson, John Clarke, and Brian Roberts, *Policing the Crisis: Mugging, the State, and Law and Order* (Basingstoke: Palgrave Macmillan, 2nd ed., 2013), 332.

60 Ibid., 339.

61 Ibid., 340.

62 Ibid., 342.

63 Ibid., 344.

64 Ibid., 348.

65 Ibid., 347.

66 Ibid., 358.

67 Paul Gilroy, 'Steppin' out of Babylon: Race, Class and Autonomy', in *The Empire Strikes Back: Race and Racism in 70s Britain*, ed. Centre for Contemporary Cultural Studies (London: Hutchinson, 1982), 287.

68 Paul Gilroy, *There Ain't No Black in the Union Jack* (London: Hutchinson, 1987), 224.

69 Ibid., 217.

70 Ibid., 217.

71 Collins and Rose, *This Is Grime*, 13.

72 Jammer, *Young Man Standing / Jammerz Birthday Bash* (DVD, Hot Headz Promotions, 2004).

73 Barnor Hesse, 'White Governmentality: Urbanism, Nationalism, Racism', in *Imagining Cities: Scripts, Signs, Memories*, ed. Sallie Westwood and John Williams (London: Routledge, 1997), 86.

74 Ibid., 87.

75 Ibid., 88.

Conclusion

1 Laurence Ralph, *The Torture Letters: Reckoning with Police Violence* (Chicago: University of Chicago Press, 2020): David Taylor, 'Chicago's Deadly Summer: Guns, Gangs, and the Legacy of Racial Inequality', *The Guardian*, 12th August 2018, www.theguardian.com/us-news/2018/aug/12/chicago-gun-violence-racial-inequality-segregation-activism.

2 'Hyperdub Release Statement on Death of DJ Rashad', *Fact*, 28th April 2018, www.fact-mag.com/2014/04/28/hyperdub-release-statement-on-the-death-of-dj-rashad/.

3 Andrew Ryce, 'Skepta Wins Mercury Prize', 15th September 2016, www.residentadvisor.net/news/36452; David Renshaw, 'Stormzy's Gang Signs & Prayer Is the No. 1 Album in the U.K.', 3rd March 2017, www.thefader.com/2017/03/03/stormzy-uk-number-one-album.

4 Ciaran Thapar, 'The Moral Panic against UK Drill Is Deeply Misguided', *Pitchfork*, 12th September 2018, https://pitchfork.com/thepitch/the-moral-panic-against-uk-drill-is-deeply-misguided/.

5 https://klein1997.bandcamp.com; https://yves-tumor.bandcamp.com; https://mhysa301.bandcamp.com.

6 https://nkisi.bandcamp.com; https://nazar.bandcamp.com; https://jlin.bandcamp.com.

Bibliography

Aggarwal, Sonali, dir. *From Jack to Juke: 25 Years of Ghetto House*. http://vimeo.com/36275353.

Akomfrah, John. 'John Akomfrah in Conversation'. Sheffield Doc/Fest 2015. www.youtube.com/watch?v=b6Mr2heCoeM.

Akomfrah, John, dir. *The Last Angel of History*. Channel 4, 1996.

Amponsah, George, dir. *The Hard Stop*. Ga Films, 2015.

Arnold, Jacob. 'Dance Mania: Ghetto House's Motown'. *Resident Advisor*, 15th May 2013. www.residentadvisor.net/feature.aspx?1806.

Auguiste, Reese, dir. *Twilight City*. Channel 4, 1989.

Baraka, Amiri. *Black Music*. New York: Akashic Books, 2010.

Barrow, Dan. 'Hieroglyphic Being and the Configurative or Modular Me Trio / *The Seer of Cosmic Visions* (Planet Mu, 2014)'. *The Wire*, no. 369 (November 2014).

Bradley, Lloyd. *Sounds Like London: 100 Years of Black Music in the Capital*. London: Serpent's Tail, 2013.

Bradshaw, Melissa. 'Slimzee: Asbos, Breakdowns and Dubplates'. *Boiler Room*, 6th July 2015. https://boilerroom.tv/slimzee-asbos-breakdowns-and-dubplates/.

Bragin, Naomi. 'Shot and Captured: Turf Dance, Yak Films and the Oakland, California R.I.P. Project'. *TDR: The Drama Review* 58, no. 2 (2014).

Bramwell, Richard. *UK Hip-Hop, Grime and the City: The Aesthetics and Ethics of London's Rap Scenes*. London: Routledge, 2015.

Bredow, Gary, dir. *High Tech Soul: The Creation of Techno Music*. 2006.

Brewster, Bill, and Frank Broughton. *Last Night a DJ Saved My Life: A History of the Disc Jockey*. London: Headline, 2000.

'A Brief History of Grime Tapes with Michael Finch and Rollo Jackson'. *Adventures in Modern Music*. Broadcast on Resonance FM, June 2011. www.thewire.co.uk/audio/on-air/adventures-in-modern-music2-june-2011.1.

Brown, Jayna. 'Buzz and Rumble: Global Pop Music and Utopian Impulse'. *Social Text* 28, no. 1 (Spring 2010).

Bulmer, Martin. *The Chicago School of Sociology: Institutionalization, Diversity and the Rise of Sociological Research*. Chicago: University of Chicago Press, 1984.

'Cameron Attacks Radio 1's Hip Hop'. *BBC News*. BBC, Wednesday 7th June 2006. http://news.bbc.co.uk/1/hi/uk_politics/5055724.stm.

Chandler, Nahum Dimitri. 'Originary Displacement'. *boundary 2* 27, no. 3 (Fall 2000).

Chandler, Nahum Dimitri. *X: The Problem of the Negro as a Problem for Thought*. New York: Fordham University Press, 2014.

Charles, Monique. Hallowed Be Thy Grime? A Musicological and Sociological Genealogy of Grime and Its Relation to Black Atlantic Religious Discourse. PhD dissertation. University of Warwick, 2017.

chukwumaa. 'Quadrillage'. Lecture delivered at Institute of Contemporary Art, Philadelphia, Pennsylvania, 16th April 2015.

Clark, Martin. 'Eski-Beat: An Interview with Wiley (Part 1 October 2003)'. *Riddim Dot Ca*, 23rd October 2009. http://www.riddim.ca/?p=232.

Clark, Martin. 'Interview with Terror Danjah'. *Riddim Dot Ca*, 29th May 2004. www.riddim.ca/?p=230.

Clark, Martin. 'The Month in Grime/Dubstep'. *Pitchfork*, 22nd June 2005. https://pitchfork.com/features/grime-dubstep/6073-the-month-in-grime-dubstep/.

Collins, Hattie, and Olivia Rose. *This Is Grime*. London: Hodder and Stoughton, 2016.

Demers, Joanna. *Listening through the Noise: The Aesthetics of Experimental Electronic Dance Music*. Oxford: Oxford University Press, 2010.

Drake, St Clair, and Horace R. Cayton. *Black Metropolis: A Study of Negro Life in a Northern City*. Chicago: University of Chicago Press, 2015.

Du Bois, W.E.B. 'Sociology Hesitant'. In *W.E.B. Du Bois: The Problem of the Color Line at the Turn of the Twentieth Century: The Essential Early Essays*, edited by Nahum Dimitri Chandler. New York: Fordham University Press, 2015.

Eshun, Kodwo. 'Jungle! Jungle! The Last Dance Underground'. *I.D.* (May 1994).

Eshun, Kodwo. *More Brilliant Than the Sun: Adventures in Sonic Fiction*. London: Quartet Books, 1998.

Fallon, Patric. 'Actress – Ghettoville'. *XLR8R*, 27th January 2014. www.xlr8r.com/reviews/2014/01/ghettoville/.

Finlayson, Angus. 'Ghettoville'. *Fact*, 24th January 2014. www.factmag.com/2014/01/24/actress-ghettoville/.

Finlayson, Angus. 'Interview: Kode9'. *Red Bull Music Academy*, 13th July 2013. http://daily.redbullmusicacademy.com/2013/06/kode9-2013-interview.

Fintoni, Laurent. 'How Fruity Loops Changed Music-Making Forever'. *Red Bull Music Academy*, 13th May 2015. http://daily.redbullmusicacademy.com/2015/05/fruity-loops-feature.

'First Sight – Pirate Radio London Kool FM'. Jungle Drum & Bass Documentary, 1996. Video, https://www.youtube.com/watch?v=d3AQ59y2t-I;.

Fisher, Mark. 'The Abstract Reality of the Hardcore Continuum'. *Dancecult: Journal of Electronic Dance Music Culture* 1, no. 1 (2009).

Forman, Murray and Mark Anthony Neal, eds. *That's the Joint! The Hip-Hop Studies Reader.* New York and London: Routledge, 2004.

Frazier, E. Franklin. *The Negro Family in Chicago.* Chicago: University of Chicago Press, 1932.

Fuller, Matthew. *Media Ecologies: Materialist Energies in Art and Technoculture.* Cambridge, MA: MIT Press, 2005.

Gaerig, Andrew. 'Actress, *Ghettoville*'. *Pitchfork*, 28th January 2014. http://pitchfork.com/reviews/albums/18946-actress-ghettoville/.

George, Edward. '(ghost the signal)'. In *The Ghosts of Songs: The Film Art of the Black Audio Film Collective*, edited by Kodwo Eshun and Anjalika Sagar. Liverpool: FACT/Liverpool University Press, 2007.

George, Nelson. *The Death of Rhythm & Blues.* London: Omnibus, 1998.

George, Nelson. *Hip-Hop America.* London: Penguin, 2005.

Gibb, Rory. 'Dark Matter: An Interview with Actress'. *The Quietus*, 5th February 2014. http://thequietus.com/articles/14423-actress-interview-ghettoville.

Gilbert, Jeremy, and Ewan Pearson. *Discographies: Dance Music, Culture and the Politics of Sound.* London: Routledge, 1999.

Gilroy, Paul. *Between Camps: Nations, Cultures and the Allure of Race.* London: Routledge, 2004.

Gilroy, Paul. 'Between the Blues and the Blues Dance: Some Soundscapes of the Black Atlantic'. In *The Auditory Culture Reader*, edited by Michael Bull and Les Back. Oxford: Berg, 2003.

Gilroy, Paul. *The Black Atlantic: Modernity and Double Consciousness.* London: Verso, 1993.

Gilroy, Paul. *Darker Than Blue: On the Moral Economies of Black Atlantic Culture.* Cambridge, MA and London: Bellknap, 2010.

Gilroy, Paul. *Small Acts: Thoughts on the Politics of Black Cultures.* London: Serpents Tail, 1993.

Gilroy, Paul. 'Steppin' out of Babylon: Race, Class and Autonomy'. In *The Empire Strikes Back: Race and Racism in 70s Britain*, edited by Centre for Contemporary Cultural Studies. London: Hutchinson, 1982.

Gilroy, Paul. *There Ain't No Black in the Union Jack.* London: Hutchinson, 1987.

Goodhart, David. 'The Riots, the Rappers and the Anglo-Jamaican Tragedy'. *Prospect*, 17th August 2011.

Goodman, Steve. *Sonic Warfare: Sound, Affect, and the Ecology of Fear.* Cambridge, MA and London: MIT Press, 2009.

Hall, Stuart. 'The Meaning of New Times (1989)'. In *Selected Political Writings: The Great Moving Right Show and Other Essays*. Durham, NC: Duke University Press, 2017.

Hall, Stuart. 'New Ethnicities'. In *Stuart Hall: Critical Dialogues in Cultural Studies*, edited by David Morley and Kuan-Hsing Chen. New York and London: Routledge, 1996.

Hall, Stuart, Chas Chritcher, Tony Jefferson, John Clarke, and Brian Roberts. *Policing the Crisis: Mugging, the State, and Law and Order*. Basingstoke: Palgrave Macmillan, 2nd ed., 2013.

Hancox, Dan. 'A History of Grime, by the People Who Created It'. *The Guardian*, 6th December 2012.

Hancox, Dan. 'The Outsiders'. *Daily Note*, 11th February 2010.

Hancox, Dan. ' "Pow!": Anthem for Kettled Youth'. *The Guardian*, 3rd February 2011.

Hancox, Dan. 'Public Enemy 696'. *The Guardian*, 21st January 2009.

Hancox, Dan. 'Skepta's Mission: Skepta's Leading Grime into the Future by Returning to Its Roots'. *The Fader* (June/July 2015).

Hancox, Dan. *Stand Up Tall: Dizzee Rascal and the Birth of Grime*. Kindle Edition, 2013.

Hancox, Dan. 'Tarik Nashnush and UKG's Most Important Label, Locked On'. *Red Bull Music Academy*, 26th April 2019. https://daily.redbullmusicacademy.com/2019/04/tarik-nashnush-ukg-locked-on;.

Hancox, Dan. 'The UK Garage Committee Meetings and the Garage Wars'. *Red Bull Music Academy*, 17th June 2019. https://daily.redbullmusicacademy.com/2019/06/ukg-committee-garage-wars.

Hancox, Dan, Tom Lea, and Mr Beatnik. 'Stand Up Tall: A Roundtable Debate about Dizzee Rascal's *Boy in Da Corner* and the Birth of Grime'. *Fact*, 22nd August 2013. www.factmag.com/2013/08/22/stand-up-tall-a-round-table-debate-about-dizzee-rascals-boy-in-da-corner-and-the-birth-of-grime/.

Harney, Stefano, and Fred Moten. 'Michael Brown'. *boundary 2* 42, no. 4 (2015).

Harney, Stefano, and Fred Moten. *The Undercommons: Fugitive Planning and Black Study*. Wivenhoe, New York, Port Watson: Minor Compositions, 2013.

Harper, Philip Brian. *Abstractionist Aesthetics: Artistic Form and Social Critique in African American Culture*. New York: New York University Press, 2015.

Harris, Laura. 'What Happened to the Motley Crew? C.L.R. James, Helio Oiticica and the Aesthetic Sociality of Blackness'. *Social Text* 30, no. 3 (2012).

Hesse, Barnor. 'White Governmentality: Urbanism, Nationalism, Racism'. In *Imagining Cities: Scripts, Signs, Memories*, edited by Sallie Westwood and John Williams. London: Routledge, 1997.

Hogg, Nico, and Martin Clark. *London: Signs and Signifiers*. London: Keysound Recordings, 2015.

Hutchison, Ray. 'Where Is the Chicago Ghetto?'. In *The Ghetto: Contemporary Global Issues and Controversies*, edited by Bruce D. Haynes and Ray Hutchison. Boulder, CO: Westview Press, 2011.

'Hyperdub Release Statement on Death of DJ Rashad'. *Fact*, 28th April 2018. https://www.factmag.com/2014/04/28/hyperdub-release-statement-on-the-death-of-dj-rashad/.

Iton, Richard. *In Search of the Black Fantastic: Politics and Popular Culture in the Post-Civil Rights Era*. Oxford and New York: Oxford University Press, 2008.

Jackson, Rollo, dir. *Slimzee's Going on Terrible*. 2014. https://vimeo.com/109801766.

James, C.L.R. *Notes on Dialectics: Hegel, Marx, Lenin*. London: Allison & Busby, 1980.

James, Martin. *State of Bass: Jungle – The Story So Far*. London: Boxtree, 1997.

Jammer. *Young Man Standing / Jammerz Birthday Bash*. Hot Headz Promotions, 2004. DVD.

Johnson, Gaye Theresa, and Alex Lubin, eds. *Futures of Black Radicalism*. London and New York: Verso, 2017.

Johnson, Imani Kai. 'Music Meant to Make You Move: Considering the Aural Kinesthetic'. *Sounding Out!*, 18th June 2012. http://soundstudiesblog.com/2012/06/18/music-meant-to-make-you-move-considering-the-aural-kinesthetic/.

Judy, Ronald. 'Special Issue – Sociology Hesitant: Thinking with Du Bois'. *boundary 2* 27, no. 3 (Fall 2000).

Kelley, Robin D.G. *Yo' Mama's Disfunktional! Fighting the Culture Wars in Urban America*. Boston, MA: Beacon Press, 1997.

Lawrence, Tim. *Love Saves the Day: A History of American Dance Music Culture 1970–1979*. Durham, NC: Duke University Press, 2004.

Lea, Tom. 'Watching Westerns with the Sound Off: Actress Interviewed'. *Fact*, 7th February 2014. www.factmag.com/2014/02/07/actress-interview-fact-ghettoville-darren-cunningham/.

Lewis, George, *A Power Stronger Than Itself: The AACM and American Experimental Music*. Chicago: University of Chicago Press, 2008.

Lewis, George. 'The Timeless Blues'. In *Blues for Smoke*, edited by Bennett Simpson. Los Angeles, CA: Museum of Contemporary Art, Los Angeles, 2012.

Lord of the Decks CD & DVD Special Vol 2. Hot Headz Promotions, 2004. DVD.

Marriott, David. *Haunted Life: Visual Culture and Black Modernity*. New Brunswick, NJ: Rutgers University Press, 2007.

McKittrick, Katherine. *Demonic Grounds: Black Women and the Cartographies of Struggle*. Minneapolis: University of Minnesota Press, 2006.

McKittrick, Katherine. 'On Plantations, Prisons and a Black Sense of Place'. *Social & Cultural Geography* 12, no. 8 (2011).

McKittrick, Katherine. 'Plantation Futures'. *Small Axe* 17, no. 3 (2013).

McKittrick, Katherine, and Alexander Weheliye. '808s & Heartbreak'. *Propter Nos* 2, no. 1 (Fall 2017).

Mercer, Kobena, ed., *Discrepant Abstraction*. London: Institute of International Visual Arts. Cambridge, MA: MIT Press, 2006.

Mercer, Kobena. *Welcome to the Jungle: New Positions in Black Cultural Studies*. New York and London: Routledge, 1994.

Moreno, Louis. 'The Sound of Detroit: Notes, Tones and Rhythms from Underground'. In *The Acoustic City*, edited by Matthew Gandy and B.J. Nilsen. Berlin: Jovis, 2014.

Moten, Fred. 'Collective Head'. *Women & Performance* 26, no. 2–3 (2016).

Moten, Fred. 'Empire, Multitude and Commonwealth: Duke Faculty Bookwatch'. 11th November 2010. https://itunes.apple.com/us/itunes-u/faculty-bookwatch/id459096499.

Moten, Fred. *In the Break: The Aesthetics of the Black Radical Tradition*. Minneapolis: University of Minnesota Press, 2003.

Moten, Fred. 'Jurisgenerative Grammar (for Alto)'. In *The Oxford Handbook of Critical Improvisation Studies Vol 1*, edited by George E. Lewis and Benjamin Piekut. New York and Oxford: Oxford University Press, 2016.

Moten, Fred. 'The Subprime and the Beautiful'. *African Identities* 11, no. 2 (2013).

Nyong'o, Tavia. 'I Feel Love: Disco and Its Discontents'. *Criticism* 50, no. 1 (Winter 2008).

Okiji, Fumi. *Jazz as Critique: Adorno and Black Expression Revisited*. Redwood City, CA: Stanford University Press, 2018.

Park, Robert E., Ernest Burgess, and Roderick McKenzie. *The City: Suggestions for the Study of Human Nature in the Urban Environment*. Chicago: University of Chicago Press, 1925.

Petty, Audrey, ed. *High Rise Stories: Voices from Chicago Public Housing*. San Francisco: McSweeny's Books, 2013.

The Police vs Grime music – A Noisey Film. Noisey, 29th May 2014. https://www.youtube.com/watch?v=eW_iujPQpys.

Quam, Dave. 'Battle Cats: From the Rise of House in the 80s to Today's Juke and Footwork Scenes, Chicago's Circle Keeps Expanding'. *XLR8R*, 9th August 2010. www.xlr8r.com/features/2010/09/battle-cats-rise-house-music-80s.

Quam, Dave. 'The Evolution of Footwork'. *Resident Advisor*, 19th November 2010. www.residentadvisor.net/feature.aspx?1235.

Quam, Dave. 'These Feet Were Made for Workin': Inside Chicago's Explosive Footwork Scene'. *Spin*, 5th July 2012. www.spin.com/articles/these-feet-were-made-workin-inside-chicagos-explosive-footwork-scene/.

'Radio Arena – Pirate Radio London Rush FM'. 1994. http://junglednbdocumentary.blogspot.co.uk/2014/11/blog-post_38.html.

Ralph, Laurence. *The Torture Letters: Reckoning with Police Violence*. Chicago: University of Chicago Press, 2020.

Renshaw, David. 'Stormzy's Gang Signs & Prayer Is the No. 1 Album in the U.K.' 3rd March 2017. www.thefader.com/2017/03/03/stormzy-uk-number-one-album.

Reynolds, Simon. *Energy Flash: A Journey through Rave Music and Dance Culture*. London: Faber and Faber, 2013.

Reynolds, Simon. 'The Hardcore Continuum or (a) Theory and Its Discontents'. http://energyflashbysimonreynolds.blogspot.co.uk/2009/02/hardcore-continuum-or-theory-and-its.html, accessed 27th February 2018.

Reynolds, Simon. 'Simon Reynolds on The Hardcore Continuum – #7 Grime (and a Little Dubstep)'. *The Wire*, no. 300 (February 2009).

Reynolds, Simon. 'The Wire 300: Simon Reynolds on the Hardcore Continuum'. *The Wire*, no. 300 (February 2009).

Rietveld, Hillegonda. *This Is Our House: House Music, Cultural Spaces and Technologies*. Aldershot: Ashgate, 1998.

Robinson, Cedric. *Black Marxism: The Making of the Black Radical Tradition*. Chapel Hill, NC: University of North Carolina Press, 2000.

Rose, Tricia. *Black Noise: Rap Music and Contemporary Culture in Contemporary America*. Middletown, CT: Wesleyan University Press, 1994.

Routledge, Paul. 'London Riots: Is Rap Music to Blame for Encouraging This Culture of Violence?'. *The Mirror*, 14th August 2011.

Ryce, Andrew. 'Skepta Wins Mercury Prize'. 15th September 2016. www.residentadvisor.net/news/36452;.

Sampson, Robert. *Great American City: Chicago and The Enduring Neighborhood Effect*. Chicago: University of Chicago Press, 2012.

Sandhu, Sukhdev. *London Calling: How Black and Asian Writers Imagined a City*. London Harper Perennial, 2004.

Saxelby, Ruth. 'Curtain Call: Ruth Saxelby on Actress' *Ghettoville*'. *Electronic Beats*, 23rd January 2014. www.electronicbeats.net/en/features/reviews/curtain-call-ruth-saxelby-on-actress-ghettoville/.

Saxelby, Ruth. 'It's Medicine – That's What Music Is'. *Dummy*, 20th April 2012.

Scott, David. *Conscripts of Modernity: The Tragedy of Colonial Enlightenment*. Durham, NC: Duke University Press, 2004.

Seely, Rachel, dir. *All Junglist: A London Sum Ting Dis*. Channel 4, 1994.

Shapiro, Peter, ed. *Modulations: A History of Electronic Music: Throbbing Words on Sound*. New York: Caipirinha, 2000.

Sicko, Dan. *Techno Rebels: The Renegades of Electronic Funk*. New York: Billboard Books, 1999.

Simone, AbdouMaliq. *City Life from Jakarta to Dakar: Movements at the Crossroads*. London: Routledge, 2009.

Simone, AbdouMaliq. 'It's Just the City after All!'. *International Journal of Urban and Regional Research* 40, no. 1 (2016).

Simone, AbdouMaliq. 'Urbanity and Generic Blackness'. *Theory Culture & Society* 33, no. 7–8 (2016).

Sivanandan, A. 'All That Melts into Air Is Solid: The Hokum of New Times'. In *Catching History on the Wing: Race, Class and Globalization*. London: Pluto Press, 2008.

Spear, Allan H. *Black Chicago: The Making of a Negro Ghetto 1890–1920*. Chicago: University of Chicago Press, 1967.

Steyerl, Hito. 'In Free Fall: A Thought Experiment on Vertical Perspective'. In *The Wretched of the Screen*. Sternberg Press, 2012.

Taylor, David. 'Chicago's Deadly Summer: Guns, Gangs, and the Legacy of Racial Inequality'. *The Guardian*, 12th August 2018. www.theguardian.com/us-news/2018/aug/12/chicago-gun-violence-racial-inequality-segregation-activism.

Thapar, Ciaran. 'The Moral Panic against UK Drill Is Deeply Misguided'. *Pitchfork*, 12th September 2018. pitchfork.com/thepitch/the-moral-panic-against-uk-drill-is-deeply-misguided/.

Tim and Barry. *I'm Tryna Tell Ya*. Don't Watch That TV, 2014. www.youtube.com/watch?v=2AlJ88YZ3U8.

Topping, Alexandra. 'Police Accused of Discriminating against Urban Music Scene'. *The Guardian*, 8th January 2012.

Vitale, Alex S. *The End of Policing*. London and New York: Verso, 2017.

Wacquant, Loic. 'Deadly Symbiosis: When Ghetto and Prison Meet and Mesh'. *Punishment and Society* 3, no. 1 (2001).

Wacquant, Loic. 'A Janus-Faced Institution of Ethnoracial Closure: A Sociological Specification of the Ghetto'. In *The Ghetto: Contemporary Global Issues and Controversies*, edited by Bruce D. Haynes and Ray Hutchison. Boulder, CO: Westview Press, 2011.

Wacquant, Loic. 'The New Urban Color Line: The State and Fate of the Ghetto in Postfordist America'. In *Social Theory and the Politics of Identity*, edited by Craig Calhoun. London: Wiley, 1994.

Wacquant, Loic. 'Three Pernicious Premises in the Study of the American Ghetto'. *International Journal of Urban and Regional Research* 21, no. 2 (1997).

Walmsley, Derek. 'Actress'. *The Wire*, no. 361 (March 2014).

Walmsley, Derek, 'Deconstructing Violence in Grime', *The Wire* (October 2015). www. thewire.co.uk/in-writing/book-extracts/deconstructing-violence-in-grime.

Watt, Paul, and Anthony Gunter. 'Grafting, Going to College and Working on Road: Youth Transitions and Cultures in an East London Neighbourhood', *Journal of Youth Studies* 12, no. 5 (October 2009).

Weheliye, Alexander. *Habeas Viscus: Racializing Assemblages, Biopolitics and Black Feminist Theories of the Human*. Durham, NC: Duke University Press, 2014.

Weheliye, Alexander. *Phonographies: Grooves in Sonic Afro-Modernity*. Durham, NC: Duke University Press, 2005.

'Welcome to the Jungle – Rude FM'. 1995. http://junglednbdocumentary.blogspot.co.uk/2014/11/blog-post_13.html;.

White, Joy. *Urban Music and Entrepreneurship: Beats, Rhymes, and Young People's Enterprise*. London: Routledge, 2016.

Williams, Ben. 'Black Secret Technology: Detroit Techno and the Information Age'. In *Technicolor: Race, Technology and Everyday Life*, edited by Alondra Nelson, Thuy Linh N. Tu, and Alicia Headlam Hines. New York: New York University Press, 2001.

Williams, Patrick, and Becky Clarke. *Dangerous Associations: Joint Enterprise, Gangs and Racism*. Centre for Crime and Justice Studies, Manchester Metropolitan University, January 2016.

Wot Do You Call It. Channel 4, 2003.

Discography

Actress. *Ghettoville*. Werk Discs / Ninja Tune, 2014.

Actress. *Hazyville*. Werk Discs, 2008.

Actress. *R.I.P.* Honest Jon's Records, 2012.

Actress. *Splazsh*. Honest Jon's Records, 2010.

DJ Clent. *Last Bus to Lake Park*. Duck N' Cover Records, 2015.

DJ Manny. *Tekfiles Vol 1*. Hoko Sounds, 2013.

DJ Rashad. *Double Cup*. Hyperdub, 2015.

DJ Rashad. *Just a Taste Vol 1*. Ghettophiles, 2011.

DJ Spinn. *Teklife Vol 2: What You Need*. Lit City Trax, 2012.

Lethal Bizzle. *Pow! (Forward)*. Relentless Records, 2004.

RP Boo. *Legacy*. Planet Mu, 2013.

Ruff Sqwad. *Guns N Roses Volume 1*. Ruff Sqwad Recordings, 2005.

Ruff Sqwad. *White Label Classics*. No Hats No Hoods, 2012.

Traxman., *Teklife Vol 3: The Architek*. Lit City Trax, 2013.

Various. *Bangs & Works Volume 1*. Planet Mu, 2010.

Various. *Bangs & Works Volume 2*. Planet Mu, 2011.

Wiley. *Avalanche Music 1: Wiley*. Avalanche Music, 2010.

Wiley. *Treddin On Thin Ice*. XL Recordings, 2004.

Index